*Love is what happens when
        you're making other plans…*

"You're wasted on him."

The words vibrated through her, shaking her awake. She did not mistake his meaning. He was saying she was wasted on the duke. Because he thought she was *with* the duke. He thought they were together romantically, intimately. He thought she had been like *this* with his brother . . . mouth to skin, their bodies straining against each other in full, heart-pounding hunger.

It was a sobering thought. It made her feel tawdry and something else. Something confusing and different and not unpleasant.

She felt desired. Coveted. And it made her heart swell inside her too-tight rib cage. In this moment she could not imagine doing this with anyone else. She could not imagine anyone except Struan Mackenzie provoking these sensations in her.

She was a sinful creature, to be sure. She never knew she could be this. So wicked. Wanton. So titillated because she had aroused this man . . . because she had stirred a need in him to take her from a man to whom she did not even belong.

This entire situation was out of control. *She* was out of control.

By Sophie Jordan

The Devil's Rock Series
HELL BREAKS LOOSE
ALL CHAINED UP

Historical Romances
WHILE THE DUKE WAS SLEEPING
ALL THE WAYS TO RUIN A ROGUE
A GOOD DEBUTANTE'S GUIDE TO RUIN
HOW TO LOSE A BRIDE IN ONE NIGHT
LESSONS FROM A SCANDALOUS BRIDE
WICKED IN YOUR ARMS
WICKED NIGHTS WITH A LOVER
IN SCANDAL THEY WED
SINS OF A WICKED DUKE
SURRENDER TO ME
ONE NIGHT WITH YOU
TOO WICKED TO TAME
ONCE UPON A WEDDING NIGHT

WHILE THE
DUKE
WAS SLEEPING

❧ The Rogue Files ❧

Sophie Jordan

AVONBOOKS

An Imprint of HarperCollinsPublishers

WHILE THE DUKE WAS SLEEPING. Copyright © 2016 by Sharie Kohler. All rights reserved. Printed in the United States of America. No part of this book may be used or reproduced in any manner whatsoever without written permission except in the case of brief quotations embodied in critical articles and reviews. For information, address HarperCollins Publishers, 195 Broadway, New York, NY 10007.

First Avon Books mass market printing: November 2016

ISBN 978-0-06222254-1

Avon Trademark Reg. U.S. Pat. Off. and in Other Countries, Marca Registrada, Hecho en U.S.A.
Avon, Avon Books, and the Avon logo are trademarks of Harper-Collins Publishers.
HarperCollins® is a registered trademark of HarperCollins Publishers.

16 17 18 19 20 QGM 10 9 8 7 6 5 4 3 2

To my mother, for blessing me with a childhood that gave me ample room to dream. I will always cherish the gift of those days.

WHILE THE DUKE WAS SLEEPING

Seldom, very seldom, does complete truth belong to any human disclosure; seldom can it happen that something is not a little disguised or a little mistaken.

—Jane Austen, *Emma*

The Shopgirl Meets the Duke

The first time Poppy Fairchurch saw him she knew.

A deep awareness swept through her, lifting her up as though she were a puppet pulled by a string as he entered the shop the first day of her employ at Barclay's Fine Flowers.

She stilled for a moment over the display of ferns she was arranging, her mouth drying at the sight of him. Clearly he was a frequent patron to the shop. The elegant cut of his garments and the way Mrs. Barclay bustled out from behind the counter to greet the gentleman alerted Poppy to the fact that he was no any ordinary customer.

Even without Mrs. Barclay fawning over him, Poppy's eyes devoured him. She knew it was not ladylike or proper, but she could not stop from gawking. She had never seen the likes of him back home. No, the village of Toadston-on-Mersey did not boast a bevy of young gentlemen.

His chestnut hair gleamed gold in places and his eyes were a clear cerulean blue—so clear that even a yard away one could detect the darker ring of blue around the irises. His elegant attire alone served as warning enough that this was a man far out of her realm. Even if she wasn't a lowly shopgirl. Even if he was not a customer. She should have known better. She *should* have known to lessen her expectations and pull her head out from the heavens.

But then Poppy Fairchurch had always been a dreamer.

When he turned his devastating smile on her, her stomach flipped and she knew her life would never be the same.

And so it was that on the seventeenth morning of May, only a month after her twentieth birthday and two days after moving into a shabby lodging house on Chess Street with her much too pretty, much too garrulous younger sister for whom Poppy was now sole guardian, she fell in love with the Duke of Autenberry.

Chapter 1

*P*oppy relished the Duke of Autenberry's weekly ventures into the shop. *Marcus.* She had learned his name from glimpsing his signature on the cards he signed and handed to her to attach to the flowers. The name suited him. A strong Roman name. She could very well see him astride a stallion, leading men into battle.

She eagerly awaited those visits, which usually fell on a Tuesday or Wednesday. She took great pains with her appearance those days—which was not saying much considering all the hems had been let out of her frocks countless times over and bore patches. She was actually grateful for the striped pinafore Mrs. Barclay provided to be worn over her dress. At least it was freshly starched.

The duke was unique in that he liked to pick out his flowers personally. He took his time browsing the available flora. He could doubtlessly send a servant for such a task, but he preferred to do it himself. Because he was that sort of a gentleman. Thoughtful and sincere in his attentions—no matter that the flowers oft went to different ladies.

She did not judge him for that. An unmarried gentleman was free to court. A handsome nobleman would surely have scores of ladies doting upon him. He might very well be a rake, but could she blame him? He simply had not met The One yet. Once he did, he would settle down into his happily-ever-after. He was far too noble a gentleman to stray. She was convinced of this. And who was to say that person could not be Poppy?

Someday they would have a *real* moment. One day he would look up at her and truly *see* her. Not as a shopgirl, but as a person. Her tongue wouldn't tie itself in knots and she would actually manage to string words together in a clever and intriguing fashion.

Then he would recognize her as a woman with a warm and giving heart. He'd have to because she knew she was not beautiful. If she was going to bowl him over with her beauty, she would have already done so. There was no self-loathing involved with this assessment. Simply self-awareness and acceptance.

Oh, she wasn't ugly. Her face was fine enough. Her eyes lovely. Papa had always said so. Even Edmond complimented her eyes on more than one occasion. Although the boy she had thought to marry also teasingly called her scrawny. Scrawny with an overly generous backside—of course, he never dared to suggest the latter. Only she knew of her unfortunate derriere. Thankfully that feature was not quite so noticeable beneath her skirts.

Just as she knew her shortcomings she knew her assets. She was smart and good-natured and loyal. Poppy winced, realizing she had just described her father's favorite old hound. Stifling her wince, she added more adjectives that would separate her from a canine.

Hard-working. Someone who did not allow despair to consume her even during the lowest moments in her life—and in recent years she had definitely had those moments. When she lost her mother at age twelve to consumption. When she lost Papa just one year past. He was tossed from a horse and never recovered from the accident. It had been a long lingering death that she wouldn't wish on anyone much less the father she adored.

Always she had stayed strong for Bryony . . . for

herself. She loved her sister and would do anything for her.

These were her strengths, and why could Autenberry not one day look at her and recognize that she was The One for him? It could happen.

In her fantasy he would freeze upon looking at her as sudden realization swept over him. Then he would glance around the store and buy every flower in the shop—all for her, naturally—in the grandest of gestures.

It was fanciful. Perhaps far-fetched.

Very well, it *was* far-fetched. But dreams often were and Papa had always encouraged her to dream large. He would smile as he reminisced about her mother, claiming that if he hadn't dreamed he could win her, then Poppy and Bryony would never have been born.

In fact, she blamed Papa for instilling such a grand imagination in her. He'd read *Gulliver's Travels* and Chaucer to her before the fire after dinner every night. Mama was no better. At least the little Poppy remembered of her. Of course, Martha Smitton, daughter to a country squire, was a romantic. A member of the gentry, she had to be in order to leave a life of comfort and status behind when she ran away and married Papa against her family's wishes. It was a story she had told Poppy at bedtime every night up until her death.

Poppy believed in love and rainbows and leprechauns. Romance and whimsy were in her blood. Life was short. She knew this from losing parents much too soon. Life was precarious and she had no wish to squander it.

She wanted to believe a grand romance waited for her. Even if, in the meantime, she was stuck working in a flower shop all day and doing needlework at night by candlelight simply to make ends meet for herself and Bryony. Someday her turn would come.

Poppy rarely worked alone in the shop. If Mrs. Barclay wasn't present, then Jenny, the other salesclerk, was in attendance. Jenny stared at her so knowingly whenever the duke visited that Poppy was sure the girl was aware of her feelings. She could do little else but gawk and fumble awkwardly around him.

Which was why she was grateful Mrs. Barclay was present when the duke called one Tuesday morning in December. Jenny was not present to waggle her eyebrows suggestively.

Mrs. Barclay was overseeing an arrangement of fresh flora that had just been delivered from one of their hothouse vendors.

The bell shook above the door as he entered the establishment.

Naturally, Mrs. Barclay greeted him. She loved

rubbing elbows with aristocracy—a perk of the trade. "Oh, Your Grace." She executed a wobbly curtsy. "So good to see you again."

He doffed his head politely. "Good day, Mrs. Barclay." He inclined his head toward Poppy, always ever the gentleman, but did not address her. *Likely he had forgotten her name.*

"What can we assist you with today, Your Grace? Tulips? These just arrived. Even in this unseasonably warm winter they are still hard to come by, even from the hothouses, but you can trust Barclay's to have them for you, Your Grace."

He thoughtfully considered the blooms. "I don't think so." He lifted his head and scanned the shop, his gaze stopping on Poppy—or rather the pair of lemon saplings beside her. "Those are lovely."

He closed the space separating them, hands clasped behind his back. The duke stopped before Poppy and leaned in to inhale the lemon saplings. The young trees were almost her height, which brought his fine aquiline nose very close to her shoulder. Her lungs ceased to draw air.

Blast, but he smelled nice.

"Would you like these?" Poppy managed to get out past her lips. Seeing that the duke was well attended, Mrs. Barclay turned her attention back to the new arrangement of flora.

"Yes." He nodded. "I think I shall take two."

"Lovely." She fixed a smile on her face. "Would you like them delivered, Your Grace, or—"

"Yes." He removed a card from his pocket and slid it toward her. "To this residence. And can you tie a ribbon and bow around the trunks or some such?" He gestured with a flick of his hand.

She nodded, fumbling for the spools of ribbon. "Of course, Your Grace."

The duke turned that devastating smile of his upon on her. "Splendid." He turned his attention out to the window, perusing the street and forgetting her.

Disappointment punched her in the chest as she fumbled with ribbon. What was she expecting? For him to lavish her with his undivided attention? She'd said nothing clever or amusing.

Think, Poppy. Be witty.

She finished wrapping each slight trunk with yellow-and-green striped bows. Following that, she marked the transaction in Mrs. Barclay's ledger so that the expenditure could be deducted from the duke's retainer.

"There we are now," she announced with a touch of too much effusiveness. *Trying too hard, Poppy. Trying too hard.*

Clearing her throat, she tried again. "Here you are, my lord." She turned and plucked a card off the counter, handing it to him to write a personal note. Her pulse kicked a little harder as their fingers brushed. He bent his head and jotted a quick message, not affected by the contact. Finished writing, he lifted his head and returned the card to her.

"It shall be delivered this afternoon," she assured him.

"Very good." He touched the rim of his hat. "Until next time."

Mrs. Barclay called farewell as he departed the store.

Poppy drifted to the storefront window and peered at his departing form between the buckets of flowers on display for passersby. She couldn't help herself. Mrs. Barclay was preoccupied and he cut such a fine figure strolling down the sidewalk that he beckoned her gaze.

The street was not yet crowded this early in the morn. She was so absorbed on him, fantasizing that he might stop abruptly, swivel around and meet her stare with his own in some epiphanic moment of recognition that she did not immediately notice he had stopped and was talking to someone.

She dragged her gaze away from Autenberry and examined the stranger in front of him.

If possible, the man was even taller than the

duke, standing well over six feet. He was a veritable giant. Broad shouldered in his great coat. Remarkably, he was without a hat in the wretched cold as though he were impervious to the winter. His dark gold hair was a rare spot of lightness amid the dreary, fog-ridden morning.

There was something familiar about him. Perhaps he had come into the shop before. He was handsome, although not as beautiful as Autenberry. Even though the stranger dressed as a gentleman he had a certain roughness to him. A harshness that reminded her of the men she'd seen working the docks. A face carved from granite. Locked jaw. Hard eyes. A brutal slash of unsmiling lips. He was not a man one would wish to cross. The thought popped unbidden into her head and she gave a small shiver, her gaze returning to her beloved duke—just as Autenberry pulled back his arm and brought it crashing into the stranger's face.

The crack reverberated through the air, finding her ears even where she stood inside the shop. Her hands flew to her mouth, stifling her sharp cry of dismay. The big man staggered back a step from the force of the blow, his head whipping to the side. He froze for what felt like an endless moment when her heart ceased to beat. When all air ceased to pass through her lips and into her lungs.

Then he moved with the suddenness of a coil sprung. He pounced, striking Autenberry in turn. The duke staggered and did not have time to recover before the stranger was on him again.

Not about to stand by whilst the duke was pounded to an inch of his life, she sprang to action and stormed from the shop.

She was not the only one to take notice. A small crowd formed. A pair of riders on horseback stopped and dismounted. Not to stop the fight, merely to observe and call out encouragement. The shopkeeper next door, a haberdasher, emerged with a gaping customer, watching as the two men clashed, delivering savage blows that elicited cringes and cries from onlookers.

Mrs. Barclay emerged to clasp her arm. "What on earth?" she exclaimed.

"That man accosted the duke," Poppy said even if that wasn't precisely true. She knew the duke had been the first one to strike, but she knew he must have been provoked.

"This is dreadful!" Mrs. Barclay cried as the duke dealt a hard uppercut to the stranger's jaw, sending him crashing into the white brick wall of the haberdasher's shop, narrowly missing the proprietor. The rotund man leapt out of the way with surprising swiftness.

Shaking his head, the stranger touched his bloodied lip. Pulling back his hand, he looked down at the crimson smear. His eyes flashed in a way that made her stomach dip. The sight of his blood apparently enraged him. He pushed off the building and charged the duke, catching him in the midriff.

The two men collapsed into the street in a tangle of bodies and blur of limbs.

"Stop it!" she cried—the only one to shout a protest. The onlookers only seemed to grow, other people emerging from shops to watch the spectacle.

Autenberry and the stranger rolled, beating each other, fists landing wherever they could make contact. It was impossible to tell who had the upper hand. They appeared equally matched, thoroughly trouncing the other with such violence that her jaw ached from clenching her teeth so hard.

Poppy turned to look at the haberdasher and his customer. "Do something!" she cried.

He shrugged helplessly without tearing his gaze from the riveting display of the two men killing each other.

Not Autenberry. Not my duke.

She shrugged out of Mrs. Barclay's grasp and

rushed over to where a trio of gentlemen watched, shouting advice and placing bets among each other on the outcome.

"Please," she beseeched. "Do something!"

One fellow sent her an incredulous look. "I'm not stopping it! I've wagered on the big one."

Shaking her head, she stepped closer to the street, one hand worrying the collar of her dress, helplessly wrinkling the fabric.

The big blond man in question managed to rise to his feet. He set his boot against the duke, shoving him back down on the ground.

She saw red.

With a cry, she lunged into the street and jumped on his back, wrapping her limbs around him.

"What in the bloody hell—" He whirled in a circle, but she clung like she did every time she had captured Papa's pig that regularly escaped its pen and fled to Mrs. Wolfston's garden.

Poppy hugged the man's hard body and squeezed, determined not to let go.

"Stop, you great brute!" She clung fast. "Leave him alone!"

"Are you daft, woman?" he growled, seizing her hands where she had locked them around his shoulders. She gasped at his rigid grip on her wrist. He was a lot stronger than Papa's pig—and determined to be rid of her.

He staggered with her sudden weight and she feared they might crash to the ground together, his greater weight crushing her. Her stomach rolled, braced for the impact. He caught himself instead, weaving an unsteady line off the road toward the building. Dimly, she thought she heard Mrs. Barclay screaming her name, but she didn't dare turn to locate her. She focused on clinging to her quarry instead.

He spun, trying to throw her off. She yelped and grabbed a fistful of his hair. The move yanked back his head and threw off his balance, launching him sideways and slamming them into the brick wall between Barclay's and the haberdashery. A stinging epithet exploded from his lips. Pain fired along her side. She would bear bruises for that.

Leaning against the wall, he gasped as though needing a moment to recover. He'd taken the brunt of the impact and was hurt. *Good.*

She slid down the long lines of his body and stepped back. Panting and trembling like a leaf, she shoved the hair back that had fallen in her face and looked him up and down. She had to drop her head back to stare up at him. He was much too tall. He was much too . . . *much.*

He clutched his arm, holding it close to his side. A grimace passed over his face.

She propped her shaking hands on her hips. "I hope it's broken! You deserve no less."

"Bloody menace," he growled in a deep Scottish brogue that she hadn't noticed before. His eyes shot hot venom as they raked her up and down. His broad chest heaved. "This is no concern of yours, lass. Step away."

Of course he would not speak like a *normal* person. Instead he sounded like a man that cracked a walnut in his teeth and bathed in an icy river every morning. Primitive and fierce. A veritable caveman.

"Look out!" Mrs. Barclay's scream tore Poppy's attention away from the heathen Scot.

She followed her employer's gaze to the street where the duke struggled to regain his footing, shaking his head as though he couldn't focus. That wasn't all she saw.

A carriage was bearing down toward him. Fast.

Her heart dropped to the soles of her shoes. It was one of those moments she'd heard described in books or by people in times of great trauma.

Everything dragged to a crawl.

She saw the carriage. The horses with their steaming breaths and wild eyes. And the duke, helpless to move out of the way, directly in their path.

No no no no no.

She didn't think. Just reacted, rushing straight into the street. The duke had just managed to rise unsteadily to his feet as Poppy barreled her body against him, propelling him safely out of the way.

She turned wide eyes to the carriage now bearing down on *her*. Cold washed through her, freezing her in place. Blast!

Then a body slammed into her. A pained cry escaped her as she flew through the air, clearing the oncoming carriage's path.

She slammed down on the other side of the street as the carriage roared past in a clatter of wheels and hooves. Hard arms wrapped around her, her savior's body cushioning her, saving her from the worst of the impact.

The horses screamed in protest nearby as their driver pulled hard on the reins, still trying to get them to stop.

She pulled back to look down at the person who had just saved her life.

"You!"

The burly Scot glared up at her, his face drawn tight in lines of pain. "Feel free to climb off me whenever you so wish. You're heavier than you look."

"Ooh!" She clambered off him, noticing that he was still clutching his arm. He was injured. She felt a stab of sympathy until she recalled he was responsible for his injury. None of this would have happened if he had not engaged in a brawl with her duke . . .

At the reminder of Autenberry, her gaze shot to where he had fallen. Several people now surrounded him. Lifting her skirts, she rushed forward and pushed through the gathering crowd, her eyes wild for a glimpse of him.

She gasped as she looked down on him still prone on the ground. His eyes were closed and there was a deathly pallor to his face—as though all the blood had been leeched from his body.

The air left her in a rush and she couldn't even make herself move for a moment. She stood there, stunned, looming over the duke, everything else disappearing around her.

Please, please, let him not be dead.

Chapter 2

*E*verything roared back to focus around her. Bodies suddenly pushed all around her to peer down at him. A man crouched beside the duke and checked for the pulse at his neck. "He's alive," he pronounced.

She exhaled deeply, the tension in her shoulders easing. That same man who declared her duke not dead pulled the cap from his head and looked up at her, his voice full of awe. "Gor, miss. You jumped in front of that carriage for him!"

She nodded distractedly, her throat clogged tight with emotion.

"Nearly got herself killed in the process," a deep voice declared.

She cut a swift glance at the speaker, recognizing that brogue. The crowd stepped aside for the glowering Scot. His moss green eyes hardly looked at her. His gaze rested intently on the duke. "He alive?"

"He's not dead." Her voice didn't sound like her own. She swallowed in an attempt to reclaim it. "No thanks to you."

He looked back at her. "And you're not dead . . . thanks to me," he reminded in his gravelly tones.

The man clutching his cap gawked. "*You* saved *her*, sir! Never seen the like, I tell you!" He looked back and forth between the two of them. "You're both heroes!"

Poppy shifted on her feet, not liking the idea of this man as heroic. He was the villain in this little drama. She ignored the voice in her head that reminded her that he had pulled her out of the carriage's path. *And* that the duke had been the one to strike the first blow. In her eyes, the brawny Scot was the wrongdoer. The Duke of Autenberry must have been provoked into striking him.

"You saved his life," Mrs. Barclay exclaimed, her hands patting Poppy's shoulders proudly.

Poppy nodded briskly. "That remains to be seen if we don't get him out of this cold and properly tended."

The man waved his cap to a nearby hackney. "I can convey him anywhere you require."

"Aye, then. Let's get him off the street," the Scot instructed as though he were in charge. *The temerity!*

Everyone scurried to action. The hackney driver and another onlooker lifted the unconscious duke between them and carried him toward the waiting carriage. Annoyance prickled through her that the stranger had achieved their instant obedience. It was as though he bore no culpability in this day's deeds. Was it merely because he was a man? A well-dressed one at that and clearly a gentleman?

She rose to her feet, delivering him a withering look. Stepping close, she hissed for his ears alone. "You've assisted quite enough here, *sir*." She let her meaning hang there, clear even if not spoken. *Take yourself off now.*

He looked at her—or *through* her, rather, for that was how it felt. A cold, emotionless stare that cut straight into her and left her chest tight, the air thick in her throat.

Then, as though she had said nothing of value to him, as though *she* was of no value, he turned and walked away toward the hack, dismissing her, still looking far too authoritative even with his bruised face, bloodied lip and arm held tightly to his side. For a fleeting moment, she wondered if he regretted saving her life.

"You should accompany His Grace home, Poppy. Make certain he is delivered to his household and into the caring hands of his staff." Mrs. Barclay leaned close to whisper with a conspiratorial air, her dark eyes shifting to the Scotsman. Apparently she was not as trusting of the stranger as everyone else. "The duke is one of our best customers. We must be all that is solicitous."

Poppy resisted reminding her that saving his life was fairly solicitous by most standards because she wholeheartedly agreed with Mrs. Barclay. The duke should not be left alone until he reached the care of his staff.

Nodding, she looked back and forth between her employer and the coach into which they were currently loading the duke. Autenberry. Her heart ached for him. He was not out of the woods yet. *Please, don't die.*

"Yes, yes, of course, Mrs. Barclay." Her nape prickled, her gaze narrowing on the broad back of the Scot as he moved to climb inside the carriage with the duke.

Oh, no, he was not!

The two men had been engaged in fisticuffs. How did she know it wasn't his intention to climb into that carriage and finish off the duke? Perhaps he would smother him with his coat the instant the doors shut? Or simply use one of his giant paws on his throat and squeeze the life from him? He couldn't be trusted alone with His Grace. That was for certain. She wouldn't permit it. She could not. There was no way she would leave the duke at the brute's mercy. Of course she would be accompanying him.

"Hold there," she called, lifting her skirts and chin in a simultaneous move she hoped looked haughty and proper. She might not be highborn, but her mother had been gentry and her father had bred her to be dignified and self-respecting. In this moment, those lessons served her well. "I'm coming with you."

He looked down at her, one eye red and puffy, fast on its way to bruising. Blood seeped from his lip and yet all combined he still managed to look imposing. Not the least bit weak or vulnerable as any other person in his condition would appear. He was attractive, she grudgingly allowed. At least some females would consider him to be. Not Poppy. "That's not necessary."

"Oh, I think it is." She climbed up into the carriage ahead of him without assistance, determined that he not leave without her and confident that he would if she gave him the slightest opportunity.

He followed, joining her inside. Since the duke was reclining on the opposite side, the Scotsman sat directly beside her, his muscled thigh aligning with her own. She recoiled from the contact.

He started to shut the door. She reached across him and put a hand on his arm, stalling him from closing the hack's door. "In fact, I don't see how it is necessary for *you* to join us."

"You don't?" he asked mildly.

"No. I don't."

"I estimate there is a lot you do not see, miss," he retorted in that rumbling growl of his.

She straightened against the squabs and twisted on the seat to better glare at him, not liking the disdain he treated her to and emboldened by Mrs. Barclay's faith in her. She would protect their patron. "You're fortunate that I don't send for the Watch for your hand in this day's deeds. Now get out." She pointed imperiously to the door.

"How soon you forget that I saved *your* life. Was that not part of this day's deeds, too?"

She inclined her head slightly. "I thank you for that, but that does not signify when it comes to the matter of your presence here with the duke."

He tried to shut the door again.

She pushed on his hard forearm, trying not to let the sensation of the ropey sinew beneath his clothing distract her.

"I'm not going anywhere," he growled. "I have every right to be here."

"Indeed?"

"Indeed," he retorted, mockery lacing that word and curling through her like burning parchment. "I am his brother, after all."

She snorted and rolled her eyes at that bit of absurdity. "Ha. Very amusing."

He stared at her in utter seriousness. Her breath froze in her chest. Dear heavens. He was not jesting.

She looked from him to the duke and back again, for the first time noting there was quite some similarity between the two men. Her stomach sank. *Oh, no.* This man was the duke's brother. She glanced down to where she clutched his arm in a vise. *Oh, no . . .*

She released her hold and blinked, falling back against the squabs. "Oh."

He slammed the door shut and rapped on the ceiling of the hack. The coach lurched forward. She swallowed the sudden lump that rose in her throat. It stung to consider that perhaps he *did* belong here. More than she.

Autenberry had a brother.

It felt wrong that she hadn't known that very basic fact about him . . . about the man she claimed to so ardently admire. She closed her eyes in a pained blink and shook her head in self-disgust.

I didn't know he had a brother.

Of course she didn't know that. She didn't know anything about him. Oh, she liked to think she knew a great deal about her precious duke, but that was all part of the fantasy in her head.

"Very well," she murmured in surrender, accepting his presence as the coach rolled into motion.

She studied him in the sudden silence, wondering why she had missed the resemblance in the first place. She chalked it up to the chaos surrounding their first encounter.

One corner of his mouth kicked up as though tempted to smile. "Very well," he echoed, sounding so blasted pleased with himself that she only felt more foolish.

She glanced at the sleeping duke and then back to his brother beside her, scooting as far as she could and craning her neck to evaluate him.

He was . . . dark. It was the first word that leapt to mind. Ironic considering his hair was a deep gold. But it wasn't his outward appearance that made her decide this. Darkness exuded from within him. He had fought Autenberry with savagery, his greatcoat whipping around his gleaming Hessians as though brawling in the streets was the most natural thing in the world to him. *Because it probably was.*

His very size set him apart from other gentlemen of the ton. Even before he opened his mouth to speak in that brogue that felt like the drag of ermine on her skin, she knew he was different.

His broad shoulders filled out his greatcoat and he seemed to dominate the space inside the coach. Her gaze dropped to his massive hands folded over his knees. Those hands looked capable of crushing rocks. Despite his gentleman façade, he looked as though he belonged working on the docks. There was a roughness to him, an edge that belied his fine garments.

With a sudden start, she realized he was studying her, as well. "You're staring," he remarked.

"As are you."

"I'm simply trying to understand your presence here. What is your involvement with Autenberry?"

She pulled back. "*My* involvement?"

He brought his face closer so that even in the airless and shadowy confines of the hack she could see the brackets lining his mouth. They might be smile lines or dimples, except she doubted he was given often to mirth.

She opened her mouth but before she could respond, he demanded, "Are you his paramour?"

"His *what*?" Heat slapped her face.

"Paramour. It means lover, a mistress—"

"I know what it means," she snapped. She

spoke three languages. She knew the definition of the word paramour. Her gaze flew to the duke in mortification, as though he might overhear his brother's outrageous line of questioning.

"You seem very invested in his welfare. You did risk your neck for him, after all."

"It's called *caring for another human being*," she cried hotly, shaking her head. "People take risks for those they care for."

"*Risks?*" he sneered. "You *care* enough about him to risk getting yourself killed. Because that's what would have happened had I not been there." He stared at her through narrowed eyes.

She swallowed, considering his accusation. He was correct. She could have died today. She should regret that. She had not only herself to think of. There was her sister. She couldn't leave Bryony alone in this world.

Moistening her lips, she tried again. "I care."

"Clearly," he interrupted, his gaze sharp as cut glass.

"That does not mean that I . . . that he and I . . ."

"Are shagging?" he finished.

Heat exploded anew in her face. Was she trapped in a nightmare? "You're vile."

"In my experience, love is a requirement for diving in front of carriages to save another person. Or at least believing oneself in love." He waved one hand, conveying the amount of skepticism he felt for that particular level of emotion. "Not that I've ever been in love, real or otherwise."

"Otherwise?" she echoed, marveling that his cynicism rivaled his vileness.

"Indeed. Infatuation is oft mistaken for love." He shrugged. "In whatever form, it drives people to act—" he cocked his head, thinking "—idiotic."

"Idiotic?" she squeaked. "Love is idiotic?"

"I didn't say that. I said love makes people *act* like idiots. Evidently you love him."

She inhaled a bracing breath and smoothed a shaking hand down her starched pinafore. She didn't know what was more insulting. That he believed her to be the duke's mistress or an idiot? "You're a confounding man."

"I've been called worse." He adjusted his long legs and one of his thighs pressed against her skirts. She jerked away as though stung.

"I can well imagine."

Indeed, it was as though he were sucking all the air inside the coach into himself, stealing it from her so that her lungs felt drawn and tight. The man unsettled her. His presence, his very words, made her pulse pound uncomfortably fast in her veins.

It was a wholly uneasy feeling. Dizzying. Faintly nauseating actually. Nothing at all like the easy warmth she experienced when in the Duke of Autenberry's company. But then not every man evoked easy warmth. Nor should she expect as much. That should be reserved for the extraordinary few.

At the thought of such a man, her gaze drifted to the duke. Marcus. His lashes rested like dark bruises on his pale cheeks. He was the only thing that mattered right now. Not his insufferable brother.

Chapter 3

*S*truan hoped he wasn't dead.

Murder would be bad enough, but killing one's own brother? Struan had committed many sins . . . done many unpardonable things in his life, but fratricide, as of yet, was not one of them.

Granted, Struan loathed the bastard on the seat across from him, but he didn't want his death on his head. Not that he had pushed him directly into the carriage's path. Nor had he even been the first to strike a blow, but it didn't matter. He'd engaged most readily once Autenberry struck him.

His mother would not be smiling down on him for this particular infraction. She had wanted Struan to find happiness. Peace. To avoid conflict.

That had been her dying request . . . in so many words.

I ken I dinna give ye all I should 'ave. I thought yer da was a decent man. I was wrong. Ye deserved more. A better ma and da. A better life. Ye go and claim it now, son. Ye deserve it. Be 'appy.

The female beside him looked at him like he was some manner of vermin—certainly not anyone deserving of anything good. Clearly, she thought the sun rose and set in his half brother. She wouldn't be the first to labor under that misapprehension. Just about everyone around Town thought that Autenberry was as fine and pleasing as cherry cordial.

Since he'd moved to London a year ago, he'd made discreet inquiries, even frequented places where his half brother would be. All so he could glimpse the son their father wanted. It was curiosity, nothing more. He certainly didn't crave a bond with one of his few living relations.

Upon first arriving in Town, he'd discovered that his father was dead. A disappointment, to be certain. He would never have that sweet moment where they came face-to-face. He'd envisioned many scenarios. The moment they would bump into each other at a ball or soiree. Or at the duke's club—which Struan had made certain to gain access to. There was nothing money could not buy, even entrance to White's. Especially when Struan possessed vouchers from some of the most admired and important men in England—men, unlike him, who didn't know when to quit. Men who played until they'd wagered everything. Their fortunes, their estates, the very clothes off their backs.

Struan had amassed a fortune in the years since his mother's death. He'd started out chasing dice in back alleys. Even without proper schooling, he had a knack for numbers, for knowing how to quickly tally them and manipulate them so that they made sense. Numbers, unlike most things in life, were reliable. They never betrayed one.

That skill helped him beat the odds at horse racing and other games of chance. By the age of twenty he'd risen from gaming in back alleys. He'd won horses and phaetons. He even once won a pair of kangaroos. Soon there was property, estates. At two and twenty, he'd won his first gaming hell. From there his empire only grew. Aside from land and houses in Scotland, he'd gained properties in the Cotswolds and the Lake District. And then came London.

Doors that had forever been shut to him magically opened, and he'd begun to fantasize about meeting his father . . . of showing him what he had become with no help from him. In these fantasies, he was in possession of a highborn wife to sweeten the pot. Someone coveted not only for her rank but her beauty. And so, that ambition had been borne.

He left for London with one clear goal: marry the most attractive, bluest blue-blooded English rose he could find and rub his father's nose in it. He would make old Autenberry rue the day he ever rejected him and called him a lowborn bastard.

Once he arrived and discovered his father dead, he continued his quest mostly out of habit. Moving through long-ingrained routine. As though he could still reach his father in the grave and prove to him that he'd been wrong—that Struan Mackenzie was somebody even though the Duke of Autenberry refused to acknowledge him as his son.

The hack hit a slight rut and the girl quickly reached across the space to clasp Autenberry's shoulder, steadying him and keeping him from falling off the seat. He felt his lip curl at her attentiveness to Autenberry.

She was a fierce little thing. Not a beauty, but there was a certain something to her. He wondered, not for the first time, if his dear brother was shagging her. There were only a few females whose skirts his brother had not lifted, after all.

She'd actually possessed the temerity to attack

him. He was twice her weight. He could crush her single-handedly and yet she'd come at him as though he were her match. What had his brother done to earn her stalwart protection? He stifled a snort of derision. He knew the answer to that. Autenberry had a way with the fairer sex.

He studied the slim line of her beneath a dress that had seen better days. He knew his brother favored his females on the curvy side, and she was a far cry from that.

Satisfied her patient would not roll off the seat, she settled back against the squabs. "You look like him a little," she admitted grudgingly. "I see it now."

"I know." He'd observed the resemblance upon their first meeting. They might look similar, but his father had claimed and doted upon Marcus. A sentiment that went both ways if the rage his brother exhibited upon first meeting him signified.

The young duke despised Struan. He was convinced that Struan wanted only to destroy the remaining Autenberry family and, like a papa bear, he was determined to protect his family. To be fair, Struan did not entirely blame him for the impulse. He might feel the same way if their situation was reversed. If he had anyone left in the whole world that cared about him. But he didn't. He had no one.

As though she couldn't resist, she leaned across the space once again, her slim fingers gently pushing a lock of hair off the duke's forehead. It was a tender move that made his chest clench uncomfortably.

Of course she doted on him. Autenberry was a duke. And handsome. Even without that to recommend him, he was charming, as well. Everyone said as much. There couldn't be too many handsome, charming dukes around. It was a bitter bit of irony that the unconscious man she gazed at with total adulation had only moments ago called Struan's dead mother a whore and him a liar before taking a swing at his face. Despite their resemblance, Autenberry liked to pretend that his father had not committed adultery and had not fathered a son he then abandoned to poverty.

It wasn't the first encounter Struan had with his half brother, but each confrontation only grew more contentious. The young duke believed Struan was after him for mercenary reasons. As though he didn't have wealth enough of his own. He could buy and own Autenberry's estate twice over—the land, his homes, the servants, his fashionable clothes and possessions. It was a pittance for him.

The first time they came face-to-face, Struan had the foolish notion that they could perhaps be actual brothers to each other. Since they were.

Well, half brothers, anyway. It annoyed him to re-
flect on that moment now. The stupid boyish op-
timism he had felt. He should have known better.
Had his father's rejection taught him nothing?
His mother was dead. The only creature on this
earth who had ever given a damn about him. He
would never have anyone love him uncondition-
ally again. Nor did he need anyone. He was fine
on his own. Rich. Respected by many. Feared by
the rest. He had women to warm his bed whenever he wished it.

After stubbornly insisting that Struan couldn't
be his brother, Autenberry ordered him to stay
away from him and his family—as though Struan
were stalking them, as though he wished the remaining Autenberry clan ill.

Only today Autenberry had taken it one step
further and insulted the memory of his mother.
*My father never strayed from his marital bed, and he
most certainly didn't father some whelp off a whore
from Glasgow—*

Their old man was dead. He'd lied and used
Struan's mother, abandoned her when she came
to him for help. He'd pushed her to her death . . .
as if he had snuffed out her life himself.

Death, as far as he was concerned, was too
good for his sire.

That said, he never intended to transfer his

hatred onto his half brother . . . but it seemed his half brother was determined to think the worst of him.

In fact, Struan had been debating returning to Scotland, selling the properties he'd accrued since moving to London and putting the past behind him for good. Or try to, at any rate.

Then they'd come face-to-face again on the street today.

Struan wasn't sure what to expect, but the venomous words had jarred him. And just like that, his thirst for revenge flared to life again. Except this time instead of exacting it on his father, he wanted his pound of flesh from the bastard's son. The *good* son. The son worth having around. The one worth keeping.

Struan had lost control. When Autenberry struck him, he was ready.

The carriage rolled to a stop. The door opened and he motioned for her to descend. "Go ahead. I'll see him out unless you mean to carry him in yourself."

She eyed him suspiciously before nodding and departing before him. He lifted the duke's not insubstantial weight, maneuvering him as carefully as he could out the door. A pair of footmen waited at the ready, arms outstretched to assist.

Autenberry's devoted little friend hovered

close, her expression fixed in concentration as she stood next to an anxious-looking woman, presumably the housekeeper, if the keys hanging from the belt at her waist were any indication.

He watched as the men carried his brother up the steps and into Autenberry's Mayfair mansion.

The gray-haired housekeeper scrutinized his face. "Mr. Mackenzie?"

He felt a small flicker of surprise that she knew him. But then of course servants talked. They knew everything, before even their masters did. As the housekeeper to the Duke of Autenberry she likely knew all about him the moment he arrived in Town.

He masked his reaction and nodded.

She surprised him further by stepping forward and closing her hand around his forearm. She gave him an encouraging squeeze. "You're the spittin' image of your father, sir. Come inside, won't you?" She motioned him inside the house with an easy smile.

He cast one final look at the girl who'd jumped on him like a wolverine, then turned his back on her. Whatever she was to his half brother, he was certain it was the last he would see of her. She hardly looked the sort to fit in among the ton—so that would exclude her from the Duke of Autenberry's drawing room.

POPPY WATCHED, WORRYING her lip between her teeth as the footmen carried the duke inside the house, scarcely listening or paying attention to the housekeeper as she addressed the duke's brother. Her heart lodged somewhere in her throat as she stood there agonizing, praying for him to survive. *Please, don't die. Please, don't die.*

The duke's half brother moved ahead of her, blocking her vision with his broad back. He looked over his shoulder at her before ascending the steps and disappearing inside the house, leaving her on the stoop, dismissing her as though she were no one of any import.

Her chest squeezed. It struck her as vastly unfair that *he* got to go inside whilst she, who genuinely cared for the duke, was left out here to wonder and worry. She let out a huff of breath and propped her fists on her hips.

"Oh, Marcus," she breathed, allowing herself the liberty of secretly using his Christian name. "Please be well. Please don't die." Her eyes stung. "I'm here for you." Her voice quavered a little. She swallowed back a choked sob and attempted a weak jest, "We're going to get married, remember?"

"Hallo, there."

She jerked and turned to face the housekeeper staring intently at her. She hadn't realized the woman was still standing outside or so close . . . or listening to her. *Blast.* Had she heard the nonsense she just spouted? If she had, she must not give it any credence, chalking it simply as the ramblings of a deranged girl.

"H-hello," she stammered, finding herself pinned by the housekeeper's eagle-eyed scrutiny. She backed up several steps. The housekeeper followed. She was a great Viking of a woman. Tall with considerable girth. Poppy felt like a sparrow in her shadow.

"What's your name?" the housekeeper asked.

"Poppy Fairchurch."

"Miss Fairchurch . . . how is it you came to be here?"

She opened her mouth to speak, but suddenly the coachman was at her elbow. "She saved his life! Jumped directly in front of the carriage and pushed him out of the way."

The housekeeper's eyebrows winged high, nearly disappearing into her hairline. "That so?"

"The damnedest thing I ever seen." The driver snatched his cap off his head. "Beggin' your pardon, ma'am, miss. It was a sight to behold. The bravest thing I ever seen."

"Indeed." She rocked back on her heels, still staring at Poppy, speculation bright in her eyes. "How fortunate. I shudder to think what would have happened if you weren't there."

Warmth crept over her face. She was unsure how to respond and still suffering acute embarrassment from the housekeeper overhearing her talking to herself.

The woman took hold of her arm and turned her toward the front door. "Come inside, my dear. I'm certain the duke will want to see you when he wakes."

She frowned, hope skimming through her. "You really think so?"

"Of course he will." Her silvery head nodded with certainty. "I'm Mrs. Wakefield, by the by."

Poppy wasn't so certain that the duke would want to see her, but she couldn't resist letting herself be guided inside the house. She wanted to know when he woke. She wanted to be there. She wanted to make certain that he was going to be well—that next week he would stroll into Barclay's Flowers and place his usual order.

Arm in arm, Mrs. Wakefield led her into the grand foyer.

Chapter 4

*L*et him hear you talking. Maybe he'll come to." The housekeeper positioned a chair by the duke's bed for Poppy.

They weren't the only two individuals in the chamber. On the far side of the enormous room Mr. Mackenzie sat on a brocade chaise. Sprawled, really. His long booted legs stretched out before him like some pasha overseeing his domain. His eyes glowed from the shadows, following her like a predator's stare.

She knew his name now. He was no longer *that rough Scotsman*. He was Mr. Mackenzie. Mackenzie.

She didn't like finding him sitting there, watching Autenberry, watching *her* as she walked across the vast chamber. Brothers or not, she still did not trust Mackenzie.

She rubbed her palms against the skirts of her pinafore, feeling very uncertain in such grand surroundings. "Thank you," she murmured.

Poppy sank down beside the bed, rationalizing that it was the least she could do until the physician arrived. Be there for Autenberry. Talk to him. Encourage him.

Mrs. Wakefield nodded in satisfaction, staring at Poppy so intently, as though she had something on her face . . . some bit of food stuck between her teeth. Poppy resisted the urge to bring her hand to her face as a shield.

"Can I offer you any refreshments while you're waiting?" she asked.

"No, thank you. I am fine," Poppy replied with a forced smile, bemused at the woman's kindness.

Mackenzie glowered from where he loomed on the far side of the room, arms crossed his chest.

The housekeeper hesitated before taking her leave. "I must say, I'm glad His Grace has you."

She floundered. "Er . . ."

"I've long wished His Grace would find someone special and put an end to his bachelor ways." She patted Poppy's shoulder approvingly.

Blast! Evidently the housekeeper had heard her ramblings, after all, and taken them to heart.

"Now have a seat beside your betrothed right here." Mrs. Wakefield patted her shoulder briskly.

Poppy's stomach dipped. *Betrothed?* Oh, sweet heaven.

She searched for the right words to correct her confusion, but Mrs. Wakefield kept on talking. She motioned to the unconscious duke. "Go on now, my dear. Let him hear you. It will do him so good." She whirled around to address Mackenzie. "If you will both excuse me. I shall wait for Dr. Mercer and escort him in the moment he arrives."

Poppy's mouth worked, seeking the right words as the housekeeper bustled from the room, moving surprisingly fast for a woman of her size. The door shut behind her with a soft click that resounded in the cavernous space.

Poppy swung around swiftly, not daring to meet Mackenzie's scouring gaze. She scooted the chair closer to the edge of the bed, peering at her unconscious duke and pretending that her lie didn't throb on the air like a giant, man-eating gnat. While she was also pretending, she tried to imagine there wasn't a third person in the room. A chore, to be certain, as she could feel his glacier stare drilling into the back of her.

Poppy patted the duke's well-shaped hand resting on the bed. She went ahead and folded it, so still and cold beneath her fingers, in her own hand and chafed it, trying to warm the chilled skin. "There now. Everything will be—"

"Fine?" That Scottish brogue spoke up from behind her. He'd risen to his feet and moved closer. "Is that what you intended to say?"

She tensed. "Why are you still here?" she snapped. Without waiting for an answer, she focused on the duke's handsome face. "Everything will be fine," she crooned, refusing to look over her shoulder and give that other man the satisfaction of her attention.

"You think so?" he asked.

She sighed. "There's no sense in being grim. That's not helpful."

"I'm being realistic."

"You're being harsh," she countered with a sniff. She recalled his hard, unsmiling face vividly in her mind as well as the savagery of his fight with his brother. Yes, this man was as unrelenting as stone and she would do well to stay clear of him. Whenever she must be in close proximity with him, she would stay on guard.

"He may never wake up, you know."

She sent him a withering look over her shoulder. She couldn't help it. At that remark, she had to look back at him. "And you'd like that, wouldn't you?"

Something flickered in his eyes . . . a brief flash of surprise. "On the contrary. Why would I wish him dead? He is my brother—"

"Who clearly cannot abide you."

He shrugged a big shoulder. Her gaze skimmed the solid outline of his physique. Did he lift boulders in his spare time? Clearly this was no dandified gentleman who required additional padding in his jacket. "A minor misunderstanding. It happens among brothers."

She scoffed and looked back at the duke asleep on the bed. "No brothers I've ever known."

"And you have great experience with brothers?"

She didn't reply, simply turned and fixed her gaze on Autenberry, and tried to ignore the sense that there was something vulgar underlying that question.

Mackenzie's boots slid closer behind her, a whisper on the carpet and a reminder that he was still there. Not that his presence was exactly forgettable. Her nape prickled and she resisted the urge to brush her hands there and chase away the sensation. "How long have you known Autenberry?"

"We first met June seventeenth." Her first day of employment at Barclay's.

"You've committed the exact day to memory?" His tone rang with derision.

"Yes." She would never forget it. The day had been a bitter thing to endure. She had thought she would live out her days in Toadston-on-Mersey as Edmond's wife. Papa was supposed to be their neighbor and live to be an old white-haired man, bouncing her children on his knees. The duke had been the one bright light in that disappointing day.

"Six months," he murmured. "That is a quick engagement."

Thankfully he could not see her face. She was certain it bloomed a fiery red at the enormity of such a lie. "Yes," she murmured, her voice surprisingly even. She was not about to confess to him, of all people, that she was not the duke's fiancée—that she was merely a humble shopgirl. He hardly struck her as the understanding sort. He'd denounce her as a fraud.

She would straighten this mess out later—after the physician arrived. There was no telling what Mackenzie would do to her. She already knew he possessed a propensity to violence. He could very well strike her. Or he could send for the Watch and have her thrown into prison. She couldn't risk that kind of trouble. If something happened to her, no one would be there to take care of Bryony.

"Yes, it was quick," she agreed. "Love is like that." Or so she'd been told. Papa ran away with her mother after a fortnight and her mother had left everything behind—her life of privilege, fancy dresses and parties—all for him.

"You must have really swept him off his feet."

She risked an uneasy look at him again, trying to gauge his sincerity. "I don't know about that," she hedged.

He closed the last few inches separating them, his moss green eyes gleaming with a mocking light, and she knew he doubted her. Naturally. He did not consider her capable of evoking that level of passion in a man. She herself doubted it. Edmond's rejection stood as proof of that.

"Or was it the other way around, then? My dear brother swept *you* off *your* feet? He just couldn't resist you, is that it?" He was definitely smirking at her now. And she wanted to slap him.

He wasn't saying it, but he might as well have been.

He didn't think Autenberry would have anything to do with someone like her. He was a duke. She was Poppy Fairchurch late of Toadston-on-Mersey, a plain, impoverished shopgirl who could scarcely afford to feed herself and her sister.

And she was a fool for fantasizing that he might think she was The One.

A fool for believing in impossible dreams.

Anger flashed through her. "Is it so very hard to believe—"

"That he fell in love with *you*?" Again with the smirk.

Righteous anger burned through her. "That does happen, you know." Just not to her. Not yet at least. "People meet. They have feelings . . . they fall in love." She waved her hand in a little circle as if that somehow illustrated her point. "Is love a sentiment you've never felt before?" She flicked her gaze over him. He was handsome as sin, for certain, but he did not strike her as the lovable sort. "Never mind."

He arched an eyebrow several shades darker than his golden hair. "What?"

"It's not so shocking, I suppose, that *you* haven't any experience with that sentiment."

His gaze raked her in turn, and she knew he was thinking something ugly and best left unsaid. In fact, she was beginning to think that ugliness was the only thing that existed inside this man. "And you do, then, Miss Fairchurch? Have a great deal of *experience*?"

She did not mistake the insult. He was implying that she was no better than a strumpet—that she had enticed the duke. Seduced him. That she was a woman with loose morals.

She inhaled thinly through her nose. She didn't know what was stronger—her sense of indignation or the flutter of gratification in her chest. He might not think her capable of winning the duke's heart but he thought her capable of seducing him. That was . . . *something*.

She was no great beauty. Did he actually think her alluring enough to trap a man like the duke into marriage? Her throat tightened. No, he likely thought Autenberry's sense of honor was at work here.

Fortunately, the physician chose that moment to arrive and she was saved from further conversation with the boorish man.

Mrs. Wakefield followed close on his heels. Brief introductions were made. Poppy winced at hearing herself introduced as his fiancée and opened her mouth, prepared to finally correct that misapprehension, but then Dr. Mercer swiftly turned his focus on the duke—as he rightly should. It did not feel right to distract him from his task, so she drifted away from the bed, permitting him to conduct an examination in relative peace. She did not want to break his concentration.

Mackenzie withdrew alongside of her. Mrs. Wakefield stayed close to the bed, ready to assist if needed.

"You were saying how you met Autenberry, Miss Fairchurch."

"No. I wasn't," she replied crisply, still gazing at the bed and ignoring the way his stare felt like an itching rash crawling over the side of her face.

"Well, then do share. How did you meet?" There was that tinge of skepticism in his voice again.

She sighed. How she longed to tell him they met at some grand ball or Almack's. That would certainly take the wind out of his sails and kill the smug way he looked at her and acted toward her. She'd love to be able to tell him she did, in fact, travel in the duke's exalted circles.

In the end, she knew sticking as close to the truth was the wisest course. "At Barclay's Flowers."

He was quiet for a long moment, his square-cut jaw locked in contemplation. Clearly he was not expecting that. "A flower shop?" he queried as though needing verification.

"Yes." She inhaled. "I'm employed there."

"You work in service?"

"I'm a florist." She straightened her spine, arms crossed snugly before her.

"Interesting."

She spun to glare at him. "And what, pray, is so interesting about that?"

"I did not realize my half brother so forward

thinking as to consider courting a female far below his social station."

She blinked, wanting to demand an apology from him, but she could not fault him for his honesty, even if he was more blunt than she would have liked. "Perhaps he believes in following his heart over the mores of class and society."

Mackenzie leaned against the wood-paneled wall, a hint of a smile hugging his lips. He really was handsome . . . if one liked the brooding, stern type. "You're describing Autenberry, are you?"

"Yes."

"Then it appears I don't know him in the least."

She didn't know him either, but she did not point that out. She was allegedly his betrothed. At any rate, she suspected Mackenzie was correct and he did not know the duke well. Autenberry's housekeeper had never met Mackenzie before, after all. The duke himself had struck a blow to him in the street. It stood to reason the two men were not on kindly terms.

"No," she replied, fairly confident that she could say almost anything about the Duke of Autenberry and he could not contradict her with any assurance. She was wagering everything on that fact. "You do not."

"But you do," he said unnecessarily, and the

censorious gleam in his eyes yet again seemed to shout: *fraud! liar!*

The physician cleared his throat. The sound rattled in the spacious chamber. He stepped back from the bed, looking to each of them with a grim expression.

Poppy stepped forward, eager for his prognosis of the duke's condition. Mackenzie pushed off the wall, his expression somber even for him.

"When will he wake?" Poppy asked, unable to hold the question at bay any longer.

"There is no way to know. He's sustained a serious injury to the head."

"Oh!" The housekeeper brought her hands to her mouth. "Will he die?"

"He's in a false sleep . . . otherwise known as a coma." His voice faded away and he glanced back at the unconscious duke with a dejected expression that did not bode well. "The longer he sleeps . . . well, it is not promising, I'm afraid."

"But he still lives," Mackenzie interjected. He waved at his brother. "He still breathes."

The physician nodded. "The body can linger long after life is viable."

"Are you saying he's essentially *gone*?" Poppy demanded, her throat closing up in horror.

The physician grimaced, glancing at each of them before looking back down at the wan duke asleep in his bed. Only he wasn't asleep. No amount of calling his name or shaking would rouse him.

She blinked suddenly stinging eyes in the thick atmosphere of the chamber. He couldn't be gone. She refused to accept that.

Chapter 5

*T*he silence was shattered when the doors flung open and a boisterous crowd spilled into the chamber. There were several of them—mostly female and as loud as a steam engine complete with a shrieking whistle. Poppy attempted to count them but they were moving so quickly they made her dizzy. Overwhelmed at their arrival, she actually took a step closer to Mackenzie.

A lovely woman led the way at the front of the group. She was unlike any woman Poppy had ever seen. Tall and regal with dark hair and eyes, her skin was a delectable golden hue that made Poppy think of warm beaches. Not that she'd ever visited a warm beach but Poppy had read about them in *Robinson Crusoe*. Dressed luxuriously in a crimson traveling dress, jewels dripped off her. If ever there was a woman created to wear jewels, this exotic creature was she.

When she opened her mouth to speak, an equally exotic accent spilled forth: "Mrs. Wakefield! What is going on here? Giles just informed me that Marcus is injured." Her gaze locked on Autenberry prostrate on the bed. She released a sharp gasp followed by a litany of Spanish—one of the languages Poppy did not speak. Had it been French or German, she could have followed her.

Too young to be his mother, but not in the first blush of youth either, she charged forward with her dark eyes snapping fire, ready to tear someone apart. The lady launched herself into the chair that Poppy had vacated moments before. She picked up the duke's lifeless hand between her own. "Marcus, *mío*. What ails you?"

Poppy shifted uneasily. Oh, dear. Her chest squeezed. In any case, all would soon be revealed now. This woman was obviously close to him. She would know Poppy wasn't his fiancée. She could very well be one of the women the duke was always sending flowers to? Perhaps Autenberry loved *her*.

"Your Grace," Mrs. Wakefield murmured, stepping closer and brushing a hand against the woman's shoulder. "You must calm yourself."

Poppy started at the form of address. She was a duchess? How could that be? She was quite certain that the duke wasn't married and it wasn't as though there were a surfeit of duchesses about Town.

"He's like a ghost," the duchess muttered, shaking her head. "My sweet stepson . . . thank the heavens his beloved father is not here to see him like this."

Ah. She was his stepmother, then? The *dowager* duchess. She scarcely looked older than the duke though. If Poppy hazarded a guess, she would place her a few years over thirty.

"Oh, Mama!" A young girl close to Bryony's age sidled close to where the dowager duchess sat. She was the very image of her mother with dark hair and eyes. "He will be well, won't he?"

The dowager nodded as though convinced, and yet doubt lurked in her dark eyes. "He's young and strong. Of course he will mend."

"How did such a thing happen?" another woman asked. She, too, had dark hair, but she wasn't the least bit exotic. She was as English as they come with milk-pale skin, gray eyes and a fine, narrow nose. Her clothing was finely made, but not nearly as bold or stylish as that of the duchess. It was difficult to determine her age with her rather stern expression.

Somehow, miraculously, Poppy's voice surfaced in that moment to answer the question. "He fell and struck his head," she explained from where she hovered. All gazes swung to her as though she possessed two heads.

The stoic-faced lady pinned Poppy with her gaze. "And how, pray, did that happen?"

"He . . ." Poppy hesitated, reluctant to betray the man standing beside her. Mackenzie did save her life. She supposed she owed him for that . . . and despite what she had accused him of to his face, she knew he did not mean for the duke to injure himself so seriously. "He and . . . another man were fighting."

"A fight!" his stepmother exclaimed in her rolling accents, pushing back up from her seat and shaking her head. "Fisticuffs! With whom?"

"With me." Mackenzie stepped forward, looking appropriately grim as he admitted this.

The dowager released a little squeak and took a hasty step back, clutching her young daughter close as though Mackenzie might turn his fists on them next.

"You?" Hot color flooded the other lady's face, enlivening her and suddenly making her appear not so stern and stoic. "Who are you?" she demanded in outrage, not shrinking away.

He opened his mouth to answer and then

paused. Angling his head, he looked at the lady strangely, as though seeing something within the tight lines of her face.

Mrs. Wakefield stepped forward and lightly squeezed her arm. "Lady Enid, it's *him*. You recognize him, don't you?"

Understanding passed over Lady Enid's face as she gazed at Mackenzie. "Ah, of course." Her voice dropped a notch softer. "I was wondering when we would meet."

"Aye," he said rather gruffly. "I'm Struan Mackenzie."

Struan. Poppy rolled the sound of his name around in her head. *Strew-an.* In her head, she heard the vibrating rumble of his brogue, especially in the first syllables, even though she doubted she could pronounce it thusly herself.

"How good to meet you," the lady replied. "This is long overdue. I'm Enid. Your sister."

His sister? And they'd never met before?

Enid turned her gaze from her brother and gave her head a slight shake as if returning to the moment. She frowned down at the duke on the bed. "Let me hazard a guess," she continued. "Marcus wasn't pleased to see you and—" She broke off with a shrug. "Well, let's just say that he said regrettable things."

The dowager stepped forward again, fisting her linen handkerchief. Poppy tensed, wondering if she would strike him. She was well within her rights. "Marcus does have a temper, but he is not given to violence. Did you do this to him?" she demanded, waving her handkerchief.

"No," Poppy heard herself quickly defend, not even stopping to wonder why she was defending him. All attention turned to her. "It was an accident."

The exotic beauty nodded, looking relieved. Then, to Poppy's great shock, she stepped forward and embraced Mackenzie. "Mr. Mackenzie . . . Struan, I've longed to meet you. We are family. Marcus has struggled to accept your existence. You can understand, I am certain. He was suspicious . . . afraid that you wanted to hurt us."

Mackenzie stood utterly still—clearly stunned as she hugged him. He lifted a hand and awkwardly patted her slender back.

Without fully releasing him, she pulled back enough to look him in the face. She clucked and touched his cheek. "You look very much like your father. I see it so clearly."

Struan's expression tightened at this, but he managed to nod in acknowledgment of what must be a compliment. Looking at the two brothers, the late duke must have been a beautiful man.

The dowager continued, "Marcus must have seen the resemblance, too. He wanted to believe it wasn't true, but he had to know." She shook her head forlornly. "It was difficult for him to accept that his father had been unfaithful. He knew his parents weren't a love match, but it's another thing to accept . . . well, you." Smiling wistfully, the dowager dropped her hand from his cheek and stepped back from Mackenzie.

A brief stretch of silence fell over the chamber. Everyone looked at the duke, still as death on the bed, willing him to wake.

With a sigh, the dowager did the inevitable and turned her gaze to Poppy. "You really saved our Marcus?"

Poppy cleared her throat. She felt uncomfortable claiming responsibility. It made her sound overly noble, so she attempted to explain it in a way that made her actions appear utterly normal. "His Grace was in the middle of the road and a carriage was bearing down on him—"

"And she saved him! Pushed him out of the way, she did." Mrs. Wakefield dove into the conversation.

"You pushed him out of the way?" the dowager

breathed, her lashes blinking over her liquid-dark eyes.

Poppy shrugged and nodded awkwardly. "Y-yes."

The dowager clasped her beringed fingers together in front of her as though in prayer. Poppy tensed, uncertain what to expect. It certainly wasn't what happened next.

Apparently deciding it was her turn now, Lady Autenberry seized Poppy's shoulders and pulled her into a suffocating embrace. "You saved his life." Astonishingly, she started to weep. "We can never repay you for saving him, but we shall try." The shoulder of Poppy's pinafore was soon damp from her tears. Unaccustomed to such public emotion, especially from the likes of a duchess, Poppy patted her back clumsily.

"I advise you not to hold out too much hope, Your Grace," Dr. Mercer interrupted, shifting uncomfortably. "The duke's life, I'm afraid to say, may yet be lost."

Still sniffling, the dowager pulled away from Poppy to face the physician. "What are you saying?" A linen handkerchief appeared out of nowhere for her to dab at her eyes.

Poppy winced. She thought the man had been perfectly clear.

The physician sent a pained glance in the direction of Autenberry. "He's in a false sleep . . .

a coma, as it were. Now while there are the rare cases of individuals who wake up after weeks in a coma, you must prepare yourselves. He may never wake again."

The dowager started bawling, dropping her face into her hands. Even her young daughter succumbed to tears. Only the stern Lady Enid maintained her composure, although her bottom lip quivered.

Struan Mackenzie didn't bat an eye, of course. His gaze was bone dry as he stared ahead.

"Is there nothing we can do?" Lady Enid asked, her voice the height of practicality. "Please? There must be something."

"Tend to him. Keep him warm and comfortable. Try to get him to take as much nourishment as you can. You don't want him to grow too weak."

The dowager and housekeeper nodded in unison. "Of course."

"And pray," he added.

Everyone nodded again, their expressions solemn. It reminded her of when Papa had died. Even weeks before his death, when he was just a wraith of himself and withering away, everyone tiptoed about her wearing expressions precisely like that.

The physician backed away as the duke's family gathered around his bedside. Poppy edged back a step, confident that this was her cue to cut a hasty retreat.

She felt Struan Mackenzie watching her and sent him what she hoped was an indifferent glance. "Going somewhere, Miss Fairchurch?" he asked.

His voice drew everyone's attention back to her.

She smiled tightly and froze. She hoped his blackening eye hurt like the devil. "Just leaving so that the duke can have some time with his family."

"Would that not include you? In a manner?" His eyes flashed with mockery.

"What do you mean?" the dowager asked. She looked back at Poppy, her lush lips dipping into a frown. "What does he mean?"

"I—I . . ." She shrugged helplessly, suddenly yearning to blacken Struan Mackenzie's *other* eye.

"Why, she's his fiancée," Mrs. Wakefield volunteered.

"His fiancée!" the duchess declared, bright color flooding her face. "How can that be?"

Voices erupted. Everyone started talking all at once, turning the room into a loud din.

"Marcus is engaged?" the youngest girl squealed, clapping her hands and in that moment reminding Poppy a great deal of Bryony.

"Why did Marcus not tell us of this?" Lady Enid demanded.

Poppy attempted to speak, waving her hands and trying to correct everyone from the misapprehension that she was the Duke of Autenberry's fiancée, but it was impossible to be heard over the clamor.

"Where is Strickland? Does he know?" Lady Enid demanded.

Poppy resisted the urge to ask who Strickland was. Her gaze slid to the chamber door that loomed open, eager to make an escape through it. When she looked back at the boisterous group, her gaze caught on Struan Mackenzie. He watched her knowingly, almost smiling, as though he knew she wanted nothing more than to make a hasty exit. As though he thought he had ensnared her.

Squaring her shoulders, she resolved to appear comfortable among the duke's blue-blooded family.

"Have you met Strickland?" Suddenly the duchess was looking at her as though she held all the answers . . . as though she had any clue who this Strickland person was. "Does he know about you and Marcus?"

Poppy opened her mouth and produced a long-drawn *"IIIIII"* sound.

Really, she needed to work on her skills of speech. "No," she finally managed. "I have not met him." *Whoever Strickland was.*

"He's Marcus's best friend," the younger lady supplied, and Poppy began to suspect she would always supply the facts that others left out.

"Of course she knows that, Clara." Enid shot her little sister a long-suffering look.

"Enough!" the duchess finally boomed in a shrill voice.

Struan Mackenzie looked on, crossing his arms over his chest as though he had all the time in the world to witness her downfall.

The duchess took several halting steps toward Poppy.

Poppy sucked in a breath and waited, certain this would be the moment she would call for the Watch or, at the very least, have her tossed out of the house on her backside.

"Our dear Marcus is alive because of you." The elegant lady yanked Poppy into her arms in a cloud of rosewater perfume. Poppy opened her mouth, but only a croak emerged as the woman petted her back and wept noisily. "I always wanted him to find someone special, and you're clearly that person. Everyone whispered when my late husband returned from abroad with me. Even though my family was an old one . . . my great-great-great-grandmother was a lady-in-waiting to the mad Queen Joanna." She nodded as though this was a great attribute, and Poppy was certain it was. Even her gentrified mother could not claim to such lineage.

The young dowager continued, "I wasn't English. I wasn't titled, but it didn't matter because my husband *loved* me."

Lady Enid snorted slightly and looked her stepmother up and down, her gaze stopping on her impressive bosom. "What's not to love?"

The dowager ignored her and held Poppy's gaze. "I know it must be the same for Marcus." She cast the duke a soft look. "He must truly love you not to care what all those Society fusspots will say of him marrying outside his class. I'm so very happy. With you to live for, I know he will make it through this."

Poppy was surrounded then, the dowager and Clara exclaiming over her as though she were their long-lost relation and not some random individual claiming to be the Duke of Autenberry's betrothed. Lady Enid held back, but there was no resentment on her face as her young stepmother and, presumably, half sister celebrated Poppy as though she were one of them—an actual member of their family.

She longed for that—to be part of a family, to belong to others. She always had. Poppy felt a pang of guilt to feel that way when she had a sister, but sometimes she felt alone even with Bryony for company.

Emotion churned in her belly and her heart warmed dangerously. These were good people and she was deceiving them.

Still crushed in the surprisingly strong hold of Lady Autenberry, she glanced over the dowager's shoulder. Her gaze locked on Struan Mackenzie.

All except him.

There was nothing good about the surly Scot— aside of his handsome face and form. She winced at the inappropriate thought and quickly gave herself a mental kick. She was *not* so shallow as to let that blind her to his true nature.

He cast a very large shadow over the room, standing with legs braced apart like a pirate on the prow of a ship—a handsome, vigorous figure as featured in so many of her girlhood fantasies. Of course, in her fantasies, he wasn't glaring at her with ill temper flashing in his eyes. She could practically feel his contempt radiating toward her.

He was *nothing* like his brother.

She sucked in a breath. And she would never forget that.

Chapter 6

*S*truan watched, enduring it as his newfound family rejoiced over his half brother's lightskirt. It rankled. How easily they accepted her . . . how easily they even accepted *him*. It wasn't right. His mother never had this. His mother had never been good enough. It rubbed him like a bur in his boot.

He didn't know what made his gut clench more. The idea that he had a family willing to accept him? Or that one of his brother's lovers (he knew Autenberry wouldn't limit himself to only one) had just been welcomed to the family? *His* family. The family he never wanted. *Because you thought they would never want you.*

He shook off the insidious little whisper,

watching as Miss Poppy Fairchurch extricated herself from the Autenberry clan, backing away to the door with promises to return even though her eyes screamed escape. Was it his imagination or did she appear eager to leave? Not about to let her depart without finishing their conversation, he made his excuses to step out.

"You're not leaving us, are you?" The dowager blinked those doe eyes of hers at him, reminding him of a wounded forest animal. Remarkable, really. She was decked out in finery and jewels enough to feed a small village for several years and yet she managed to look vulnerable.

"I will be back," he assured her, wondering where that promise had come from. He owed her and the others nothing. He wanted nothing from them. He should not become embroiled with this family.

They were merely in shock and sought to cleave to him in this time of trouble. The golden son was gravely wounded. They would later regret inviting the black sheep into their fold. As soon as Autenberry awoke from his coma, he would make them see the error of their ways. Struan was not of their ilk. For all his money and aping of their manners, he was not one of them.

Turning, he strode from the room. He wasn't entirely certain of his intent, only that the moment the shopgirl departed the bedchamber he was on his feet and after her, his blood pumping in a way that insisted he go, move, follow. He'd spent a lifetime trusting his instincts, so he didn't question his need to pursue her.

Her plain skirts whipped around her ankles. She was a quick little thing as she advanced on the front door, her hand reaching out for the latch. The valet stationed in the corner shifted on his feet, his eyes wide, clearly uncertain whether or not he should step forward to open the door for her as she charged ahead with all the doggedness of a rushing bull.

She was the sort of female to dive in front of carriages and rescue dukes, after all. His chest clenched. He couldn't say why, but the sudden thought irritated the hell out of him. *Foolhardy chit.*

In any event, he beat the valet to the door, stepping around her and blocking her exit. "How do you intend to get home?" he asked.

She blinked, her expression startled. It was a frequent look on her face. As was the flash of distaste that crossed her face as she looked him up and down. It was a look he'd experienced before—that expression of disdain. As though he were a bit of filth beneath her boot. As a boy, he had been treated to that expression frequently enough. He never cared for it. Not then. And he especially didn't care for that look coming from her now.

"I was blessed with two perfectly functioning legs. I can walk, sir," she said stiffly as though he were somehow deficient of intelligence.

He stared at her, looking her up and down in turn, not missing the shabby dress beneath her starched pinafore. If she was Autenberry's fiancée he would eat his boot. "Do you live close?" He would wager she did not. Not in Mayfair or in any of the surrounding areas. Too rich for her blood.

She hesitated, dipping her gaze and shaking her head. It was all the confirmation he needed.

"Come," he said brusquely. "I'll hail a hack for the both of us."

"That's not necessary—"

He took her by the elbow and led her out the front door, ignoring her protests. "Come now. We are family . . . or soon to be, are we not?"

Family. He'd meant the words to be partly jesting, but as he stared down at the lass, the word reverberated through him with dishonesty and he faced the glaring and uncomfortable truth. He had no family, least of all *her*.

He might have just exchanged civil words with a chamber full of people who he could rightfully call family, but they were far from kin to him. It took more than a blood connection to be family. His father had taught him that painful lesson well. No, he was quite alone in this world.

Her lips pressed into a flat line. He expected to hear her resounding refusal, but she surprised him by agreeing. "Very well, then. Thank you."

The driver from earlier still waited at the edge of the drive. Struan was surprised the man hadn't left yet to find other fares. He hopped from his perch as soon as he spotted them. Snatching his cap off his head, he bobbed a greeting. "Hallo, there." He motioned to each of them. "I 'spected one of you might need to be conveyed elsewhere . . ."

"That's very good of you." Struan nodded with approval.

The driver hurried to open the door and drop the step for her to ascend. "I hope his lordship is faring well."

"His Grace has not yet woken," she offered.

The driver tsked his tongue. "I'll be saying a prayer for him. Me and the missus will tonight."

"That's very kind of you," she said, and Struan could not help but notice she used a much gentler tone of voice when addressing the hackney driver than when she spoke to him.

Unbidden, he wondered what tone of voice she

used with his brother. Undoubtedly sweet. She probably even smiled—something he had yet to see her do. And why should she? The man she claimed to be her fiancé was in a false sleep as a result of their brawl in the streets. Naturally, she didn't feel like smiling at him.

She supplied her address and the driver shut the door.

He settled across from her, watching her as the hack started rolling forward. "Will you return tomorrow?" he heard himself asking.

She opened her mouth and then closed it with a snap, clearly uncertain how to reply.

"Foolish question. I am certain you will," he went on to answer for her. "You will be much too worried to stay away."

She turned to gaze out the window, dismissing him. He began to suspect she wouldn't say anything at all when she suddenly declared, "He'll mend, you know." Defiance tinged her voice—as though she expected him to argue the point.

"I do hope so," he replied.

She jerked her head around to look at him, her gaze narrowly sharply. "He will. He will wake. I know it."

"Do you now?" He folded his arms across his chest, arching an eyebrow at her. "Are you blessed with the sight?"

She snorted. "I am no seer."

"Ah. Just burning conviction, then?"

"It's merely something I feel." She pressed a hand against her heart. He casually surveyed the starched pinafore covering her chest. It was impossible to measure her assets hidden there, but it didn't quell his curiosity to do so. He wanted to see. He wanted to peel back her layers. He wanted to know what his brother knew.

She continued, "I can't explain it." She shook her head, disgusted with herself or him, he wasn't certain. "I don't need to explain it. Not to you as you sit there laughing at me."

He pointed a finger to the straight, unsmiling line of his lips. "Do you see a smile here?"

She shook her head. "No. I see no smile. I've yet to see you smile at all."

"The same can be said of you," he countered.

She lifted her chin with a little sniff. "We're simply two people who don't rub well. It happens. Not everyone can like everyone."

"True," he remarked, still assessing her, trying to read her, and wondering why it should bother him that she didn't *like* him. Most women did. He wasn't arrogant thinking so. It was simply truth. He'd always had a face and form women desired, even if he was rough about the edges. "How old are you?"

She frowned. "Don't you know it's impolite to inquire a lady's age?"

"Five and twenty?" he baited, knowing she was younger.

Her eyes flared wide. "I am twenty!"

"So very young?" he mocked. "You seem older."

"Why? Do I look so very haggard?"

"No. You merely act like it."

Her lips snapped shut, and he knew she was chewing that over, trying to decide whether or not she was offended.

As they rolled to a stop, he glanced out the window at a four-storied house with a crooked sign out front that proclaimed Gibbons Lodgings.

He opened the door and hopped down before the driver could disembark from his perch. Turning, he held a hand up for her.

She hesitated before finally placing her hand in his. As soon as her feet touched down she snatched her hand back as though she feared he might wish to keep a grip on her. Was she so very assured of her allure? Had snaring his brother filled her with such confidence?

No woman was so irresistible. Just as no single woman was irreplaceable.

He addressed the coachman. "A moment, if you will."

The man nodded.

Hot color bloomed in her cheeks. She gestured at the waiting hack. "I left my reticule back at the shop, but I should like to recompense you for the—"

Annoyance shot through him . . . along with something else. He was intrigued. No woman of his acquaintance had ever offered to recompense him for anything. On the contrary, he was a man of considerable means that they wanted to squeeze for everything they could. He didn't even begrudge them that. He well recalled what it felt like to go to bed hungry. There was a time when he was every bit as mercenary as any of them.

She, however, annoyed him. Why couldn't she be like every other female of his acquaintance? The more she mystified him, the more irritated he felt with her—and, to some degree, with himself.

Perhaps this is why Autenberry fancied her. For her very uniqueness? He snorted. There was no chance of that. His brother was much too shallow and concerned with position and rank to allow himself to do more than shag her a time or two. Whatever she was to Autenberry . . . she was *not* his future wife. He would wager his fortune on it.

"That's unnecessary," he said. "I don't need your money."

She looked on the verge of arguing and then

inclined her head, clearly deciding not to dispute the point.

"Well, then. I thank you." She shifted awkwardly. "For escorting me home . . . for saving my life." She looked like she was sucking lemons, clearly reluctant to voice her gratitude for that latter part. She blamed him for this day's deeds and that much hadn't changed in their short drive together.

A wiggle of something that felt uncomfortably like guilt wormed through him. For all he felt toward Autenberry, he did not wish him dead, and he wondered if he could have done something differently. Something that did not result with the duke being unconscious in a bed right now.

Damn her for thinking the worst of him. And damn him for caring one way or another.

"I'm certain we will meet again," he said, wondering why that rang ominously to his ears. What did he care if he ever saw his brother's doxy again?

She nodded once brusquely and then presented him with her back. He followed her up the path to the stoop of her lodging house with measured steps. She registered his steps and whirled around. "What do you think you're doing?"

"Walking you to your door. It's the gentlemanly thing to do. Certainly you are accustomed to such treatment from my brother." He arched an eyebrow.

She inhaled, lifting her slight chest. "You needn't escort me." She stood elevated two steps above him, which enabled her to look down her slim nose at him. "You may go."

She was a contrary female. She might be a shopgirl, but she had all the air of a queen. How had his brother ever managed to seduce someone so prickly?

He was a duke.

Little else mattered in the minds of most females. In that respect, she was no different from any other chit, easily felled when the man was rich enough, handsome enough, powerful enough.

Except staring at her, he felt lost in her eerily wise eyes. She didn't seem like any other chit. She appeared not in the least put off by his stern mien. Not his great size. Not his coarse accent. For God's sake, she'd pounced on him like an angry mama bear only hours ago.

He felt lulled, mesmerized. She did not seem like someone to be so caught up in the superficial trappings of an individual. Not a woman with shoes as scuffed as hers, or with a frayed hem peeking out beneath her pinafore.

"Poppy!"

At the shrill shout, Miss Fairchurch looked up.

Poppy. So that was her name. Somehow it suited her.

He followed Poppy's gaze. A girl hung out the window, waving wildly at them.

"Bryony!" she chastised. "Don't hang out the window! You'll fall!"

The girl did look like she might tumble the two stories if she took too great a breath. "Who's that there with you, Poppy?" she called down excitedly.

Miss Fairchild sent him a pained look. "My sister," she explained. "She's an excitable girl."

"I see that," he murmured.

"Hello, there!" The girl continued to wave wildly, her reddish hair a halo around her. "Who are you, sir?"

He lifted his fingers in silent greeting.

"Are you coming inside?" Bryony called down eagerly as though he were a long-lost relation and not a complete stranger.

He thought he heard Miss Fairchurch mutter something that sounded suspiciously like, *Providence save me.*

"I best hasten before she drops on her head before us." Her lips twisted wryly. It was the closest thing to a smile he had caught on her face and a small hum burned through him at the sight of it—which was utterly peculiar. She wasn't to his tastes. Not in the least. "Trust me," she added. "It could very well happen."

Before he could respond, she turned and rushed up the path with quick strides, moving with surprising spryness. There was certainly nothing demure about her. She was a ball of energy.

He watched as she ascended the last step leading inside. He surveyed the house a final time. It appeared drooping and tired in the winter air—the complete opposite of Miss Fairchurch. As tightly wound as she was, she buzzed with life and vitality. *Fire.*

Perhaps this was what Autenberry had seen in her. Clearly there was more to her than one might first perceive. Something had to be there for his brother to have noticed her initially. He was well aware of the type of women his brother was typically drawn to and it wasn't their inner beauty that attracted him. He liked his women beautiful and with bountiful curves. Not unlike Autenberry's young stepmother he had just met. *Not unlike their father's taste in women.* He cringed and shoved the thought of his father away.

So what was it about Poppy Fairchurch that had ensnared his brother?

Shaking his head, he decided that he didn't know. But he intended to find out.

Turning, he climbed back up in the hack. Once settled inside, he found himself looking out the coach at the window he knew to be hers. It wasn't until the carriage started moving that he faced forward again.

Chapter 7

*S*he took a bracing breath as she cleared the landing that led to the room she shared with her sister. She knew she was in for a thousand questions and after the day she had it was going to be a struggle to maintain her patience throughout all of them.

On an average day, Bryony was inquisitive. After spotting Poppy with a strange gentleman, the questions would be endless.

It turned out she didn't even need to open the door. As she rounded the corridor, her sister was waiting in the open doorway, bouncing lightly on her bare toes.

At the sight of Poppy, she rushed out into the

corridor, her pretty face flushed with excitement. "Who was that man?"

"Struan Mackenzie," she replied, because it was the truth and an answer she could give without disclosing anything too revealing. The last thing she wished to do was chronicle this day's events for her sister. She could not pinpoint the precise moment when she had erred, but she was certain she had. Greatly. Grievously. Otherwise, the duke's family wouldn't believe she was betrothed to Autenberry. She closed her eyes in a long blink and rubbed at the center of her forehead where it was beginning to throb. All whilst the hapless duke was in a coma. It was a blasted nightmare.

"Struan Mackenzie . . . that sounds Scottish. Is he Scottish?"

"Yes. He is."

Bryony's lovely chocolate brown eyes bulged in her face. "Did he escort you home?" The way she asked the question signified how scandalized and titillated she was at the very notion.

Poppy stepped inside their humble room and closed the door behind them. Bryony followed close behind, breathing down her neck as she peppered her with question after question. "Oh. La! Do tell, Poppy!"

"Very well. Yes. He did." She lifted the pinafore

over her neck and hung it on a peg, brushing out the barely there wrinkles.

"Poppy!" Bryony shrieked. "Do you have a beau?" She clapped her hands together and bounced again, her auburn curls dancing like gleaming sausages over her shoulders, grazing the tops of her generous bosom. It was a strange sight she was not yet accustomed to seeing. Her baby sister was in possession of breasts twice the size of her own and enviable hair that made her own wheat-colored hair look every bit as plain as it was.

Strange, yes, but she did not resent it. She admired her sister's beauty. Much like a parent, she even took pride in it. Not that it was achieved through any great accomplishment. It was a twist of fate, a blessing of birth, but she was still proud of Bryony nonetheless.

"Don't you dare tell me you've been keeping such a momentous thing from me! The way you moped around after Edmond ended things, I feared there would be no one for you and you would die an old maid!"

Poppy closed her eyes in a pained blink. Her sister was never one for tact. Hopefully that would come with age and maturity.

Bryony started hopping on her toes again. She had the energy of a toddler. Heaven knew staying cooped up all day in this house wasn't good for her, but there was no way Poppy could unleash her pretty sister into the wilds of London. It was a recipe for disaster. This city would gobble her up. She had wrought enough havoc in their tiny village. The vicar's two sons had engaged in fisti-cuffs merely to see who would be allowed to walk her home after church. She could not be let loose in this city.

Thankfully the proprietress of the house was willing to keep an eye on her. Poppy knew Mrs. Gibbons and Bryony spent a good portion of the day doing needlework in front of the fire, and that was hardly the most riveting way for a young girl to pass her days, but there was naught Poppy could do.

Once a week the harpist that also let rooms from Mrs. Gibbons gave Bryony a lesson in ex-change for Poppy giving her day-old flowers. The woman claimed they made her dreary little room feel like a home. Poppy wasn't certain it was a fair exchange, but she gladly accepted the arrange-ment. She wanted to provide an education and culture for her sister, as Papa would have wanted. And yet education and culture were no easy feat when they lived on a mere pittance.

Mrs. Gibbons was also kind enough to take Bryony with her when she went to market, so her sister did step out often for fresh air. Things could be worse. This was what Poppy told herself when she found herself grieving for Papa and feeling sorry for herself and bemoaning her old life when they had a roof over their heads. Food. A garden to tend. Countryside to roam.

Bryony was fifteen. Poppy would have to do something to start readying her for the future. With any luck, Poppy could find Bryony an apprenticeship or position as a nanny or governess. Perhaps a lady's companion. Any number of situations Poppy herself could have found if she didn't have a younger sister to bring up in the world.

She winced as she gazed at Bryony, who was now curling a lock of her hair around her index finger. She hardly seemed ready for the world. Her sister might possess the face and body of a full-grown woman, but she was very much still a little girl.

"I'm not being courted by anyone. Rest easy, Bry. Nothing as exciting as that." Stepping forward, she pressed a quick kiss to her sister's cheek. She smelled of rose talcum. It was Mrs. Gibbons's scent and proof that she had spent a good deal of her day in the widow's rooms.

"Posh!" Bryony crossed her arms and stomped her foot. "Nothing exciting ever happens. If I worked in Mayfair, I would have a score of exciting things to report. You should let me take a position. We could use the funds."

The notion of her too-pretty sister in Mayfair made her wince. Even if she wasn't so dewy-fresh, the shrill volume of her voice alone would draw attention. The purpose of any good employee was to discreetly serve their master without calling attention to oneself. Bryony would never manage that. At least not right now. Perhaps with more maturity, it could be accomplished. One day. That was Poppy's hope.

"Did you eat already?" Poppy rubbed again at the center of her forehead where the beginning of a headache was taking root.

"Yes, with Mrs. Gibbons. She made a stew. Do you want me to fetch you something from the kitchen? While you eat you can regale me with all the details of your day." She jiggled her eyebrows up and down. "If you're not being courting by Struan Mackenzie, then who is the man?"

"I will go downstairs later. For now, I merely want to rest." She plopped backward on the bed they shared.

Once upon a time Poppy had a bed all to herself—in her very own bedchamber with a gabled ceiling and window that overlooked a garden. Before Papa died. Granted the chamber had been small, but it had been all hers.

She hadn't known that was such a unique thing at the time. It was all she had ever known. As a little girl, she would play with her dolls and look out the window to spy on her mother happily toiling in the garden. She could still hear Papa reciting Latin to his pupils in the library below.

Now that she realized she might never have that again, she pulled those memories out every day, stroking them and turning them over and loving them so that they would never be lost to her.

How her life had changed. Now she slept with Bryony, who kicked like a mule and talked in her sleep.

Her sister dropped beside her on the bed. "Very well. Then tell me . . . who was that man? He was dressed very finely. I've never seen a gentleman dressed so well even in Toadston-on-Mersey. Not even Mr. Heppleton or his son and they were the richest family in the village. The lighting was poor, but he looked handsome. And tall. He looked handsome *and* tall. Is he handsome, Poppy? Tell me! Is he? Is he?" Before Poppy could even answer, Bryony plunged ahead. "Papa was handsome. Maybe the most handsome man in Toadston-on-Mersey. Mama was a beauty, of course. Everyone said so. Even Mrs. Heppleton. Remember when she said that? But then like goes with like. Is that not the saying?" Bryony took a breath.

Poppy rubbed at her forehead, hoping her sister's diatribe had finally come to an end. It was too much to hope for. Bryony continued, "Of course, your Edmond had a fine face. You were a worthy match. Not that it should matter, dreadful cad that he is." Poppy closed her eyes, hoping that would somehow blot out the sound of her sister's voice.

Still she chattered on like a magpie. "He'll not find a future wife with eyes as fine as yours, I daresay. Poppy!" Her voice turned into a full-fledged whine at this point. "Are you sleeping? Why won't you tell me anything about that man? I've a right to know!"

"Bryony!" Her eyes snapped open. "If you hold your tongue, I'll tell you everything."

Well, most everything. She'd leave out her fabrications. Merely thinking about her deceit made her head pound harder.

Bryony pressed her lush lips shut—a true challenge, to be sure.

Sighing, Poppy continued, "Today at Barclay's, one of our very prominent customers, the Duke of Autenberry—"

"Gor, a duke! What's he like? And why have you never told me about him before?"

Because he was something that Poppy had wanted to keep to herself. A secret dream that she alone knew about. Selfish of her, but there it was.

Bryony continued, "Was he dressed in gold brocade and dripping in jewels—"

At Poppy's quelling look, Bryony fell silent again.

"Today, upon leaving the shop, he met with an unfortunate accident."

"Oh!" Her sister clasped her hands together.

"He nearly perished before the wheels of a carriage."

"No!" Bryony exclaimed, slapping her hands to her apple-round cheeks. Papa always said that Bryony looked like their mother. He never said that about Poppy. It wouldn't have been true and they both knew it. Poppy wasn't certain who she looked like. Herself, she supposed. Not that that had won her any prizes. It certainly hadn't won her Edmond.

Bryony knotted her hands and bunched them in the folds of her skirts. "No fair." She pouted. "You get to leave every day and have these adventures whilst I'm stuck with Mrs. Gibbons—"

"Oh, come now. You like Mrs. Gibbons—"

"I would like an adventure *more*."

It was going to be difficult to keep her sister contained for much longer. Mrs. Gibbons couldn't watch Bryony every hour of every day. Sooner or later, she would grow bold enough to sneak out from under Mrs. Gibbons's care.

Then what would Poppy do? She couldn't resign from her position to watch over her sister. They needed a roof over their heads. Food in their bellies. Her sense of helplessness gave way to longing. If she truly were the duke's fiancée she would have the resources to see Bryony properly brought up. She wouldn't be another lost soul who fell prey to the vices of London. And Poppy wouldn't have failed her parents in seeing Bryony well situated in life.

Why couldn't it be real? Why couldn't she truly be the duke's betrothed? Almost instantly she felt awful for wishing that. Her problems weren't the duke's responsibility. He was gravely ill. She only wished him whole again.

Poppy would be fine. Bryony would be fine. She sniffed and rubbed at the cold tip of her nose. Everything would be fine. They had each other. They were young and healthy and those were the important things. Her silly fantasies and longings were of no account.

Poppy held up her hand and pointed at a bundle of cracks in the plaster ceiling. "That looks like a basket with loaves of bread." It was a game they had oft played. Either with clouds or twigs on the ground, Poppy had always turned the shapes of things into familiar objects.

Bryony giggled until the sound quickly cut off into a snort. Poppy remembered then that Bryony was trying to act more like a sophisticated woman these days. "Oh, Poppy, you are such an odd duck."

"I'd rather be an odd duck than like everyone else," she replied automatically. It was something Papa had always said. *Better to be different than the same as everyone else.*

Apparently her sister remembered that about him, too. "You sound so much like Papa when you say that." For a moment, her baby sister sounded almost grown-up.

Poppy elbowed her in the side. "Go on. Your turn. What do you see?" She pointed at another intricate pattern of cracks.

"You know it's a sad state of affairs when we can make a game out of our dreary living conditions." Even following that remark, Bryony concentrated on the pattern before finally sighing. "I don't know. A rabbit? Right there." She pointed to where the cracks formed a shape that could be construed as a pair of rabbit ears. If one squinted. Evidently she interpreted Poppy's hesitation to mean disagreement and sighed in defeat. "I don't know. I'm never any good at these dumb games of yours. You know I'm not smart, Poppy. Not like you."

"Stop it," she chided. "Don't say that. You are smart."

"No. I was an atrocious student. Even Papa said so. But I don't care. It doesn't matter. I'm going to marry a gentleman who won't care about such things." Her pert little nose shot up.

Any sympathy she felt for her sister died quickly at that reply. "You think so?" she asked tartly. "And where do you plan on meeting such gentlemen?"

"I will eventually. Once you let me out of this room and away from that watchdog Mrs. Gibbons."

Poppy shuddered and resisted telling her that would never happen.

"I suppose you're never going to tell me about this mysterious Struan Mackenzie, then?"

"I am not. Because there is nothing to tell."

Bryony sighed. "So you say."

Poppy stifled a smile. Apparently Bryony was not as unclever as she claimed. She knew there was more to tell, and she sensed that Poppy wasn't telling it.

After a few moments, she rose to her feet. "I'm going downstairs to get something to eat."

"I suppose I'll join you. I haven't anything

better to do." She rolled her eyes dramatically. "As usual." Bryony flounced ahead of her out of their room.

As far as Poppy was concerned, her sister wouldn't have anything *better* to do for a good many years. Especially as her sister's idea of something *better* involved all manner of activity unfit for a young lady of fifteen.

It was a healthy reminder. She needed to keep her priorities straight. She needed to stop engaging in silly fantasies. As soon as this matter with the Duke of Autenberry was straightened out, she would forget about him. Her mind flashed to another face. Moss green eyes. Lips tantalizing even when hard and unsmiling. A deep Scottish brogue.

Yes. She would forget about him, too.

Chapter 8

The next morning Poppy arrived early at Barclay's to make up for missing yesterday afternoon. Not that she feared reprisal for her absence. Mrs. Barclay had, after all, insisted she accompany the duke home and the woman, above all, was always exceedingly fair with Poppy. The one time Bryony had been sick for two days with a terrible ague she hadn't blinked an eye over Poppy's absence, insisting she nurse her sister and not become ill herself.

Even so, Mrs. Barclay was already there, bustling around the shop and setting everything to order for the day. Jenny did not always leave things the most tidy when it was her turn to close up for the day.

"How is the duke? Is he well?" Mrs. Barclay asked anxiously, stepping forward as Poppy entered the shop.

Poppy reached for one of the fresh pinafores hanging from a hook in the back room. "I haven't seen him since early last evening. I stayed as you suggested—"

"Yes, yes, of course." Mrs. Barclay waved her hand anxiously, encouraging her to keep talking, clearly not concerned over Poppy's absence. "He is awake, then?"

"When I left him, no, he was not awake." She exhaled a shaky breath. "The physician said the longer he slept, the less likely it is that he shall ever wake."

Mrs. Barclay shook her head sadly. "How dreadful. Well, take these." She reached for a bouquet of fresh tulips sitting near the counter. "Deliver these personally this morning and see how the duke fares. Offer our sympathies and see if there is anything else that we can do."

Poppy hesitated. While she appreciated the sentiment, she hated to intrude on the family. And what precisely did Mrs. Barclay think they could do? He was surrounded by loved ones and receiving the best of care.

She had nursed her father in the last couple weeks of his life and it was terribly awkward whenever someone called upon them. She knew they meant well, but being forced to attend them in the parlor whilst she could be looking after her father or the household or shepherding her sister (who was in chronic need of shepherding) was the height of discomfort.

"You want me to leave? Right now?" She glanced around. "What about the shop—"

"It will be fine. Jenny will be here in a little while. Lord Autenberry is our most loyal patron. I won't be remiss in our respects. You must go and represent Barclay's so that when—" she paused and winced slightly "—*if* he recovers, he shall hold our shop only in greater esteem."

"Of course, Mrs. Barclay." Poppy inclined her head and avoided pointing out the self-serving nature of her employer's motivation. She knew Mrs. Barclay was not an unfeeling woman. However, she was also a businesswoman with an infirm husband to look after. Poppy could not fault her.

She deposited a coin in Poppy's hand for fare and shooed at her with her hands. "Go now. Off with you."

In a matter of minutes, Poppy was in a hack and on her way to the Duke of Autenberry's home. Again.

She clasped the fragrant bouquet between her

fingers and inhaled its delicate scent. She tried not to let where she was going fill her with panic. A difficult feat knowing everyone in that house believed her to be someone she was not. She was perpetuating a lie. *Living* a lie. She wasn't certain how severe the offense ranked in the grand scheme of offenses. Surely she couldn't go to Newgate for such a thing? Sudden fear pumped hard in her veins. What, then, would become of Bryony?

She reined in her racing thoughts. She needed to compose herself before she succumbed to a fit of apoplexy. She'd never succumbed to such fits before but there was a first time for everything. She gazed out the window.

It was still early and the streets weren't too crowded. An icy gray draped the air. The hack made excellent time to the duke's residence, and she was soon standing before the grand double doors of his town house, gripping the bouquet in suddenly sweating palms, her breath fogging in front of her. Yesterday seemed almost a dream, when the Autenberry clan had welcomed her so warmly. Surely today they would see the error of their ways and adopt Struan Mackenzie's attitude toward her and expel her from their orbit.

Deliveries always went around back, as with most aristocratic residences. It was tempting to drop off the flowers at the back door with a note and beat a hasty retreat, but she knew Mrs. Barclay expected a status update on the duke. In addition, the household believed she was his fiancée. It would be ludicrous to walk around to the back like any ordinary delivery person, deposit the bouquet and leave.

Still, standing there in the morning cold, waiting for the doors to open, it was hard to pretend she was anything other than ordinary. Woefully ordinary Poppy Fairchurch.

Pushing the sobering thought away, she knocked one more time on the door and risked a glance over her shoulder. A nanny was pushing a pram, passing the front of the duke's residence.

Poppy felt conspicuous and out of place—as though a giant sign were painted on her back that read FRAUD.

At last the door opened. The footman from yesterday stood there. Before she even had a chance to introduce herself, he ushered her inside, tsking over the dastardly cold.

Out of the chill and standing in the warm foyer, the footman did not move before the housekeeper appeared.

"I thought I heard the door. Hello there, Miss Fairchurch. How good to see you again. So sorry you had to brave this bitter cold. I hope you were able to sleep last night."

In truth, she had slept poorly and, for a change, it had little to do with Bryony's kicking. She'd slept fitfully, half awake, half conscious. Images of the duke and a speeding carriage with wild-eyed horses and lethal hooves chased her. And then there was Struan Mackenzie. His glowering face intruded, too, hovering at the edges, threatening to take over completely and shove everything else out.

"I managed to sleep," she lied. "Thank you." She nodded to the flowers. "I brought these. My employer, Mrs. Barclay, made the arrangement herself."

Mrs. Wakefield accepted the flowers. "Oh, lovely, and how thoughtful of her. I shall put them in a vase and set them in His Grace's room so that he may see them when he wakes."

Her heart sank. "He's not awake, then?"

On the way over she had been hoping, praying, for a miracle. Why not? Miracles happened every day. Why could they not happen for the duke?

The housekeeper's face settled into grim lines. "Sadly, no. No change." She nodded with sudden cheer. "Come. This way. Perhaps now that you're here he'll respond."

And that only made Poppy feel all the more wretched. There was nothing about her arrival that would bring about his swift recovery.

The duke's bedchamber door was slightly ajar. Mrs. Wakefield pushed it fully open and motioned her inside. "Have a seat and spend some time with him. The others are still abed. Not early risers as you are, Miss Fairchurch." She hesitated and took a breath. "If you forgive me for being so forward, I must say it's refreshing that the duke chose you. Speaks to the depth of his character that he can see beyond rank to the heart that lies within a woman. Trust me, there has been a great deal of pressure over the years for him to marry one lady or another. And yet he chose you."

And yet he did not choose me.

It was a rather ridiculous prospect. Something told her that if the duchess had been anyone else, anyone other than the eccentric she clearly was, she would have laughed Poppy straight out of the house yesterday.

A clatter in the distance drew Mrs. Wakefield's attention away. "The new girl has clumsy fingers," she muttered. "Best go see what she destroyed now. I vow I should never have taken her on, but she's my niece. S'pose I can't give her the sack. I'd never hear the end of it from my sister." She shook her head ruefully. "Make yourself comfortable. I will give you some time with him." She patted Poppy's shoulder. "It's right . . . for both of you."

Then she was gone, leaving Poppy standing in

the doorway and staring at the great big bed in the center of the room. It could sleep an army but only one man reclined in the center of it, as still as stone . . . much as he had been when she last saw him. He didn't look as though he had moved, but she knew he had been tended to and must have been moved at least a fraction.

Taking a breath, she crept toward the bed, her steps a hushed whisper on the carpet.

The chair she had occupied yesterday was still there, an indentation left upon its cushion from previous occupants. She sank down onto it.

"Hello," she greeted into the vacuum of the room. Silence greeted her back.

"It's me again." She winced, knowing he didn't know her. Not truly. Weekly visits to a flower shop where he purchased flowers from her hardly constituted *knowing*—never mind however much she felt that *she* knew him from those occasions. "Not certain you remember me. I'm Poppy Fairchurch."

Leaning forward, she started to touch his hand, but then pulled back. No one was here. It wasn't necessary for her to perpetuate this farce. It seemed somehow presumptive to do so.

"I know you don't know me outside of Barclay's Flowers, and this will seem wildly, well . . . *mad*, but there was some confusion the day you were hurt. As it turns out . . . well. I'm your fiancée. At least that's what your family believes."

Continued silence.

She sucked in a breath. If that wasn't enough to spring him from his false sleep nothing would.

She grimaced at the misplaced thought. He would wake. *He must.*

"I know I should have corrected the misapprehension by now, and I will. I promise. Just as soon as everyone wakes today." She moistened her lips.

More silence.

"It's just . . . well, this is rather mortifying to admit, but I've never been betrothed before." She glanced down at herself in her plain pinafore that hid only a plainer dress. Her gaze caught on the toes of her scuffed boots. "Not such a surprise." She released a pained laugh that she felt to the depths of her.

"There was a time when I came close," she admitted. "It's strange to think about that now. To consider how, if my life had taken a different turn, I could be a married woman now. Perhaps even a mother. But that's neither here nor there." She took another deep breath. Talking about this, saying the words that needed to be said even to an unconscious man, was more difficult than she expected, but now that she had started it was as though a dam had been opened. She couldn't stop. The words surged forth in a torrent. "The fact is . . . I've never been truly betrothed to anyone. *Almost* doesn't count, does it? But when I imagined myself married . . . when I imagined myself with the man of my dreams . . . he was always you." She felt the heat of her blush score her cheeks. "At least ever since I met you."

She was wringing her hands so tightly now she hardly felt them anymore. The blood had ceased to flow, but she couldn't help herself from squeezing. It was a strange echo of another time when she had sat vigil at the bedside of her father. When she wasn't holding Papa's hands or wiping his brow or forcing sips of broth or water past his lips, she had squeezed her hands to the point of numbness. As though the force of her own grip could imbue fresh life once again into her sire and bring him back to her.

Shaking off the memory, she reached for the cup of water near the bed, glad for something to do. A cloth sat beside it. She picked it up and dipped it inside. Without wringing out the fabric, she brought the wet end to his mouth and dribbled water between his lips. He wouldn't last long if he didn't have water and sustenance. Mrs. Wakefield seemed sensible and attentive, but Poppy didn't know how experienced she was with nursing the sick. She would ask if he had taken any broth. She might as well impart what knowledge she possessed. Her father had been beyond saving, but the verdict was not yet decided for the duke. Despite what the physician said, he could yet wake. As long as he didn't starve in the interim. She wasn't giving up on him.

"There you are now," she crooned approvingly. "You must think me daft. Infatuated with you when you've given me no encouragement other than treating me with kindness and respect each time you came into the shop. That can't be common for a nobleman of your rank though." She hesitated. "You always made my heart a little lighter . . . brought a little happiness into my day. For that, I'm grateful. I won't abuse your kindness. I promise to straighten this mess out soon."

After several minutes of feeding him slow sips of water, she put the cup and cloth down.

She swallowed against the sudden dryness of her throat.

The full impact of her admission sank in like a slow-sinking rock in her stomach. Even unconscious, she had just confessed her infatuation to the object of her . . . infatuation. She had never imagined such a mortifying thing occurring.

Her hands resumed their death grip. "I know it's impossible. Naturally, I understand that. Someone like you could never love someone like me. You're a duke. I'm a shopgirl. But I want you to know that I don't admire you for your rank. I would have admired you even if you were naught but a man." She gave her head a small shake. "A baker. A blacksmith. From the moment you entered Barclay's, everything about you charmed me."

More humming silence, and that only seemed to compel her to talk more, to fill the awkward quiet.

"Of course, you're handsome, but you're kind, too. The way you thoughtfully consider all of the flowers, ask questions and listen to my suggestions. I know you purchase flowers for different ladies and that you're not devoted to any one of them. Some might say you're a rake." She shrugged. "But you care enough to send flowers and you put thought into the cards you write. You extend courtesy to everyone . . . from a lowly shopgirl to the boy with barely enough coin in his pocket. Do you remember that? I do. The boy came into the shop to purchase flowers for his ailing grandmother. You told me to put the flowers on your account."

Again. Silence.

"Forgive me for blathering on. It's nice to actually talk to someone for a change . . . even if you can't talk back. You'll wake up. I don't know how

I know it, but I just do. You're strong and young and your time on this earth isn't over yet."

She sat in her chair, wrapped up in the silence of the room, gazing at the beautiful duke with a yearning in her heart that was twofold. Yes, obviously she wanted him to recover and wake up. But there was still the old selfish longing, too. For love and acceptance and companionship—somehow in her mind he had come to represent all of that to her. Despite her avowal to let go of that longing and focus on rearing her sister, that indomitable craving crept in again.

Lifting one hand, she brushed a lock of chestnut hair off his brow, unable *not* to touch him. Just this once. Just to see. To feel. The lock rebelliously bounced back into place. Oddly, she felt nothing at the contact and she frowned. No ripple of awareness. No zing along her nerves as she always imagined she would feel at first contact with him. His hair merely felt like . . . hair. Likely it would be different if he was awake and hale and inviting her touch. A sigh welled up and escaped her lips.

Suddenly a deep voice spoke. "I don't know if he's quite as admirable as all you claim, but regardless, he's fortunate to have you."

Poppy yanked her hand back from the unconscious duke with a stifled shriek, nearly losing her balance and falling from her chair. She hopped to her feet and positioned herself behind the chair, clenching her fingers along the back of it.

A man stood in the threshold, his shoulder propped against the doorjamb, arms crossed casually across his chest.

"Who are you?" she demanded. He was handsome and young and looked quite at ease in the duke's home and not the least shame-faced to be eavesdropping.

He considered her, a speculative gleam in his eyes. After a moment, he stepped forward, his lean frame closing the distance between them with easy strides. "I'm Lord Strickland." He nodded at the duke. "And I've known Marcus since we were lads in knickers."

From the fine cut of his clothing—to say nothing of the fact that he happened to be in a duke's bedchamber—she could have surmised he was a nobleman.

"O-oh," she stammered, glancing from the duke and back to Lord Strickland, wondering how much he had overheard. "Have you been standing there very long?"

"Long enough." His eyes glinted knowingly.

Oh, dear. Cold washed through her. She swallowed against her suddenly thickening throat. "I c-can explain." She held up a hand in supplication.

"I think you did. When you were talking to Autenberry. Quite the enlightening conversation even if very one-sided." He frowned slightly and looked down at his friend, the concern he felt for him evident in his eyes.

She dragged in a heavy breath. There was no doubt now. He knew. He knew everything. "I'm going to tell everyone . . . the dowager, his sisters, just as soon as they—"

"No. Don't do that."

"What?" She blinked. "You don't want me to tell the truth? Why not?"

Lord Strickland nodded slowly, still staring at Autenberry. "It will only upset them. Last night when I called upon them they spoke so highly of you. You were their one bright light in an otherwise dark day. Don't take that from them. Not now." He lifted his gaze to her again. "And I liked what you were saying. It was honest."

Except she was lying to everyone else. She shook her head. "But that's what I'm trying to be . . . honest."

"Time enough for that later. When Marcus wakes." His gaze crawled over her face, assessing. "The dowager already speaks of you with such affection." He looked to the duke again, then back to her, his gaze turning speculative.

"I—I . . ." Would she never cease to stammer?

"I'm beginning to see why." Nodding, he continued his scrutiny of her. "I think you might be just what this family needs. You're very kind and guileless."

She winced at that description. She did not feel very guileless.

"Why not?" he continued with a shrug.

"Why not *what*?"

"You and Marcus. Why not? He needs someone." He scoffed a little. "Desperately. Even if he doesn't realize it, he has needed someone with a good heart for a while now."

Was he jesting with her? She stifled a snort and shook her head. He could not think she might be a legitimate match for the duke. He was a *duke*! She was merely . . . Poppy Fairchurch.

"I'm sorry, my lord. You're not making any sense. I should go now."

He held up both hands. "Don't let me scare you away. That was not my intention."

"I need to go now, my lord." She tried to move around the chair, giving him a wide berth. He stepped closer. It was going to be hard to bypass him in any direction without being within arm's reach of him. Given as she was questioning his sanity, it seemed like a good idea to stay out of his range.

"You were all they talked about. Well, aside of their fears for Marcus, of course."

She nodded. "Of course."

"Even Enid had nice things to say about you, and she can be rather taciturn. You gave them something else to focus on besides their fear. They were so thrilled that Marcus finally decided to wed . . . and to such a nice girl."

She winced. "And yet you said nothing? As his friend you had to know he was not engaged to anyone."

He shrugged. "I didn't say anything because I didn't want to upset them further. And I wanted to meet you first. See this 'nice' girl for myself."

She dropped her head guiltily. "I'm a fraud."

"Yes, you are," he agreed. "But you're quite the loveliest person I've ever met and you saved his life." He motioned to the bed with an elegant wave of his hand. "And everything that I overheard you say?" Her face warmed at the reminder. "You're so sweet you make my teeth ache."

Her gaze flew back up to his. "I beg your pardon, my lord?"

He nodded his head once decisively. "We shall not utter a word to the family. You will be whom they believe you to be."

"I—I cannot do that!"

"It brings them some measure of happiness and right now they deserve that. I love this family. The dowager is . . . she's a rare gem." He rubbed at the back of his neck. "Generous and accepting to a fault. Autenberry often criticizes her for that, but then he can carry the role of arrogant noble a bit too far. Not his fault, I suppose. The old duke raised him to be that way." Dropping his hand from his neck, his stare fixed intently on her face. "I'll not have them hurt. Understood?" For a moment the soft friendliness of his gaze hardened, and she saw a glimpse of an entitled nobleman accustomed to getting his way. "If Marcus—" he caught himself and amended "—*when* he wakes, this can be sorted out. No one will care then as they'll be so overjoyed that he is alive and well. If he doesn't wake . . ." His voice faded. "Well. Then your little subterfuge won't matter."

"He *will* wake."

He stared at her for a long moment. "I don't know why, but I believe you. Despite what the physician says. Foolish, perhaps, but I do."

"You have to believe it." Somehow, in her mind, his recovery was linked to this—to the fact that none of them gave up on him.

"Now." He clapped his hands lightly and rubbed them briskly. "We're in accord. No disappointing the dowager or the others with unwanted confessions?"

It was perplexing to think that the truth could cause more harm than good. "Very well," she agreed. "When His Grace awakes we shall confess everything."

He beamed. "Very good, Miss Fairchurch. You'll see. This will be for the best."

"What of the duke's brother?" The man was never far from her thoughts. "He doesn't believe me. He practically said as much to my face."

"Mackenzie?" He chuckled lightly. "No, he wouldn't. He's one surly scoundrel."

"He doesn't like me."

Lord Strickland chuckled even harder at that. "Don't take it to heart. I'm not sure the man likes anyone. He doesn't seek the good in people. It's not in his temperament to do so, and I suppose with his upbringing, or lack thereof, it should not be expected of him."

As intrigued as she was at the reference to Struan Mackenzie's upbringing, she resisted inquiring more about him. She shouldn't *want* to know more about him. Her only thought should be for the duke.

"He's a wretch." If her words sounded sulky, she hoped Lord Strickland would not notice. She crossed her arms over her chest in a huff. "Did you know Mr. Mackenzie was fighting with His Grace before the accident? They were brawling in the streets like a pair of ruffians." She deliberately failed to mention that Autenberry had thrown the first punch.

Lord Strickland shook his head. "Well, to be fair, Marcus has been obstinate when it comes to his half brother. He hasn't exactly thrown open his arms in brotherly love and acceptance."

She sniffed, not to be dissuaded in her dislike of the man. She would *not* feel sorry for the wretch. "Have you *met* Struan Mackenzie? I'm certain he deserves some of Marcus's aversion. I've not met a more unpleasant individual in all my days—"

"Fret not, Miss Fairchurch. I'll handle him."

She chafed her hands up and down her arms, feeling unaccountably cold and not the least reassured. She somehow doubted the agreeable Lord Strickland would be able to discourage the offensive lout from sneering at her and proclaiming her a liar. She'd rather stick pins in her eyes than endure another confrontation with him.

If she was to maintain this farce, another encounter with Struan Mackenzie seemed probable.

But endure it she would.

Chapter 9

*H*e couldn't sleep.

Struan told himself it was not because he was worried about a brother who didn't want him, a brother who would just as soon plant his fist in his face than greet him on the streets of London. He told himself it was not because of the words some prickly shopgirl had flung at him, blaming him for Autenberry lying unconscious on his bed.

It was neither of those reasons. Neither one should matter to him. Neither reason should prompt him to rise and dress. They shouldn't guide him from his bedchamber in the middle of the night and out of the comfort of his house and across town to Mayfair.

He'd avoided paying a call throughout the

day, but somehow with the fall of night, without the business of day to blind and distract him, he couldn't stay away.

Standing in front of Autenberry's town house, he paused, burrowing his hands into his pockets. It was cold but he was accustomed to that. He'd spent many a winter night sleeping in a Glasgow alleyway after his mother died. He knew cold. And pain. And suffering.

Why are you even here? Don't you have anything better to do than go to places where you are not wanted?

The answer smacked him solidly in the face as a sleepy-eyed groom granted him admittance and led him upstairs—the dowager's warm reception of him earlier guaranteed his ready admission into the house. His father had never claimed him. Nor had his brother. And yet the Dowager Duchess of Autenberry treated him like the prodigal son returned.

The groom left him and he stood just inside the opulent bedchamber, gazing across the stretch of space to the still and silent figure in the bed. Apparently no. He did not have anything better to do. That was the only explanation he could give himself as he stood inside his half brother's bedchamber.

Miss Fairchild's accusing eyes flashed in his mind. Damn her. Was she correct? Could he have said or done something differently? Something that wouldn't have prompted his brother into attacking him on the streets and ultimately ending up in the path of that coach?

He moved closer, stopping at the foot of the colossal bed. His brother was only a year older, but staring down at his pale and relaxed features, he looked far younger.

Marcus had everything Struan never had. A roof over his head—*roofs*. All the food he wanted. Servants. More clothes than he could ever possibly wear. And their father. More precisely, the love of their father.

He glanced around the elegant chamber before his gaze returned to the sleeping duke. He had the life he'd desperately craved as a boy.

Struan's mother had filled his ears with fanciful stories of the life that awaited him when his father came to claim him. It had taken him years to realize that would never happen. Ignorance would have been far sweeter than the truth. His father could have eased their suffering and saved his mother from an early grave, but the bastard hadn't lifted a finger for either one of them.

Unfortunately, he couldn't unlearn that knowledge. Or erase the memories of going to bed with an aching belly, his body sore from a beating he'd endured on the streets. The world was full of predators and he'd had to fight his way from becoming their prey.

He crossed his arms, gazing at the face so similar to his own. Autenberry might never wake. Maybe he had wanted this on some deep level? No. He wasn't that broken that he wanted his brother dead.

Her voice whispered through him. *You didn't have to strike him back.*

True, he'd spent his entire life never backing down, never giving up an inch, but would it have been so impossible to simply take the hit and walk away? Could he have not found that strength of will within him to turn his cheek?

Gazing at his brother who looked pale and vulnerable in the bed, resentment still bubbled beneath the surface like acid. He couldn't deny that it had felt damn good to crush his knuckles into his brother's face.

He moved away from the bed, not particularly liking himself right then. He sank into a chair in the corner in the room, buried deep in shadows where he could watch his half brother.

Sighing, he dragged a hand over his jaw, waiting, watching, searching for some flicker of movement. Something that signified the bastard wasn't dead. That *she* wasn't right about him, that the way she looked at him, like he was some bit of filth beneath her shoe, wasn't justified.

SHE COULDN'T SLEEP.

Her thoughts churned. Halfway across Town the duke slumbered in a fairy-tale-like sleep and there was no magical kiss that would wake him. And even if a kiss could wake him it would not be from her—contrary to the fact that his family thought she was the love of his life. She cringed and buried her face in her hands. How on earth had she let Lord Strickland persuade her into continuing this farce?

Perhaps because you want it to be real.

It felt good to be wanted, and the duke's family made her feel wanted—excluding Struan Mackenzie, of course. But she hadn't had to see him this morning. No, she and Lord Strickland had been joined by the rest of the duke's family, all of whom had insisted she take breakfast with them before returning to the flower shop. They had been warm and lovely, plying her with sticky buns and kippers and the most delicious chocolate she had ever consumed. It slid like ambrosia down her throat. In addition to the wonderful fare, they had been genuinely interested in her—asking questions about her life that made her feel human again and not simply a machine that functioned day to day, eking out an existence to keep both she and her sister one step out of the gutter.

Light from the grate cast dancing shadows over the walls and ceiling of their small chamber. The smell of wet leather drifted to her nose. It had rained earlier in the day and she'd been caught out in the deluge on her way home from Barclay's. Her boots sat near the grate in the hopes that they would dry by morning.

She rolled onto her side with a soft groan. She couldn't stop wondering if they were giving the duke enough water and broth. Perhaps she had been too soft with Mrs. Wakefield when she stressed that he needed proper sustenance through his convalescence.

Foolish, she knew. Loved ones and a houseful of servants surrounded him. He didn't need her. Even if his family believed they were affianced, the best thing she could do was keep her distance.

She told herself that for several moments, her laced fingers thrumming over her chest. He was fine. There was nothing she could do. Her presence wouldn't help him.

Her fingers thrummed faster.

Blast!

She wasn't going to fall asleep. Giving up, she rose. Flinging back the covers, she left her warm bed where her sister tossed and turned, encroaching onto Poppy's side of the bed.

She slipped on her garments, dressing warmly for the bitter night. After checking her boots and finding them still damp, she slipped into her sister's boots. They were only slightly too large, but they would suffice.

With one last glimpse at her sister asleep in the bed, her arms flung above her head and lost in all her lovely auburn hair, Poppy departed the room, closing the door gently behind her. Not that her sister was a light sleeper. It took an avalanche to wake her in the mornings.

The light in Mrs. Gibbons's downstairs parlor glowed onto the hall floor. She paused outside the cracked double doors, glimpsing the widow inside, sitting before the fire with her knitting.

"Mrs. Gibbons? I'm going out for a bit," she said as she wrapped her wool kerchief around her throat. "Bryony is asleep. I doubt she will awake."

Mrs. Gibbons slid her spectacles up the bridge of her nose. "Is anything amiss?" She glanced to the mantel clock. "The hour is late to venture out."

"No, nothing amiss. Just something I forgot to do that needs to be done before the morning." She deliberately let her words imply that it was a work-related task. In no way would she explain what she was really about at this late an hour. She wasn't certain she even could. She could scarcely explain it to herself. To explain what she was about, she'd have to disclose her deception.

Mrs. Gibbons pursed her lips disapprovingly as she observed her. Poppy pulled her cloak around her shoulders. It had belonged to her mother. Once the height of fashion, it was trimmed with ermine and lined in velvet. She could almost imagine Mama wearing it before she turned her back on her family and married Papa.

"Go if you must, but be careful." Mrs. Gibbons tsked with displeasure.

Poppy's lips twitched in amusement. She, of course, did not point out that she did not require Mrs. Gibbons's permission. Mrs. Gibbons had adopted a maternal role not just with Bryony. It was rather nice. Except when it wasn't. As in right now when the woman fixed her gimlet stare on Poppy.

"I'll be careful," she promised.

"All manner of riffraff turn up at night," she called as Poppy made her way through the small foyer. "Mrs. Huxley down the street said some beggars accosted her last week. Tried to filch the bread right out of her basket. Don't know what the world is coming to when good God-fearing women can't walk the streets—"

"I'll be cautious," Poppy called behind her, burrowing into her cloak as she stepped out into the night.

Her borrowed boots rang out over the air, clicking over the cobbled walk as she walked a steady line, doing her best to ignore the sliding of her heels inside Bryony's shoes. The streets weren't completely deserted. A steady flow of carriages passed and she surmised that the theater located a half dozen blocks away had let out for the night.

It wasn't a short walk, but she didn't relish using her precious earnings on the price of a hack. Even at this late hour. Even with boots that didn't quite fit. Even in the cold.

For some reason, Struan Mackenzie's glowering face rose up in her mind. She knew the arrogant man wouldn't approve and at that thought she reminded herself that his approval didn't matter. He was a boorish brute, and she had been taking care of herself long before she met him. So what that he escorted her home yesterday. That didn't make him a gentleman. Nor did it mean that she should care for his good opinion.

She sniffed against the cold wind and reminded herself that she didn't mind walking. When she lived at Toadston-on-Mersey, she spent many hours walking the countryside. At least before her father fell ill. It had been one of her favorite pastimes.

Upon reaching the duke's residence, she knocked tentatively at the door, hoping she didn't wake the entire household. It was opened quickly by the footman standing sentry in the foyer.

She opened her mouth, ready with an explanation as to why she was here so late, but his stern expression lightened the moment he saw her. He apparently remembered her from her previous visits. "Miss Fairchurch. All the family is abed. Mrs. Wakefield, too. Is there anything amiss? Anything I can assist you with?"

"No, nothing to fret over." She shifted uneasily on her feet. "It's only that I couldn't sleep. Would it be possible for me to sit with the duke for a bit? I won't disturb anyone." It still felt odd to suggest such a thing even though no one had questioned her presence on her prior calls. Indeed, it even seemed expected that she call on him.

The man nodded kindly. "I understand. You must be beside yourself with heartsick." He clucked sympathetically. *Because he believed her to be Autenberry's fiancée. Because he believed she had a right to be here.* "Of course, come in. I'm certain His Grace would like that." He motioned her inside. She stepped into the foyer and removed her cloak, passing them into his waiting hands.

"This way." Turning, he started escorting her.

She stopped him with a hand on his arm. "I know the way. No need to trouble yourself."

"Are you certain? It is no trouble—"

"Stay at your post," she assured.

He inclined his head in a slow nod. "Very well. I'll be here if you need anything."

With a parting smile of thanks, she hastened up to the second floor.

The door was ajar as before. She moved into the room with less hesitation than this morning, more comfortable in her surroundings and in the knowledge that the family was asleep and would not happen upon her here. She would not have to continue the charade for their sake. At least not tonight.

She stopped at the side of the bed, peering down at him.

His color looked a little better. He wore a different nightshirt and the sight made her feel slightly better—and silly. Of course he was being well cared for. He didn't need her looking after him.

"Hello, again," she murmured as she sank down in the chair. "Sorry to call on you so late. I couldn't sleep."

Her fingers played in the folds of her skirts for a moment before she lifted an arm and covered his motionless hand with her own. She hissed at the chill of his skin.

"You look better," she murmured, chafing his hand under her own, trying to warm the skin.

Her gaze traveled his face, traveling the well-memorized lines. If she was a decent artist, she would attempt to immortalize him on canvas. She wouldn't do him justice if she attempted the task with her less than notable talents.

His hand was starting to feel warmer. She turned her attention to his other one. "It will be Christmas soon," she said, her voice ringing cheerfully. In her head, she heard Mrs. Wakefield's voice encouraging her to talk to him. "Perhaps you'll be awake before then and can celebrate the holiday with your family."

A voice spoke into the thick silence. "You really think so?"

With a gasp, she spun around, her gaze flying to the doorway, half expecting to see Lord Strickland there again, even though something deep and primal struck her at the core as that voice rippled over the air.

The doorway was empty. She twisted in her chair, searching the room, her gaze landing on a person sitting in a shadowed corner, his big frame dwarfing a wingback chair, booted feet stretched out into the fall of light.

Her gaze traveled up those boots and legs. Big

hands clasped the chair arms as the body leaned forward, bringing a face out of the shadows.

"You," she croaked, and just like that her stomach dropped to her too-big shoes. Of all the faces she wanted to see, Struan Mackenzie's was the last, and yet there he sat, looking at her with equal displeasure and sending her heart into palpitations.

"In the flesh," he returned, his gravelly voice sending a rush of goose bumps over her flesh. Suddenly, she was acutely, achingly aware of how alone they were. It was just the three of them. Her lips twisted wryly.

Considering one of them was in a coma, it was more accurately the two of them.

Chapter 10

"Miss Fairchurch," Struan greeted stiffly. In fact, all of him was as rigid as a board sitting in the chair, watching her from his corner. The only movement was the tapping of his fingers against his thigh.

From the moment she had entered and taken position at Autenberry's bedside, tension thrummed through him, vibrating along every nerve. He felt his lip curl as he observed her decidedly one-sided exchange with his half brother. It was sweet and endearing and he despised it. He despised her.

No, that wasn't true.

He felt something other than dislike for her. That much he couldn't deny. There was an irrefutable stirring in his cock as his gaze fixed on the fine arch of her throat, the soft wisps of light brown hair that grazed the soft skin at the back of her neck. Unbelievable. His bouncing fingers increased their ticking, picking up speed. It was a definite first. Never had a woman's nape managed to arouse him.

He shouldn't have felt anything at the display. Truthfully, he had no stake in either one of them. Not his brother. Certainly not her. And yet the sight of her bent so dotingly over Autenberry, chafing his hands as though she could will life back into him, stabbed him with annoyance.

He wanted to cross the room and pull her from her position at his brother's bedside. He wanted to run his hand down that throat, force her around and press his open mouth to the back of her neck and sink his teeth there in a primitive display of dominance.

He sucked in a sharp breath and tried to shake off the unwanted image, willing his hardening cock to slumber.

To say that his train of thinking would scandalize her would be an understatement. Even as Autenberry's paramour, she couldn't be accustomed to proclivities such as his. He was no gentle lover. Born of the streets, his tastes ran to rougher bed sport than was common among blushing, milk-skinned females.

He chose his partners carefully, and with reason. No tender misses for him. Experienced women he didn't have to seduce or ply with gentle words. That was usually his preference.

Usually.

"You should have alerted me to your presence." Her soft voice was full of accusation.

Aye, he should have, but he'd held silent, watching. He did not bring himself to speak, hoping to learn something of her that she would not willingly reveal.

"And miss any potential bedside declarations?" he mocked, finally reclaiming his voice.

Her features tightened.

"Don't fash yourself, lass," he assured. "You didn't say anything inflammatory. More's the pity. In fact, I was quite bored sitting here." The lie tripped easily off his tongue. He preferred boredom to watching her moon over Autenberry. If he had to endure any more of that he might put a fist into a wall. He scowled, telling himself what she did and said—with Autenberry or any man— shouldn't affect him.

"What were you expecting?" she demanded.

"Oh, I don't know, kitten. A titillating profession of love. Some naughty reminisces of sweeter times?"

Her shoulders squared. "You're perverse."

Again, he felt his lips threaten to break out in a smile. She had no idea what he was, but he imagined the truth would horrify her.

"I've been called worse things than that, kitten." Although usually not by the fairer sex. Even before he'd amassed his wealth, females had always favored him. His mother called it the one blessing Providence had seen fit to bestow on him. *Yer face has been touched by angels, lad. Don't let such a thing go to waste.*

"Don't call me *that*." She hissed the last word as though it were something dirty.

"What?" he asked, all innocence, enjoying the flash of fire in her cheeks and imagining what other activities might produce that same fire in her.

"You know . . . *kitten*!"

He pushed to his feet and strode toward her, his pace unhurried. "Oh, you don't like that? That's what you remind me of. Soft and small with big eyes and tiny sharp teeth and claws. Just like a kitten."

"It's much too intimate, sir," she reprimanded, those tiny teeth and claws at work as she glared at him.

He stopped a few feet from her. She remained sitting, her hand pushing against the chair back but not moving as she looked up at him. "And what does your duke call you?" He nodded to the bed. "Miss *Fairchurch*?" He could not stop the sneer from curling his lips. He knew his half brother's proclivities. They were all the gossip. He did not maintain *platonic* relationships. He doubted his brother called her *Miss Fairchurch* as he plowed between her thighs.

That image settled like boiling acid in his stomach. He did not like it. He did not *want* it. He banished it from his head.

Still, he could not deny the truth of it. If this girl was tangled up with Autenberry, their relationship was definitely in the realm of *intimate*. She needn't act so prudish or pretend with him. He knew what Autenberry was.

Consequently, he knew what she was. She was low-hanging fruit, ready to be plucked. So why shouldn't Struan be the next man to pluck her?

At the mere idea, his blood rushed south, straight for his cock.

"That's none of your business," she snapped in answer to his question.

Even in the dimness of the firelit room, he marked the deepening rush of color to her face. "Come now. Does he call you by your Christian name? Or some endearment?"

She released a huff of breath. "You are the only one so bold as to use a nickname."

"Am I?" The idea pleased him somehow . . .

even though it ought not to. He wanted to be different. He wanted to make his mark on her.

"Your brother is far too circumspect for that."

At that, he chuckled. "Autenberry? Circumspect? That is one adjective I've never heard applied to him." Arrogant. Boorish. Smug bastard.

"Perhaps you don't know him," she challenged.

"Perhaps you don't," he returned.

Especially if she believed his half brother would actually marry her—a lowly working class girl. Never in this lifetime would he do that. Autenberry was too much of a snob. He was a product of his father and his class.

Struan would be doing her a favor if he convinced her of that. If, by the time Autenberry woke up, she was no longer enamored of him, then all the better. She wouldn't be crushed when he gave her the boot.

"That is quite enough, sir." She shot a quick glance to the door. "It isn't seemly for us to be alone in here at this late hour. You should go."

He glanced at Autenberry, scratching his chin as though in deep contemplation and ignoring her demand. "He doesn't strike me as a deep thinker." Of all the things he'd heard about his brother, no one ever called him clever. "I'd wager he calls you something unoriginal. Is it 'darling'? Or 'sweetheart'?"

She stood abruptly, her face still hot with color. Initially, he thought her unremarkable in looks, but now he could see her appeal. She was comely with her ire up. He imagined it would be the same effect in bed—her eyes bright, cheeks flushed, mouth parted with arousing gasps. His cock hardened anew.

"If you won't leave, then I shall," she huffed.

He stepped sideways, blocking her retreat. For a moment they brushed, her softness colliding with his body. He heard her breath catch . . . felt his own breathing stop and hold. She need only glance down to see the evidence of his arousal . . . here beside his coma-stricken brother. Then she would really think him perverse.

To little surprise, she took a hasty step back, as though fearful of their contact.

"We're practically family," he said. "No need to rush away."

Her expression turned almost comical. She looked as though she just bit into a tart apple. Her nose wrinkled and her lips worked. "Family? You? And me?" She glanced again to where the duke slept. "That status is built on the fact that you and His Grace are in actuality family." She laughed a touch sharply. "From all accounts, your relationship is strained."

True, and the reminder of how precisely unbrotherly their relationship was stung as it shouldn't.

"Oh? Listening to gossip, Miss Fairchurch?" A sinister thread wove through his voice. "Who has been filling your ears? The staff?"

"I witnessed proof enough of that with my own eyes."

He shrugged. "A mere spat. Not uncommon among family."

"Not *my* family." Bryony might make Poppy want to pull her hair out at times, but she loved her sister and she had no doubt that her sister loved her back. They would never strike each other.

"Then you've led a sheltered existence."

She narrowed her gaze at his mocking tone and crossed her arms. "Why are you even here, Mr. Mackenzie?" She paused and flicked a glance to the duke's bed. "You aren't feeling guilty, are you?"

"Guilty?" He started. Of all things he thought she might say it wasn't that. "For what?"

"For your role in all of this." She waved toward where his brother slept.

There it was again, that prick of something in his chest—a tight, twisting pinch. She was closer to the truth than he liked to acknowledge.

"*My* role? And what of your role?"

Her eyes flared at the charge and her voice escaped in a sharp squeak. "Me?"

"Yes. You." He took another step forward and she backed away one to match. He followed with another. "You were the one that shoved him out of the way, after all."

Her breath escaped in a hot rush. "Out of the way of a charging carriage, you mean!"

"Yes, but if you hadn't attacked me, I would have been there in the street with Autenberry. I could have pulled him safely away without knocking him to the ground . . . where he then struck his head."

Her mouth parted, lips trembling as she stared at him, as though trying to understand what she was seeing . . . what he was saying.

And suddenly he felt like the biggest bastard. It wasn't her fault. He knew that. He simply didn't like her placing the blame on him so he flung it back on her. And let's face it. Everything in him bristled around her with the need to lash out. He couldn't stop himself. It was primal in nature. Almost the same as his urge to grab her and pin her beneath him. To unwrap the camouflage of her pinafore and see just what she hid beneath the trappings of her garments.

She at last recovered her voice. "By that logic, *sir*, you could also blame yourself for starting the fight that put you both in the street."

An angry breath huffed out of him. "For the

last time, I did *not* start that bloody fight, as you well know. You saw it begin."

"Since when are you so concerned with the truth?" She waved to the bed, her bright eyes snapping with emotion. "According to you, I'm responsible for putting him in that bed, remember?" Her chin went up. "You made it abundantly clear that I'm culpable. If he dies, it's on me, you . . ." Her lips worked, searching for a foul enough epithet. She arrived at, "Beast!"

Before he could form a reply, she dodged past him and fled the room.

He stood there for a full minute before releasing a foul curse and giving chase, not about to let her have the last word—and not about to let her leave here with that bit of guilt hanging over her head. Never mind that he had been the individual to plant it in her head to begin with. For some reason, the notion of her in any kind of anguish was unacceptable.

Chapter 11

*H*e was horrible. An absolute wretch! How could he possibly even be related to the honorable Duke of Autenberry? It didn't seem possible that they shared any bloodline at all. There wasn't a scrap of decency to him.

She'd been battling her own demons, questioning if she had really saved the duke when she pushed him out of the carriage's path. Her efforts had only caused him damage, after all. And then Struan Mackenzie had come along and only confirmed her suspicions.

How dare he so accurately pinpoint and give voice to her most private fears?

How dare he take no responsibility for his part in all of this?

How dare she *care* so blasted much what he thought?

She scarcely uttered a farewell word for the footman as she stalked out into the wintry night, wrapping herself more fully inside her cloak. Nonsensical mutterings fell from her lips as her boots bit into the walk.

She walked at a clipped pace beneath the gaslight cast from the sconces at the gates of Mayfair mansions, her anger notching higher and higher with every stride she took.

Gradually, she left Mayfair behind and her surroundings altered to darkened shop fronts closed up for the night. Her steps rang out, echoing on the air as she made her way home.

Eventually, she became aware of steps thudding behind her. Her heart quickened and she shot a quick glance over her shoulder, marking a figure in the distance following her. She quickened her pace and it seemed that the person followed suit. Mrs. Gibbons's words drifted back to haunt her. Could it be a ruffian looking to filch her purse?

Her racing heart steadied at the sight of a small group of people walking across the street. It was comforting to see she wasn't entirely alone out in the night. She need only shout out for help if necessary. She darted one more glance behind her.

The person behind her was much closer now

and passing directly under a streetlamp. She had no difficulty identifying the familiar features of Struan Mackenzie.

That fine edge of alarm she first felt when she heard the footsteps tapered into annoyance. She should have known he would follow her. He was persistent that way. Her gaze darted across the street again. The trio of people rounded a corner, leaving both she and Struan Mackenzie alone on the shadowy, fog-shrouded streets.

She stopped and spun around, propping her fists on her hips. "Why are you following me?"

"You shouldn't be walking out here this late alone." His voice drew closer as he advanced.

"Leave me alone or I'll call for the Watch," she threatened, feeling full of dramatic flair and a bit like her sister in that moment. Especially considering she didn't see evidence of a watchman—or anyone, for that matter. Now that the people had rounded the street it felt as though she and Struan Mackenzie were the only two people left in the world. It was rather eerie. A call for help would likely go unheeded, swallowed up in the viscous night.

Feeling slightly threatened at that realization, she turned and hastened on her way. Not that she thought he would physically harm her, but there were other ways to do damage and she was quite positive Struan Mackenzie could easily, effortlessly, damage her.

His voice followed, hard and fast. And much too close. "Look around you. Do you see any solitary ladies strolling about?" She stubbornly stared ahead and increased her pace. The sooner she reached home, the sooner she would be rid of him. "Come back to the house and we'll take my coach. I'll see you home."

"No. Thank you."

"Stubborn chit—"

She whirled around. "I'd appreciate it if you did not call me names simply because I won't let you order me around. Such intimidation won't work with me."

Mackenzie slid a step closer and she managed to hold her ground. "Perhaps you require being ordered around."

"By you?" she scoffed. "I managed twenty years without you in my life—" Her indignant speech died away as two dark shapes stepped out of the alley bisecting the street directly behind Mackenzie.

"Well, what 'ave we here? A toff and 'is lady?"

Mackenzie turned slowly to face the strangers while placing a hand on her hip and shoving her behind him. In that moment, she didn't even mind that hand curled around her hip. Not the bold intimacy of it. Not how very large his palm and splayed fingers felt against her. All sense of propriety flew to the winds as the air thinned to something that felt cold and clammy on her skin. In this instance, his touch offered solace.

Standing on tiptoes, she peered around Mackenzie's great body to scrutinize the men. Suddenly all of Mrs. Gibbons's warnings flooded back and she tasted coppery fear in her mouth. She hated that the woman was correct.

"Good eve, gov'nor. Why don't you 'and over your purse and anything of value and we won't 'urt you or the lady."

Poppy blinked. It was harder to remember to breathe, however. Her chest squeezed.

Mackenzie appeared, however, to have no problem functioning. He reached into his coat and pulled out his pocketbook. With a flick of his wrist, he handed it over. No hesitation. No comment. No objection.

"Just like that? You're giving it to them?" The question squeaked past her lips before she could consider the wisdom of it.

She expected him to offer some modicum of resistance. A great big man like him? She thought he might at least *appear* menacing.

One of the men laughed and elbowed his partner. "Got a feisty one 'ere. More mettle than the big lad." He chuckled. "She 'as a point. Perhaps we should be calling the big lad a lass."

Mackenzie showed no outward reaction at the insult to his manhood.

The other scoundrel nodded, his narrow face reflecting none of his friend's amusement. The thin, gaunt lines of his features made him appear practically cadaverous in the murky night. "What else you got? Besides that pocketbook?" His turned his gaze to Poppy and gave her a slow once-over.

Her chin lifted. "I haven't any money."

She felt his gaze continue to scan her in the feeble light of the streetlamps. "What's that there on your finger? A ring? I'll 'ave it."

She immediately covered her mother's wedding ring as if she could erase the memory of it. It was a simple silver band, etched with her parents' initials. Aside of her memories, it was all she had left of her mother. She shook her head vehemently. "No."

"It's not worth the fight. Give it over," Mackenzie growled without turning to face her.

"It's worth it to me," she argued, clutching her hand tighter, glaring at the back of him. "I'm not giving it up." She turned her glare to the pair of villains with their avid, feral eyes. "It's not even gold. Worth nothing—"

"Then give it over," Mackenzie bit out.

"It's sentimental," she argued. Blast him! Whose side was he on?

"Very sweet," Cadaver-face uttered, stretching out his arm and flicking his long fingers impatiently. "Now give it to me before I 'ave to take it from you myself. You don't want me to do that, poppet. Trust me there. You might find me taking something else for me troubles."

Mackenzie turned his face to the side and addressed her through lips that barely moved. "Damn it all. Give over the ring and hold your tongue, girl."

She puffed out an angry breath of outrage. No one spoke to her like that. Not even her father used that tone with her. "Just because you're willing to roll over and play coward does not mean I am!"

With a curse, he turned and grabbed her hand.

"What are you—" she sputtered as Mackenzie seized her finger and worked the ring up the digit. It caught at her knuckle. Still sputtering, she tried to yank her hand away, but his grip was like iron. He twisted the band until it finally slid free.

"How dare you!" she screeched, punching his arm several times. His bicep felt like a slab of solid meat. Impenetrable to her puny blows. She wondered if he even felt her. "You're as bad as they are!"

He ignored her and faced the ruffians, tossing the ring up in the air. Cadaver-face caught it neatly in his hand and her heart sank, dropping to her feet.

He faced the men again. "You've got what you want. Now go," he said as though he had not just handed over a keepsake that meant so much to her. As though he had not cut out a very important piece of her heart. She blinked burning eyes. Her thumb swept over the back of her finger, marveling at how it suddenly felt so strange and bare there, like the slick, smooth skin of a scar.

She couldn't help herself. She made a sound of disgust and crossed her arms. For all his air of menace and brawn, Struan Mackenzie was about as imposing as an iced biscuit.

Cadaver-face pocketed the ring and stepped to the side with all the idleness of a man strolling the park. He peered at her where she stood with her arms crossed. "Never would 'ave expected a small package to possess such fire. I like 'er. What about you, Cam? What do you think?"

Her crushing disappointment over losing her ring flowed into something else, something razor-sharp and icy as her gaze darted between the two men. She felt like a hare facing down a pair of hounds. Mackenzie already proved he would offer nothing in the way of protection. She had only herself to rely upon.

"Well, if you like 'er." Cam lifted an arm,

stretching past Mackenzie to touch her shoulder lightly. "Maybe the big chap won't mind if—"

Mackenzie's hand sliced through the air with stunning swiftness and wrenched Cam's hand from her. "You have my money and the ring. Take them and go."

Cadaver-face moved with a swiftness that matched Mackenzie's. He brought a blade up, waving it before Mackenzie's face.

She gasped, but Mackenzie didn't even flinch. His big body didn't move. Nor did his hand loosen from Cam.

Mackenzie stood as still as a column of stone, hard and immobile, only his voice rippling over the air like a warm current. "I won't warn you again."

Cam snickered at the whispered threat, clearly not worried. "If I were you, I'd lift your 'and off me before Kenny here decides to use that there knife and—"

Mackenzie moved in a blinding flash.

She didn't think someone of his size could move with such speed. In a maneuver she couldn't even process, he disarmed Kenny, seizing the knife from him and bringing it down in an arc and driving it into Cam's arm.

There was a moment of absolute stunned silence.

Poppy froze, gaping. Then Cam started screaming, registering the pain of the knife embedded in his arm.

"Oh?" Mackenzie queried in that deep brogue of his, his manner eerily mild. "Hurts, does it? Aye, I've been stabbed before." He blinked with mocking innocence. "Would you like me to remove this wee blade from your arm, then?"

Cam nodded and started pleading and blubbering amid his sobs.

Kenny made a move as though to do it for him, but Mackenzie waved him away and turned the hilt of the blade, twisting and digging it deeper into his cohort's arm, producing a fresh wave of sobs. Kenny watched, frozen and wearing an expression of mingled fear and dismay.

"Mackenzie," she murmured, not sure what she was asking. She only knew she didn't like the situation. The tinny smell of blood in the night air. The violence. The fear. Hers or theirs, she wasn't even certain anymore.

Mackenzie looked at her beneath hooded eyes and her heart tripped. He looked like some fierce Viking with his glittering eyes and hard expression. "Yes, kitten?"

"Please." She shook her head, unsure what she wanted to say. What she wanted him to do. He held her gaze and the pulse at her neck continued its wild tempo, threatening to break free of her skin.

She only knew that she had misjudged him. This man was no coward. She wasn't certain what he was, but he was not that.

Mackenzie grunted and looked away from her. He reached inside Cam's pocket and fished about until he pulled out her ring. He brandished it in the air between thumb and forefinger, offering it to her.

She hesitated only a moment before snatching it from him with a happy cry and slipping it back on her finger. "Thank you."

He gave her another one of those enigmatic looks and turned his attention back to the would-be thieves. "I'll take my pocketbook back, too."

Kenny hesitated and Cam shouted at him, panting and perspiring now, his face in a perpetual grimace as he suffered the blade in his arm. "Gor, give the man what 'e wants!"

Kenny fumbled for the purse and practically threw it in their direction. Mackenzie caught it nimbly and slid it back inside his jacket. Without removing his gaze from the pair of thugs, he slid the knife from Cam's arm like it was nothing to him. A task he did all the time. Plucking a flower from a vase.

Cam collapsed against his friend, clutching his arm and gasping.

Mackenzie's deep brogue rolled over the air. "Now you two disappear before I call the Watch. And don't let me ever see your faces again."

Their heads bobbed. "Y-yes, guv'nor. Apologies to you and yer lady." They shuffled away, eyeing Mackenzie as though he might change his mind and spring at them.

Poppy watched them flee down the alley where the shadows were the deepest. They turned at the far end until they were out of sight. Only then did she realize her mouth sagged open. She closed it with a snap and swung her gaze back to Mackenzie. She'd been wrong about him. She shook her head slightly, still perplexed. He'd simply been restraining himself the entire time.

His fingers lightly brushed her elbow. "Are you well? I don't need to fetch the smelling salts, do I?"

She inhaled and that only made her head spin with the scent of him. She hadn't noticed it before. Masculine and woodsy. How he smelled woodsy in the midst of London she could not begin to fathom.

That hand on her elbow drifted up, trailing along her arm to curl over her shoulder. "Your heart is racing."

"How can you know that?" Her voice came out in a scratchy rasp. He couldn't feel her racing heart. God willing, he could not hear it pounding like a drum. No, he couldn't know how it pounded.

As though he could read her mind, he said, "I can see your pulse here." His gloved fingers brushed the patch of skin visible at the base of her throat. Her breath quickened at the sensation. "It's fighting against your skin."

She swallowed and nodded jerkily, wishing she could blame it on the fear of moments ago. Their brush with danger. And yet it wasn't that. It wasn't those men. He was more dangerous to her than them.

It was this. *Him.*

Chapter 12

*T*reacherous thoughts flitted across her mind. She batted them away, but still they hovered, threading their way under her skin and into her blood.

What would it feel like to have his fingers on her without the gloves? His mouth? She fought to swallow against her suddenly thick throat as she stared into Struan Mackenzie's deep gaze.

She had allowed Edmond certain liberties. Oh, she was still a maid. Nothing too intimate had transpired between them, but she was no stranger to kisses or a man's touch.

She had known Edmond all her life. It had seemed acceptable, on occasion, to indulge in a few kisses and caresses. She had thought they were to be married. She was her parents' daughter, after all. Like them, she believed in passion and following one's heart.

Over kisses and mild petting, Edmond had whispered fervent promises of marriage. Those words had persuaded her to shove aside her reservations. And yet in all their trysts, she had never felt this breathlessness. This pooling heat in her belly. It was a heady sensation.

She moistened her lips, trying not to notice the way his gaze followed the trail of her tongue along her bottom lip. "I'm not going to swoon if that's what you're so worried about. I'm not that manner of female," she whispered.

"No?" His boot scraped against the ground as he stepped closer. "And what manner of female are you, Miss Fairchurch? I confess it has been a point of curiosity for me ever since we met." The purr of his voice dragged over her skin.

She swallowed against the giant lump in her throat. "I'm not that squeamish."

"No," he agreed. "You are not."

"Nor am I the sort of person to disarm a street ruffian with my bare hands." She shook her head, her voice tight and breathy . . . still in awe of him. "But you, apparently, are. One moment you behaved as a coward and handed over our belongings with nary a blink, and then you did that trick with the knife. However did you do that?"

"Those two men?" He jerked his head toward where they'd disappeared, still keeping his gaze trained on her face. "I didn't think they were truly dangerous." He lifted one big shoulder in a scant semblance of a shrug. "And I was right."

"Then why hand over your purse in the first place? And my ring?" She bristled, recalling that point with the most indignation.

"Because you were here."

"Me?" She pulled back slightly. What did her presence have to do with anything?

He stared at her a long moment before elaborating. "I didn't feel the need to risk your safety."

She stared at him blankly, struggling to process his words.

He released an exasperated breath. "I was attempting to protect you. Not that you were any help in that endeavor, Miss Fairchurch. A paltry bauble isn't anything to risk your neck over . . ."

"It wasn't a mere bauble to me." Her spine shot straight. "It was more than that to me." Her father didn't have much. As a tutor, he had scrimped and saved to buy her mother that ring. Their meager home and everything within it was gone, lost to them. All she possessed was that ring.

Suddenly she noticed the muscle ticcing madly in his cheek. He was angry, and that only discouraged her. He didn't understand. He couldn't. He was a man accustomed to having his way. He wouldn't know what it felt like to be her . . . to have so little, to want to cling to what little was left to her.

"What were you thinking?" he bit out. The velocity of his words propelled her back a final step, forcing her against the wall of the alley. The scratchy brick scraped at her mother's old cloak and she hoped it wasn't snagging the already worn fabric.

She forgot about the cloak when his hands came up on either side of her head, caging her in. She gasped and looked left and right at the hard arms on either side of her head.

He continued, "A token from your lover isn't worth calling attention to yourself . . . and that's precisely what you did when you refused to give that ring up."

"A token from my lover?" Is that what he thought? He was wrong. So wrong. Was that why he cared so little about giving away her ring? She longed to smack that smug condescension off his face. Her lips worked, but her outrage blocked anything coherent from forming on her lips.

"Am I incorrect? Did Autenberry not give you

the ring?" he sneered as though he were deliberately trying to be cruel. As though he wanted to hurt her. Like the mean girls back home who took jabs at her once it became clear that her sister far outshone her. When Bryony was eleven years old her beauty was already glaringly obvious. "I admit it's rather modest. I'd expect something more extravagant from him." A certain thickness entered his voice as he demanded, "A different lover, then?" He leaned in, his breath on her cheek sending ripples of awareness through her.

"You cad," she charged. "The ring was from no lover. It was my mother's ring."

He fell silent at that, just the fall of his breath so close on her skin.

"An apology would be the gentlemanly thing to do at this point," she got out past her clogged throat.

One corner of his mouth curled. "I'm a bastard born to the streets of Glasgow. Never mistake me for a gentleman."

"Duly noted."

"Did you not hear me warn you to keep quiet?" he growled, evidently moving on to the next subject.

"Indeed. I seem to recall you *ordered* me to hold my tongue. Maybe if you had not spoken to me like a senseless child—"

"Should I have taken a few minutes to politely and gently explain to you that I did not want to draw undue attention to your person in front of those ruffians? Rather counterproductive."

He was maddening, trying to make her feel dense. And foolish! True, he was succeeding but damn if she would let him know it. Her eyes burned but she blinked the fire from them.

His head canted in a way that reminded her of a predator right before it pounced on its victim. "I've saved your life twice now in so many days, Miss Fairchild. How on earth have you managed to arrive at your age unscathed?"

She breathed through her nose, controlling her ire. She'd never been a temperamental individual, but this man brought out the worst in her. "You know as well as I do that they weren't about murder. Nothing as dire as that," she said in an attempt to make light of the night's brush with danger.

These words only seemed to enrage him. His eyes went black. He thrust his face closer, his voice a hiss as he lifted one hand from the wall by her ear and lightly circled her bare throat. Not strangling, although she imagined he would like to do that very thing. No, his touch was gentle, his thumb brushing the side of her neck in the most distracting manner.

"What are you—" she started to say.

He cut her off. "You cannot be that naïve. How could you mistake their intent when they said they *liked* you?" His gaze traveled over her insolently. Not that he could see much of her beneath her voluminous cloak, but she felt stripped naked. "They sought to relieve you of something far more valuable than a mere bauble. I'm certain that clever brain of yours can surmise to what I refer."

She did, but she wouldn't humor him with a response.

He continued, "It's one thing to let them take your ring and my money . . . another thing entirely to let them put a hand on you."

Her breath hitched at the sudden deep timbre of his voice. She read menace in his eyes.

He sounded—and looked—as though he could kill for her. She'd never felt that before. Never felt that there was anyone out there who would go to extreme lengths for her. It was strange. It filled her with an anxious giddiness and that terrified her. She did not need to be feeling that way. Especially not with him.

"Poppy?" The hushed whisper of her name— the first time she had ever heard him say her Christian name—only made that giddiness spread through her in the most awful, traitorous way.

"That's Miss Fairchurch to you," she reprimanded, her voice gentle and lacking all heat.

He lowered his head. "Poppy," he repeated as
though she had not corrected him. More than
likely he simply did not care. She knew that he
put little value into her wishes.

If he cared about honoring her wishes, then
he would not be with her at this moment. But
he was. And his presence here might very well
have saved her. Again. The fact only irritated her.
Absurd, she knew, but there it was nonetheless.
She was now indebted to him for her life no less
than two times.

Her pulse hammered at her throat. No doubt
he could feel it with his hand on her. His fingers
moved again, grazing her skin, his touch warm
through his gloves. Hot actually. She felt singed,
burned at his caress. Any attempt to speak was
impossible in that moment. Not with him looking
at her as though he wanted to strangle her.

Or do something else to her.

He truly must hate her. No one had ever
touched her thusly. Or addressed her so boldly or
looked at her with such intensity. His green eyes
looked dark. Black eyes. Pirate eyes.

"No more," he warned. "No more venturing
out alone at night."

Her chest swelled on an indignant breath. Who

did he think he was? "I don't take commands from you."

"Hell's teeth, woman. Do you ever simply admit you've made a mistake and back down?"

"To you?" she scoffed, glaring at this bossy male before her and wondering how it had come to this. Yes, he had a point. She wasn't typically stubborn, but glaring up at his angry face, she couldn't give an inch. Everything inside her rebelled at the notion.

A few days ago the Duke of Autenberry was merely a fantasy and this brother of his not even known to her.

"You are no one in my life," she said in a voice fraught with tension. "You cannot tell me what to—"

"Oh, I can," he bit out, his voice a gravelly purr that abraded her skin and sparked something inside her. His hand slid around her nape and hauled her closer. His pirate's eyes swallowed her up and forced all the air out from her lungs in one great rush. "I will."

She opened her mouth to protest, but his mouth covered hers. Claimed her. It was the only word for it. This was a taking.

And she the taken.

Chapter 13

Struan Mackenzie smothered any words she might have thought to say.

In fact, thoughts were wild and fleeting once his mouth touched hers. Sensations and emotions, however, abounded.

Shock. Outrage. The utter strangeness of it all.

Her head spun. She'd been kissed before. This shouldn't feel so totally foreign to her. But kissing had never been *this* before.

She gasped and he took full advantage. His tongue slid inside her mouth.

Warm. Slick. Wet.

Astonished, she stood frozen, motionless, letting him have his way with her mouth. Plunder at will. Appropriate for a man with pirate's eyes.

His thumb nudged under her chin, forcing her head back and that only deepened the kiss. Made it wetter. Hotter. *Better.*

Heaven save her. She was getting squirmy all over. That had never happened before either. What was happening? What was she doing? What was she *letting* him do?

She hated him. And yet she had this mad impulse to fling her arms around his shoulders. Wrap her legs around him. Outrageous.

Not at all how she should feel.

Certainly not with him. She hated him. *He* hated her.

Didn't he?

Of course, he did . . . no matter what his mouth was doing to her. No matter how his gloved thumb grazed the side of her neck. They had done nothing but quarrel from the start. Ever since she saw him battering her poor duke. Rightly so. He was a brute. Rude and insulting.

And yet it was a strange thing to reconcile hatred when his mouth was moving so expertly over hers. Men did not kiss women they did not like.

Immediately a voice rose up inside her to contradict.

Well . . . some men did kiss women for whom they felt nothing. She wasn't so naïve that she didn't know men weren't above using women. Especially women they felt were somehow *less*. Indeed, it was those very men that Poppy guarded Bryony against. It was her duty to make certain no man looked at Bryony as a meaningless vessel and decided she was a female who didn't matter.

She pulled up hard. Did Struan Mackenzie think she was that sort of woman? That she did not matter? The notion made her sick. She brought her hands up between them. She pressed both palms flat against his chest—a definite distraction *that* chest. It was muscled and hard. She didn't know gentlemen could feel so very . . . solid. Shaking off the thought, she gave him a hearty shove. The kind of shove she imagined would succeed in budging him. And it did.

His lips lifted from hers with a strange puff of sound that resembled words. In his gravelly brogue, she translated it to mean, "What did you do that for?" She couldn't be certain. Just the sound of that voice stroked something deep inside her. His voice seduced. It wasn't fair.

His pirate's eyes fixed on her, mesmerizing. All at once she wasn't pushing so hard at his chest anymore. Her hands relaxed, palms softening against him.

His head dipped toward her, moving slowly,

his intent clear as his eyes drifted over her face. She had all the time to move, to protest, but his sinful eyes mesmerized her. His mouth touched hers again, soft at first and then more firmly.

She forced herself to remain utterly still as he nudged her lips apart. Not an easy feat. Her lips yearned to react and all her lady parts hummed and throbbed in the most delicious yet painful manner. Strange how one could feel both pain and pleasure.

"Come, Poppy," he murmured against her mouth, his tongue gliding along her bottom lip and igniting a tremor through her. "Kiss me back."

She gave the barest shake of her head and he chuckled, the sound dark and rich. "So stubborn. You know you want to," he coaxed. "I can feel your heart pounding."

Oh, he was ruthless, but she would resist him.

He pulled her bottom lip between his teeth, and her core clenched in response.

She would. She must.

Suddenly he bent his knees, crouching his great height so that their faces were on level. He wrapped his arms around her waist and lifted her off the ground as though she weighed nothing at all. She squeaked, her hands flying to his shoulders.

"What are you—"

"Lock your legs around me."

With their faces level, she stared wide-eyed at him.

She opened her mouth to refuse, but that brogue of his filled the space between them, hard with command, yet husky with something that spoke to all the tender and aching places inside her. "Do it, kitten."

She obeyed, hopping up slightly until her legs locked around his hips. He brought his big hands to each of her thighs, fingers digging through her skirts and adjusting her so that her sex met directly with the stiff bulge of his manhood. Even through the fabric of her skirts she could feel him and she had to stop herself from rocking into the beckoning ridge.

It was like she was outside herself. A voyeur looking down at this woman she didn't know who followed the lead of a man much too masculine, whose brutal beauty and hypnotic voice robbed her of all sense.

He withheld his mouth from hers. Waiting. Waiting for her.

His warm breath gusted her cheek. His mouth was so close. Tantalizingly close. She caught a whiff of the heady scent of him again. Her gaze darted from his lips to his eyes, so dark and compelling. They pulled her in, muddied her thoughts. She leaned in slightly, forgetting everything, wanting that mouth even though everything about this was wrong. She couldn't think.

He rocked his hips and a bolt of lust shot through her body.

Desire licked through her. Her breathing hitched. She leaned forward slightly, tasting him with her tongue, the barest, swiping stroke, and his eyes went black with heat. He closed the fraction of space between them, his chest grazing the front of her chest. Her breasts grew heavy and tight, aching.

Sweet heavens, he was going to kiss her again. Yes, yes, please.

He pulled back slightly and growled against her lips. "Kiss me, Poppy."

Her name on his lips broke something loose inside her. Ignited her. She leaned into his mouth, finally kissing him back, starved, touching her tongue to his.

He made a deep growl of approval, his hands gripping her thighs tighter and hefting her higher. She squeaked and gripped his shoulders.

"I'm not dropping you," he rasped on her mouth. "That's not happening."

Her heart tripped as his big hands slid around, holding her up by her bottom. Her mouth devoured him, tongue tasting and exploring, savoring.

He lifted his head and the air left her in a rush as she looked up into his starkly handsome face. His gaze drilled into her. "Who knew the little kitten could kiss like that?"

"Oh," she croaked, half expecting him to lower her to the ground now. It had to end. Reason and sanity had to surface eventually.

But he didn't move away. He stared down at her, his eyes dark and full of something she couldn't read.

She pushed the tendrils of hair that had come loose off her face. She moistened her lips, reaching for her composure—the last of which fled as she watched him glance down at the bare amount of flesh peeking above her bodice. His eyes smoldered at that scant sight of her skin.

His words brushed over her, murmuring, "You want my mouth again?"

She nodded jerkily.

He rocked against her, rubbing his hard length along the core of her that was covered up with far too much fabric. He lowered his head and brought his mouth against her neck, directly beneath her ear. She felt his words vibrate against her skin. "Good. Because I want to taste you here. Now pull your cloak wider for me."

She nodded even though a part of her rebelled at being told what to do. Her hands curled around the edges of her mother's cloak, exposing herself for him. In this moment, he wielded total control over her and she reveled in it. For the first time she felt like she could let go.

His mouth dragged down her neck in a trail of searing kisses. Lips, grazing tongue and softly nipping teeth. She gasped and whimpered, wiggling against him, need pumping through her. His lips reached where her neck and shoulder met. His warm breath fanned in the hollow there for an agonizing moment. Anticipation zipped through her as she waited for more. She trembled, holding her breath for his kiss there.

Finally it came. A savoring, openmouthed kiss followed by the slight scrape of teeth. His lips moved against her skin. "You taste so good, Poppy. Like there's nectar buried in your skin."

She shivered at his words and his teeth sank deeper, marking her, claiming her. A choked gasp ripped from her as her bones liquefied and a rush of heat pooled between her legs. Her eyes flew wide and she gasped. She had no idea that a bite could affect her so pleasurably. That she would like such a wicked thing so much. That she would feel it so deeply.

He pulled back, laving the tender flesh with his tongue.

Her head spun, chest lifting with ragged breaths.

His eyes gleamed down at her. "See? We can get along."

"Wh-what—"

"There are benefits to being more . . . amenable."

"Amenable?" she echoed, attempting to shake off the fog of desire. "Oh!" She pushed at his rock solid shoulders.

His hands adjusted on her, leveraging her so that the hard ridge of his manhood thrust harder against her—deliciously so. She gasped and bit her lip in an attempt to cut off the sound and not appear the total wanton. *Little late for that, Poppy.*

"Wouldn't you rather be doing this than fighting? You and I would fit together just right, lass."

She shuddered. Yes . . . *yes.*

She was damp directly where she rode him, his hardness rubbing deeply against her. Dear heavens. Shame washed over her as an invisible band coiled tighter and tighter in her belly. He could probably feel how moist she was between their clothing. As much as that mortified her it didn't stop her from whimpering and moving against him, seeking something near and yet elusive.

His lips returned to her throat and she was helpless against arching into that mouth. "You're wasted on him," he growled against her skin.

The words vibrated through her, shaking her awake. She did not mistake his meaning. He was saying she was wasted on the duke. Because he thought she was *with* the duke. He thought they were together romantically, intimately. He thought she had been like *this* with his brother . . . mouth to skin, their bodies straining against each other in full, heart-pounding hunger.

It was a sobering thought. It made her feel tawdry and something else. Something confusing and different and not unpleasant.

She felt desired. Coveted. And it made her heart swell inside her too-tight rib cage. In this moment, she could not imagine doing this with anyone else. She could not imagine anyone except Struan Mackenzie provoking these sensations in her.

She was a sinful creature, to be sure. She never knew she could be this. So wicked. Wanton. So titillated because she had aroused this man . . . because she had stirred a need in him to take her from a man to whom she did not even belong.

This entire situation was out of control. *She* was out of control.

Jarred, she blinked and looked around, seeing the alley in which they stood. The cloak of night with its shifting mist. His body pressed against hers. Her legs wrapped around him. *This* was depraved. She'd gone mad.

Stark. Raving. Mad.

"Stop." A single word but he lifted his mouth from her neck.

He released her. Her legs slid back down, feet landing on solid earth—right alongside her judgment.

She looked up into his eyes. They were a dark forest, the green lost to the night, unreadable as they crawled over her face. "This was a mistake," she whispered, looking down at herself, smoothing a hand down her rumpled cloak.

He snorted and she cast him a sharp look. "A mistake," she repeated.

"You weren't saying that moments ago. You were as hot for it as any lass I've ever had. I must confess a little surprise. I didn't think you would be quite so . . . proficient."

Angry heat stung her cheeks. Why shouldn't he think she would be good at . . . at . . . amorous endeavors? As soon as the indignant thought entered her head, she slapped it away. A lady shouldn't take offense over such a thing. *Indeed, a lady would never have permitted a rogue like Struan Mackenzie such liberties.*

He continued, "Although I suppose I should have surmised a certain aptitude from you since you've secured my brother's interest."

That's right. He thought she was Autenberry's lover. How could she have permitted herself to kiss the wretch? To *more* than kiss him? She'd responded to him as she never had with Edmond.

Not trusting herself to answer him, she pushed off the wall and started down the narrow alley, shaken and rattled, her body still throbbing in places where it should feel nothing.

She heard him follow behind her. "Poppy," he started to say, one hand closing on her arm, forcing her around.

"You two there!"

Startled, she jerked, her gaze colliding with a figure looming at the mouth of the alleyway. She scanned the big-bellied man, marking his uniform. Mackenzie stepped beside her to face him, as well.

Now the Watch appeared? Earlier, when his presence could have been useful, he was nowhere to be found.

"Constable." Mackenzie nodded circumspectly. "Just walking the lady home."

Mackenzie slid a hand against the small of her back, guiding her out of the alley.

The man looked her up and down as though skeptical that she was in fact a lady. Granted, they were emerging from an alley. Doubtlessly, her hair and wardrobe were mussed. She could guess at all his lurid thoughts. The man's gaze returned to Mackenzie, who stared back at him with a stony expression that seemed to dare him to disagree at the veracity of her virtue.

The man cleared his throat, resting his hand on the butt of the baton secured inside his belt. "Carry on, then. All manner of questionable characters out and about this late."

Indeed. All manner.

Poppy held her tongue, her steps a quick staccato on the walk as they hastened home. She didn't even attempt to shake off his hand against her back. It had been a long evening and she was tired of fighting. Besides, she could feel the Watchman's stare fixed on the back of them and the sensation of Mackenzie's big hand against her felt somehow comforting.

They turned the corner and she murmured, "You needn't escort me the rest of the way. He can't see us anymore. I can take myself home."

"That is not happening," he replied. "You're daft if you think I will let you walk the rest of the way unescorted. Now if you had shown some sense and taken a hack in the first place or—"

"I can't afford it," she blurted, her arms swinging as she walked. It was so easy for him to assume that she had other choices—that she could simply hail a hack whenever she chose. This world, this life, held a decided lack of choices for women without family and means.

He fell quiet. For once, she had silenced him.

Heat crept over her face as her admission sank in. Only now did she feel embarrassed and vulnerable that she had admitted such a thing to him. In his eyes, in the eyes of a man who was clearly as rich as Croesus, it felt like a weakness. She felt small and pitiable, and she hated that. She hated being on the receiving end of anyone's pity.

She had endured enough of that in her life. After her father's death. After Edmond's rejection. After every time people met her stunning sister and then looked at her, comparing her much plainer looks to Bryony's and finding her lacking.

"It's a matter of funds?" he demanded.

She groaned and increased her pace, forcing his hand to fall from the small of her back. He followed, his steps matching hers.

"You say that as though it's an issue of no concern," she accused. "For some of us it is."

"I find it hard to believe that Autenberry's paramour would be living short on funds."

There it was again. That insulting and erroneous

assumption. He thought she was Marcus's lover. Even after the way she had just kissed him and let him touch her. He thought she was his brother's lover.

Instead of bothering to correct him, she cut him a swift glance. "Last time I checked, your brother is in a coma."

"And you have no nest set aside? No pin money from him?"

He made her sound like a kept woman.

"No." It was the only word she could manage.

He made a sound. "Not much of a protector, my brother."

His words rang in her head and she shivered. *You're wasted on him.* She knew he was thinking that again.

"Can we not discuss this?"

"He's more like our father than I realized. Shagging with little thought to anything else. To *anyone*." She glanced back at him, stumbling slightly. He caught hold of her elbow. His gaze cutting and direct, his implication was clear. *With any thought to you.*

"Oh, and you would never do such a thing." Her voice trembled, betraying her. "You who claim to be no gentleman."

His fingers tightened marginally on her. "I am

no gentleman." He tugged her closer, his mouth a hairsbreadth from her own. "But I take care of what's mine."

Her stomach quivered at his pronouncement. She felt his words as deeply as she had felt his teeth on her flesh.

She swallowed and twisted her arm free. He let her go, watching her as though he would very much like to take a bite out of her again. She moved ahead of him. As predicted, he followed.

It took two blocks for her to recover her voice. "Let us just forget this happened."

He didn't reply for some moments and she felt something akin to relief. Perhaps she need say nothing more. Perhaps they would carry on and forget that kiss—forget all of this—had ever happened between them.

"Can you do that?" He angled his head as though interested in her response. Not that he gave her time to reply. "You're lying if you say you can."

"I can," she insisted.

"Then I can't."

She sent him a startled glance. Clearly he didn't mean that.

She snapped her face forward again, looking

straight ahead. "I am your brother's fiancée." Now seemed as good a time as any to cling to that particular falsehood.

"Are you?"

There he went again with the mocking skepticism. She stopped hard for a moment and glanced up at him before resuming walking, her pace as brisk as ever.

"You know I am." She lifted her chin, hoping to appear confident and not defensive.

"Then why did you kiss me back?"

"Did I?" she challenged, and somehow didn't choke on that prevarication.

He chuckled. "Not at first, perhaps. Once your surprise ebbed away you most definitely kissed me back. I wouldn't call that the behavior of a woman happily betrothed to another man, but don't torture yourself. I won't tell anyone. And it was nice. Unexpectedly so."

They turned onto her street. *Nice.*

That shattering kiss was simply nice for him?

She seethed inside, feminine pride she didn't know she possessed stinging. It had been more than nice. Every other kiss she'd experienced paled beside a kiss from this wretch of a man.

She stopped before her lodging house and turned smartly on her heels to face him.

He was busy looking at her residence, his forehead knitting as he took it in. "This is where you live?"

She squared her shoulders, perfectly aware of her humble dwelling. But seeing it now, through his eyes, she felt suddenly embarrassed. "Yes. You know as much."

"Autenberry lets you live here?"

"No one *lets* me do anything . . . even Autenberry. I make my own decisions."

He looked back at her curiously, and she couldn't deny that it must look odd that the Duke of Autenberry would be affianced to someone who lived in a place like this.

"Doesn't sound much like Autenberry."

"Perhaps you don't know your brother as well as you think you do."

He shot another quick glance to the boardinghouse. "I think I may know him better than you do. I know a side to him that the world rarely sees." A strange, pensive tone entered his voice and she wondered what he was thinking. She would hazard that it had to do with whatever rift stood between them.

She cleared her throat and he turned his attention back to her. "It's late." She motioned to the door. "I should go in. Thank you for—" *driving me mad, insulting me, accosting me,* kissing *me* "—walking me home."

"I didn't give you a choice."

"No." She gave the barest smile. "You didn't."

"No more walking alone at night."

Instead of arguing or exchanging sniping words, she lifted the hem of her cloak and started up the steps leading into the house.

"Miss Fairchurch." She looked over her shoulder at him. He stood with his legs braced, a pirate at the prow of his ship gazing up at her. "I look forward to seeing you again."

Her pulse spiked at his words. Turning, she ascended the final steps and entered the house, shaken, furious. Furious with herself for letting things go so far with Struan Mackenzie. Furious that she had reveled in every moment of it.

What would he think, what would he *do*, when he found out the truth? The prospect made her shiver. A man like Struan would not appreciate being made a fool, and she was certain that's how he would feel. He'd feel deceived, perhaps even mocked. Her skin broke out in goose bumps.

She couldn't see him again. Even if a small part of her wanted to.

She sighed. As long as she was living this subterfuge, it was bound to happen. She would see him again whether she wished it or not. It was the last thing that should ever happen, but it would.

She simply needed to make certain that they were never alone again, that they never did any of the things they'd already done. She'd forget what it was like to be with him . . . to kiss him, to touch him and be touched by him. And then she wouldn't feel so shaky and unsteady inside anymore.

Chapter 14

*H*e wanted her.

Struan gazed after her as she disappeared into the substandard boardinghouse and knew this to be true with a sense of grim disgust. It was the truth and he needed to decide what he would do about it. Rather, he had to decide if he would do anything at all about it.

His attraction to her had simmered since their first meeting, even though she was not to his usual taste. Poppy Fairchurch was much too difficult a female, and he did not make it a habit to pursue prickly women. Why bother with those who did not look upon him with invitation? Miss Fairchurch was all barbed words and glares.

Nor did he waste time on women attached to

other men. There were too many available lasses eager for his company. Why trouble with the minor few who were not?

Because she's a challenge. He shoved aside that annoying whisper wending inside his head. That was too pedestrian for him. Weak men ruled by base desires would want her for such a reason. Struan was not weak. He did not need the conquest of a woman to inflate his ego.

So then why do you want her so badly?

For a while, when he first arrived in London, he'd considered marrying. He set his sights on one female in particular—the Duke of Banbury's sister, Lady Aurelia. She was comely and her family's lauded position in Society had appealed to him for wholly self-seeking reasons. It would have been nice to rub Autenberry's face in the fact that he'd wed a duke's daughter.

He'd moved on from her, however, when it became apparent that her heart lay with another. Since then he had lost the whim to marry some blue-blooded chit simply to aggravate his half brother.

Although what better way to irk him than to seduce his woman?

Inhaling, he rubbed at his jaw where stubble was starting to grow and gave a small shake of his head. He was lying to himself if he wanted to pretend that was his motivation. There was no revenge plot tangled up in his hunger for her.

She belonged to Autenberry, and that fact should have repelled him. He didn't long for anything his brother possessed. He had made it a point to feel that way. Struan had amassed wealth enough that he would never want for anything. He was as rich as Croesus. In good health and possession of all his teeth. He didn't need anything his brother held claim to—especially his latest paramour.

And yet she was different.

She wasn't a title. Or something as intangible as prestige. She didn't symbolize acceptance into the ton. In fact, she would never bring him status.

He stared up at the house, at the window he knew to be hers, as if it held the answer to life, the secrets of the universe.

She was in there now, readying for bed. Presumably with her sister.

Would you follow her and finish what they'd started if she resided alone?

He imagined himself walking through the front door and up the stairs as if he had every right. He envisioned himself striding unannounced into her private room, invading her sanctuary and stripping off her clothes. *Invading her.*

Would she demand he leave?

Of course she would, but he could persuade her otherwise. It wouldn't be too difficult. He'd tasted her lips, felt the hitch of her breath and the press of her body. She was ripe for it. He could have her. Whether she realized it or not, she wanted him, too. She'd responded to him. She was a woman of intense passions. And he could have that passion for himself. He could. At least for one night. He could satisfy this need for her and move on.

He gave the building one last look and turned away, tucking his hand casually inside his pocket. He only had to decide if he would do it.

Was he so lacking in conscience that he would take his brother's woman?

POPPY SPENT A miserable night tossing and turning in the bed she shared with her sister. She could still feel Struan Mackenzie. His lips. His hands. The way his brogue rumbled on the air, the sound infusing her body with heat.

If it wasn't too late when she returned home, she would have dragged out the hip tub for a bath. Perhaps that would rid her of the memory of him—if she could scrub him off her body. By the time she fell asleep dawn was already tingeing the sky.

It was the only excuse she had for sleeping in so late. An hour and a half hardly amounted to a good night's rest. She hurriedly stabbed the pins into her hair. There would be no time for breakfast. She would have to go directly to the shop.

She had just finished with the last button on her dress when the door to her chamber was flung open—no thanks to Bryony. Her sister had left it unlocked after she stepped out this morning to visit the washroom. Bryony squealed at the sudden intrusion from where she sat in front of their dressing mirror, dropping the ribbon she had been trying to weave into her plait.

Poppy spun around to face their flush-faced landlady. The woman might be a busybody, but she had always granted them a semblance of privacy and at least knocked before entering their rooms.

"Mrs. Gibbons!" Poppy planted her fists on her hips and leveled her with a stern look. Boundaries. They needed to discuss their boundaries.

The lady practically danced in place, indifferent to Poppy's disapproving stare. "Come! Come at once!" She waved her hands furiously. She looked fit to apoplexy.

"What?" Bryony jumped up to her feet from her chair, evidently sensing something epic was on the verge of transpiring. "What is it?"

"A grand carriage with a footman riding in the back! Heavens! It has a coat of arms on it. I don't know the house, but I've never been very good at keeping such things to memory."

A sinking sensation started in Poppy's stomach. Something epic indeed.

"It stopped here?" Bryony hopped and clapped, catching some of Mrs. Gibbons's enthusiasm.

"Yes, and they want to see you, Poppy! They wait in the parlor."

"They?" Bryony demanded, stopping her hopping to swing her gaze to Poppy. "They who?"

"A duchess! I confess after I was told her title I heard nothing beyond that, although there was a string of names."

"Poppy!" Bryony clapped her hands in a frenzy. "There's a duchess calling on you!"

Poppy nodded absently at her sister's stupefied expression. "Yes, I heard that." She didn't need to be told the string of names to follow the duchess's title. She knew who it was. Currently, there was only one duchess in her life. Poppy pressed her hands together and twisted her fingers. "I, uh, shall go downstairs, then."

Both her sister and Mrs. Gibbons nodded eagerly. "Yes, do hurry! Don't keep her waiting."

She smoothed her hands over her dress and walked with far more composure than she felt down the stairs and into the parlor. Mrs. Gibbons and her sister refrained from following and she knew that must have been a true feat for the both of them.

Indeed, the duchess was there, waiting in the parlor. As well as her daughter and stepdaughter. All three were elegantly attired for traveling, their hands delicately folded in their laps.

"Your Grace. Ladies." Poppy executed what she hoped was an adequate curtsey.

"Ah, there you are, dearest!" Her Grace rose from Mrs. Gibbons's shabby sofa and crossed the room to embrace her, the sensation of her slim, beringed fingers patting her back still strange and bewildering.

Poppy closed her eyes in a long blink and patted the lady's back in turn, still marveling over how she ended up in this situation.

"Poppy?"

She pulled back and turned quickly at her sister's arrival in the parlor. Her stomach sank. So much for her staying put.

"Bryony," she returned. "This is the Duchess of Autenberry and her daughter and stepdaughter, the Ladies Clara and Enid."

Bryony, never at a loss for words, was speechless. She could only gawk, her head bobbing up and down as she assessed the three ladies in all their finery and elegant coiffures. They were resplendent in colorful dresses, the drab background of Mrs. Gibbons's parlor all the more dreary as it framed them.

"I didn't know you had a sister," the young duchess exclaimed, stepping forward to assess Bryony with keen, interested eyes.

Bryony pressed a little closer to Poppy's side, for once appearing almost shy. "I didn't know you had a duchess," she whispered for Poppy's ears alone as she in turn assessed the ebony-haired beauty.

The Dowager Duchess of Autenberry stopped directly in front of Bryony, her dark eyes softly reprimanding as they settled on Poppy. "How remiss of you. What a stunning creature! How old are you, dear?"

"Fifteen, ma'am, I mean, my lady," she stammered, and performed a clumsy curtsey.

Poppy leaned toward her ear. "Your Grace," she corrected.

"Your Grace," Bryony chirped, color suffusing her face. "I mean, Your Grace."

The dowager clapped her hands together and held her palms pressed together. "Charming," she pronounced in her heavy accent. "You're near the same age as my own sweet daughter." She motioned to Clara. "I am certain you will be fast friends."

The girl stepped forward and nodded in greeting at Bryony. Bryony's wide eyes traveled over the girl in her stylish pink-and-blue striped muslin trimmed with matching fur.

"How delightful," Poppy murmured.

"It will be nice to have two girls of like age in the family."

"Yes," Lady Enid chimed in drolly. "Perhaps I won't be the only one to endure the little magpie now."

"Oh, posh! Your life would be a dreadful bore without me, Enid. You love me," Clara insisted with easy conviction, flashing a dimple as she grinned.

"They shall have a grand time together," the dowager continued with certainty, nodding as she looked between her daughter and Bryony. "It shall put some joy into the season. All things considered, we could use a bit of joy."

Bryony swung her gaze to Poppy. Accusation gleamed brightly in the blue depths along with the sudden realization that her sister possessed a life apart from her—a life of which Bryony knew very little.

Bryony shook her head slightly and sent each of their guests a confusing look. "Forgive me, I don't understand."

Of course she didn't understand what was happening. Poppy could scarcely understand it herself.

"Poppy!" The dowager tsked and shook her head "Don't tell me you haven't told your sister? Why have you kept such a thing secret? She should share in your happiness and good fortune."

"Told me what?" Bryony demanded.

Suddenly, Poppy found it difficult to breathe. Had the parlor become overly hot? She tugged at her modest collar.

From the corner of her eye, Poppy glimpsed Mrs. Gibbons hovering near the parlor doors. Naturally, she would want the gossip to impart later. The entire neighborhood would be told of the dowager duchess's visit. No detail would be left out of her report.

Poppy shrugged lamely. "I wanted to surprise her."

She had not thought her lie would ever reach her sister. She didn't imagine it would affect Bryony, but now here she stood facing the duke's family with her sister at her side. Her lie had caught up with her . . . had collided directly into the reality of her world. She wanted to flee upstairs and hide under the covers of her bed.

"Your sister is betrothed to my stepson, the Duke of Autenberry." The duchess blinked, still looking mildly surprised that Poppy's own sister did not know such a monumental fact. As she should.

The color drained from Bryony's face. "P-Poppy? Engaged to a duke?"

Poppy glanced reproachfully at the fire crackling in the small fireplace, blaming it for the sudden suffocating heat of the room.

It was unavoidable. *Lying* to her sister had become unavoidable. Her lips parted to speak. "It's true." She smiled weakly. "We've made no formal announcement yet . . ."

Because there was no actual engagement. Because she was caught up in this insane deception and had promised Lord Strickland she would not reveal the truth.

"You're betrothed?" Bryony clearly could not wrap her head around this. Poppy could not fault her for her bewilderment. "To a d-duke?"

The dowager duchess clasped her hands together before her, the light catching the gemstones of her rings. Rings that would probably see Poppy and her sister through a lifetime of meals. "The reason we're here is because we decided to return home for the holidays. We always spend Christmas at Autenberry Manor. This year Marcus suggested we spend it here in Town, but we should never have broken with tradition. If he'd been on his way home, perhaps . . ." Her voice faded away. "That's neither here nor there now, is it?" She smiled shakily. "Of course we want you there with us. You belong with us." The duchess shot a glance to Bryony as an afterthought. "Both of you, of course. We're family now."

Poppy could scarcely draw a breath in the over-heated room. "You want me to leave Town? With you? What of His Grace?"

"We've secured Marcus in a coach and made him as comfortable as possible. He's already left for the country." The dowager explained this as though it were the most normal of things. Poppy blinked at the odd image of this—the duke in a coma, strapped inside a carriage and bumping along on the way to his country home.

The dowager must have read some of her thoughts on her face. "Dr. Mercer said it was fine to do so," she said with a touch of defensiveness.

Poppy recalled the physician's face. Of course he'd sanctioned such a thing. He behaved as though the duke were already dead.

"Lord Strickland is with him. He will make certain all is well," she added as though this made it all acceptable. "Strickland spends every holiday with us," she explained. "He has no family him-self. It's just us. Has been ever since the boys at-tended Eton together." The dowager's eyes grew shiny with moisture. "It is for the best. Marcus belongs at home right now. I can't help thinking it might help him recover."

Poppy nodded. Yes, the dowager was unconventional, but perhaps she was correct. Perhaps the duke would heal better at home. "Of course."

"And you belong there, too." The dowager nodded once, bobbing her glossy dark head, her dark eyes gleaming with determination.

"Poppy." Bryony hissed her name and tugged on the cuff of her sleeve, clearly insistent on letting her know her thoughts on the matter. She wanted to go to Autenberry Manor. Of course. Who wouldn't want to spend Christmas at a duke's manor?

"I can't just leave. I have a position." Poppy shook her head. They were quite busy this time of year at the shop. "I can't hare off to—"

"I've already spoken with Mrs. Barclay this very morning. She's the one who told me where you live." The duchess sniffed and paused to flick a disapproving glance around the shabby parlor, reminding Poppy of Struan Mackenzie in that moment when he had first assessed her home and so obviously found it lacking. "She insisted you come with us. She said for you to take all the time you need."

Now it was her turn to be speechless. Until logic settled over her. Of course Mrs. Barclay would want her to go. She valued the duke's business. She would never refuse a duchess's request for anything.

"I—I'm not certain, Your Grace. We'd hate to impose."

Bryony inched closer and squeezed her elbow, communicating her desires. She, of course, wanted them to impose.

The duchess stepped forward and closed her hands around Poppy's arms, giving her a squeeze. "Poppy, first of all, call me Graciella. Or Ella. We are past formal titles, no?" She glanced at her daughters to confirm this. Young Clara nodded happily. The stoic Lady Enid offered a single nod that seemed to say: *I've learned not to resist.* "Now no more protests. It's no imposition. Family needs to be together over the holidays and especially in times of hardships—"

"But—"

"Do not deny me in this. Back home, I had so many cousins, aunts and uncles. I could not count them all! I miss having a big family. I've longed to see our own grow and I'm thrilled it is finally happening." The dowager duchess's dark eyes took on a steely glint. "Think of Marcus. He needs you there. If he's to recover, he needs the woman he loves at his side."

The Duchess of Autenberry—Graciella—was

clearly a romantic at heart. And yet she was not without sense. The duke was gravely ill. He might not even survive. Of course his betrothed would want to be at his side. She *should* be there. That was only natural and right. Refusing to go would appear illogical and insensitive.

And truthfully, she wanted to go.

She was worried about the duke. She cared. She wanted to be at his side. A voice whispered through her: *Wouldn't it also be nice to spend Christmas with these kind ladies away from Town?* It wouldn't be just Poppy and Bryony anymore. They would be part of a family. At least for a little while. She couldn't deny it would be a treat for both of them. For a short time, she could forget all about her responsibilities.

She could forget about Struan Mackenzie and her unconscionable behavior with him.

Her face heated and it wasn't from the overly warm room. No, it was with the memory of Mackenzie and the liberties she'd permitted him. The delightful sensation of his mouth and hands on her. The memory of her wanton response to him.

She sucked in a sharp breath. It wouldn't hurt to remove herself from Town for a bit and any chance encounters with him. Indeed not. Perhaps that would be the wisest, safest course of action.

She shot a quick glance at her sister, whose

eager gaze fixed on her, pleading and conveying her most fervent wishes.

Poppy sucked in a breath. "Yes, thank you for your most kind invitation," she heard herself saying. "We would love to join you for the holidays."

Chapter 15

The coach was crowded with the five females and it quickly became apparent that five was too many. Clara and Bryony were incessant chatter-boxes. Seated to the left of Poppy, their animated discussions spilled over into their actions. It wasn't long before Poppy was pressed up against the carriage wall, jostled from the movements of their bodies.

When they stopped to lunch at a village en route to Autenberry Manor, Poppy practically tripped down the steps in her eagerness to be free of the coach. The duchess was right. Bryony and Clara had become fast friends.

"I need a cool compress." Lady Enid pressed fingertips to her temples. Clearly Poppy was not the only one overcome from the girls' constant babbling. She grimaced. Enid should try sitting beside them. She'd need more than a cool compress.

"Don't sound like such an old lady," the dowager admonished. "You're still young. You should be giggling with the girls."

"I'm not *that* young," Enid said as they were escorted into a private dining room where they took their seats and ordered drinks and food.

"I don't think Enid has ever giggled," Clara snickered.

Outside the wind howled, and Poppy watched small flakes of snow churning in the air through the large mullioned window. Winter had arrived in earnest. They would have snow by Christmas.

"Wait until you taste Cook's mint jelly and roasted lamb," Clara was telling Bryony. "It's divine. She prepares it every Christmas eve."

"Sounds wonderful," Bryony exclaimed. She met Poppy's gaze. Flags of color marked her cheeks, partly from the cold, partly from her excitement. She was happy and the sight made Poppy's chest swell a little. It had been a long time since Bryony looked truly happy. "Does it not sound wonderful, Poppy?"

"Indeed it does." She opened her mouth to comment further, but her gaze was snared by the gentleman who suddenly entered the room. The innkeeper escorted him to a smaller table near the crackling fireplace.

Everything inside her seized hard. She couldn't breathe. No. No. *No.*

Struan Mackenzie in the flesh. Every hard inch of him. His moss green eyes prowled the room and landed on her.

What was he doing here?

"Struan!" the dowager exclaimed, although there was no actual surprise in her voice. At least not to the degree that Poppy felt at seeing the duke's half brother stroll into the room. She motioned him over with an elegant wave of her hand. "How nice that we've bumped into each other. I'm so glad you accepted our invitation to join us for Christmas."

She had invited the blasted Scotsman, too? Her stomach plummeted. He would be spending the holiday with them at Autenberry Manor?

Suddenly the delight she had been feeling at leaving Town behind and spending the holidays in the country vanished. Mackenzie would be there for every moment of it. Watching her with those pirate's eyes. Scowling at her. His big body swallowing up all the air in every room and drawing her attention in a manner entirely inappropriate—especially considering she was to marry another man.

How would she bear it? Surely the others would notice. Her sister, the duchess, Lady Enid . . .

Dear heavens. Her lungs felt suddenly too tight. Air impossible to inhale. Just being in the room with him was disconcerting her.

Her gaze strayed to the large mullioned window as though contemplating escaping through it.

Struan Mackenzie approached, his boots scraping the floor as he stopped and bowed slightly at the waist, nodding to each of them. She forced her gaze back up to him.

"Ladies." Did she imagine that his gaze lingered on her? "Good to see you all again."

Bryony leaned into her where they shared a bench seat, her bright eyes traveling over Mackenzie, missing nothing. "It's *him*," she whispered indiscreetly.

Poppy rolled her eyes and did not bother answering her.

The dowager motioned to the table. "It's growing frigid out there. They recommend the stew. It sounded quite reviving. I imagine it will warm you right up."

"He's Scottish," Enid chimed in. "I am certain he is accustomed to far colder climes than this."

Clara motioned to the space at the end of the table, directly beside Poppy. "Join us, Struan. Plenty of room."

Poppy stiffened. There was not *plenty* of room. A child's body could fit in that scant space, perhaps. Not a body the size of his. Still that did not stop him from sinking down on the bench beside her—his thigh pressing against hers.

"Yes!" the duchess added in her gushing tenor. "We are so looking forward to becoming better acquainted. It's thrilling that our family had suddenly grown in size. In Spain, my family was quite large. I've missed that dearly." She gestured dramatically to Poppy. "Once Marcus awakes and you are married, we shall work on expanding our number ever more, yes?" She smiled blindingly at Poppy.

Poppy managed a single nod, achingly aware of Mackenzie's stare on the side of her face. The crawl of his gaze felt like a beam of heat on her skin. His thigh against her practically burned.

She scooted as close as possible to her sister, but his great, muscled thigh seemed to follow her, pressing alongside her skirts. Unfortunately, the wool of her dress wasn't as thick as she would have liked. She felt the heat of that leg distinctly bleeding into her. She shivered.

"Chilled, Miss Fairchurch? You are trembling."

"A bit, yes. It's far colder here than in Town." A plausible explanation.

Conversation flowed around them. For that she

was grateful. She acted interested, contributing very little and taking great interest in her stew when it arrived, which was as warming as the proprietor promised. A fact that only made her feel more flushed and uncomfortable as she sat beside Mackenzie.

When everyone finished eating and rose to their feet to resume the journey, Lady Enid groaned. "I am not looking forward to returning to that cramped carriage for the remainder of the journey."

Poppy blinked and resisted pointing out that she was the one squished on the seat with Bryony and Lady Clara.

"Crowded are you?" Mr. Mackenzie inquired.

"Extremely." The dowager duchess sighed and then perked up. "I've an idea. Why don't one of you ride the rest of the journey with Struan so that we have more room?"

Her mouth dried as the duchess scanned all of them. Clara and Bryony clung to each other as though the idea of being separated terrified them. The dowager duchess laughed at the picture they made. The proprietor appeared to help the dowager slip on her cloak. "Have no fear," she assured. "I wouldn't dream of separating you two, nor would I punish Struan by sticking him with you both."

Don't look at me. Don't suggest me.

Her gaze stopped on Poppy. "Poppy," she proclaimed.

Poppy winced. She had been afraid she was going to be called out. It was just her misfortune to be stuck with the one man she had vowed to avoid.

"Why don't you join Mr. Mackenzie for the remainder of the ride?" Even though she posed it as a question it did not feel as such.

"Uh—"

"Excellent idea." Lady Enid nodded. "We shall have more space now."

"That sounds like a splendid idea," Bryony seconded as though her opinion held any weight.

"That would be fine," Mackenzie's deep voice intoned, his gaze falling unerringly on her, but there wasn't a flicker of reaction on his face. "My carriage has plenty of space."

Poppy avoided looking at him. She feigned great fascination with everyone save him.

"We shall follow directly and see you all there soon," Struan rumbled in that gravelly burr of his.

Poppy knotted her hands together in front of her in an attempt to quell their shaking. This couldn't be happening.

The dowager duchess nodded. "Very good. Tell your driver to mind the bends in the road as we near the manor. If the weather worsens he needs to be especially careful." As they stepped outside, she tugged on her fur gloves and squinted up at the snow falling gently from the overcast sky.

"I'll do that," Mr. Mackenzie agreed, his hand very properly coming to rest on the small of her back.

The ladies waved cheerfully at them as they made their way to the waiting carriage. "See you soon!" Bryony called.

Poppy watched helplessly as her sister trotted alongside the Dowager Duchess of Autenberry and her daughters. She swallowed thickly as Mackenzie's hand at her back increased its pressure, turning in the direction of his carriage.

"This way." His free hand gestured to the carriage sitting on the other side of the yard. This one was even more magnificent than the dowager's carriage. Poppy knew that he was a gentleman of some means, but it had not occurred to her that he might be wealthier than Autenberry. Not that it mattered. It wasn't the duke's pocketbook that attracted her. The man's character and inner qualities drew her.

None of which Struan Mackenzie possessed.

But Struan's good looks were certainly equal to the duke's. Some might even favor Mackenzie's looks. If one preferred the rakish Viking effect.

Not Poppy, of course. She inhaled through her nose. No. Not at all. Not in the least.

Her face and throat suddenly burned. She pressed the back of her gloved fingers against her flushed cheek as she strode through the cold.

To be certain, the Duke of Autenberry had never pressed her against a wall and wrapped her legs about him. *He* had never touched her throat. Never kissed her. Never bit her neck. Never said bold or shocking or rude things. No, that was reserved for Struan Mackenzie alone. She frowned. All reasons he should repel her. He *should*.

She suddenly felt hot and achy inside. She called a halt to such provoking thoughts, desperate to banish them. It was wrong to compare the two brothers. They were night and day. She walked a bit faster so that his hand fell away from her back, severing their contact.

Only one man deserved her affection and he was lost to a coma.

Chapter 16

*S*truan imagined this was what it felt like to be a spider when a tasty bit of prey stumbled into its web. He watched Poppy settle herself on the seat across from him. She shifted several times as though she could not find a comfortable position—all the while avoiding his gaze. It almost made him smile.

He had her alone again. He knew she had not anticipated his arrival—she especially did not anticipate he would be joining them for the holiday at Autenberry's family seat. He'd seen the brief flash of shock on her face when he entered the room, followed by panic.

She thought she was done with him. She

thought she wouldn't have to see him again. She had hoped that. Even if she didn't want it.

She stared out the window, fidgeting and pushing an errant strand of hair back off her cheek. She might think she wanted that, but he knew better. Last night had not been a chance occurrence. It had been real. She'd wanted him as much as he wanted her. Tension still hummed between them. Even now, watching her, his gaze narrowed on the madly thrumming pulse at her neck. She was aware of him. She only wanted to appear unaffected. He simply had to show her that pretending around him wasn't going to work.

She might belong to Autenberry, but she wasn't immune to Struan.

And Autenberry wasn't here. He was.

He cleared his throat. Her gaze remained fixed on the window.

"Miss Fairchurch?"

He scowled. She still didn't look his way. Stubborn chit.

If he didn't want her to look at him so very much he would find humor in the situation. His irritation grew. She'd avoided looking at him during lunch, but he thought that would come to an end once he had her in his carriage. He had plans for them during this carriage ride and it didn't consist of silence between them. Deciding to provoke her into looking at him, he said, "I imagine spending Christmas at Autenberry Manor will be quite the treat for you, Miss Fairchurch."

He succeeded.

Her gaze snapped to his and he felt a hot zing of triumph.

"Whatever do you mean?" she demanded hotly.

"Just what I said. Christmas at Autenberry's family estate . . . quite the coup for a girl who works in a flower shop."

She released a huff of breath. "I am sure it will be quite lovely. Not as lovely as it could be if the duke himself were *present* for it."

He arched an eyebrow. "I agree. That would make it far more . . . interesting."

Her eyes narrowed. "Indeed. I can just imagine the two of you together. Singing carols. Trimming the tree. The best of friends. Brothers."

He chuckled at her sneering tone. She meant to bait him in return. Little did she know that he had ceased to suffer years ago at the hands of his family—if he could even call them such. His father's rejection had been the deepest cut. What was one half brother's rebuff?

"It would be an occasion, to be certain," he agreed mildly, his gaze sliding over her. She was modestly attired, covered in that worn and threadbare cloak. He remembered the weight of her thighs in his hands, even through all the voluminous fabric of her dress, and felt a stirring in his cock. "We shall have to endeavor to have an *interesting* time while he recuperates."

Her nostrils flared. "That will be challenging." Her voice came out tight and offended.

"I think we can do it." He let the words hang between them, his double meaning clear. "In fact, we can begin, if you like, by making this carriage ride more interesting."

There. Now she knew. He wasn't so loyal to Autenberry that he would not pursue her. In fact, he wasn't loyal to Autenberry at all. It wasn't in his nature to deny himself something he wanted. And he wanted her.

"You're incorrigible." She let out a huff of breath and wrenched her gaze back to the window.

He chuckled again, satisfied that he had planted the seed in her mind. It would grow.

The invitation was there. She need only take it.

ALONE IN A carriage with Struan Mackenzie was every bit the bad idea she feared it would be. It was too late, however. Her sister was already gone in the carriage with the duchess and the other girls. Unless she wanted to jump from a moving carriage, Poppy was stuck. Alone with a man who was much too dangerous to her senses.

And he *was* dangerous. Just because she didn't fear for her life did not mean he posed no threat. There was more than one way to pose a danger. She had their time in the alleyway to serve as a constant reminder of that.

Shivering, she burrowed deeper into her cloak.

"Here." He lifted the great fur blanket off the seat beside him and unfolded it. Shaking it out slightly, he draped it over her.

She shook her head. She wasn't shivering because of the cold, but she wasn't going to tell him that. "You don't have to—"

"Don't be stubborn. I can hear your teeth clacking. You need a new cloak. This one is worn thin."

"It was my mother's." She lifted her chin, an undeniable edge of defensiveness creeping into her voice.

"Sentimentality is good and well until you take chill and sicken."

She choked back the impulse to tell him the truth—that she couldn't simply go purchase a new, warmer cloak. That kind of expenditure would require setting money aside for months. And right now Bryony had needs that came before her own.

They rode in silence for a good while and some of the tension began to ebb from her shoulders. Perhaps they could pass this journey in relative peace and without incident, after all. She stared out the small crack in the curtains, at the sliver of world awash in winter gray.

"Where's your mother that she does not need her cloak?" he asked suddenly.

She started, her gaze returning to his. Was he interested in such things about her?

"She's gone," she said after a few moments. Conversation with him made her uneasy. *He* made her uneasy. He seemed to enjoy discomfiting her. She didn't know what he would do or say next. "For twelve years now," she continued. "My sister's birth was . . . difficult. She was never very strong after that. Every cold, every ague, took its toll and left her weaker. She finally succumbed to consumption."

The coach swayed with a comforting rhythm. Her hands stroked the velvet squabs restlessly.

She had never been in so fine a carriage. Even her brief time in the duchess's carriage had not treated her to such luxury—and she had thought that was the finest carriage she would ever grace. Her fingers stroked the fine seat. Struan Mackenzie might not be highborn, but he certainly had wealth to spare if he could possess a coach the likes of this.

"I lost my mother, too," his deep voice rumbled across the space between them to confess. "When I was ten and four . . ."

Awkward silence fell.

"I was two years younger than that," she volunteered into the quiet. "I still remember her voice . . . things she said and did. How she liked to garden. In the spring she would smell like the soil, loamy and floral. But her face is less clear to me. That's the most unsettling thing. I search my memory for her face and it's always hovering, just beyond my reach."

"Have you no portraits or sketching of her?"

"Sadly, no." She gave a wobbly smile and looked down at her hands. "But the reverend's wife says I favor her."

"Then she was beautiful," he quickly returned, almost as though the words had been unthinking on his part.

Her head whipped up at that. No one had called her beautiful before. That was reserved for Bryony.

He looked at her only a moment before turning his gaze to stare out the crack in the curtains that had held her attention earlier, almost as though he regretted uttering the compliment.

Poppy didn't know what to say. She studied him for a moment. Hoping to change the subject, she inquired, "What happened after your mother died? Did you go to live with your father—"

His face hardened. "The Duke of Autenberry

didn't want anything to do with his lowborn son. I only met him once. A few months before my mother died. He was visiting friends on the estate my mother once worked as a maid." His fingers clenched on his thigh, clearly recalling bitter memories. "They sacked her when she began increasing with me. Can't have an unwed girl cleaning the chamber pots." His lip curled. "Never mind it was their houseguest who pursued her as relentlessly as a bloodhound. It was she alone who bore the burden. My father ruined her and then left her. No family would take her in after that. She was soiled goods." If possible that lip only curled further, revealing a flash of white teeth within the shadowy interior. He reminded her of a wolf. She shifted uneasily where she sat across from him.

She trembled, listening raptly, horrified as an image of his childhood in all its ugliness took shape before her. "Then what happened?"

"She made her living the only way she could. As so many before her have."

"You grew up like that? With her . . ." It was too wretched to say. Although it was not something that hadn't crossed her mind before. The constant strain of pinching pennies, fretting about the future for both herself and Bryony. How could such a fate that befell on so many hapless females lacking finances or protection *not* have crossed her mind as a dreaded fear?

"Aye, different men." He nodded, his eyes taking on a faraway quality. "A slew of them coming and going . . ."

She sucked in a sharp breath.

He shook his head with a muffled curse. "My apologies. It's not a fit subject. I don't know why I'm telling you this." He sounded bemused. "I've never talked about it with anyone. Perhaps it's because of those eyes of yours."

"My eyes?"

"Aye, they beg a man to spill all. Everything. Hold nothing back."

"They do?" Her fingertips brushed her upper cheek. The afternoon was a day for revelations, it seemed.

"Aye," he repeated. "That is when they're not flashing as though you wish to maim me."

She gave a small grunt of laughter, stifling it. "Well, you do wage a good argument for justified maiming." She sobered, picking at a fraying thread along a seam in her dress. "I don't mind you talking about your mother. Perhaps you do so now for the very reason that you never have. Everyone should have someone to confide in."

"And you want to be my confidante, Miss Fairchurch?" His voice adopted a husky pitch that made her stomach roll. If possible, it seemed that the air grew thicker, the confines of the coach tighter.

"It's something to do to pass the time during the journey," she said with forced brightness.

"I could think of other things to do."

Her face burned, understanding precisely what things he referred to.

They lapsed into awkward silence for some moments and she feared she had killed the impulse in him to confide in her.

And then he began talking again.

She released a small anxious breath.

"One of my earliest memories is taking care of her after one of her gentlemen *callers* decided he needed to rearrange her face." He tapped the edge of his nose, and she wondered if he was even aware that he was doing that. Or was he seeing his mother, seeing her face when it had been *rearranged*.

Poppy winced, visualizing him as a little boy trying to help his mother, the one adult who should have taken care of *him*.

"I'm sorry," she whispered, her voice shaking.

He turned his attention from the window and fixed his stare on her once again. He stared at her for a long time, his gaze deep, curious, as he assessed her. "What do you have to be sorry about?

You were a little girl then, caught up in your own world doing little-girl things. Even once your mother was gone, I presume there was a father there for you?" At her nod, he continued flatly, "My own father is dead now. He was the reason I came to London."

She frowned. "How is that?"

"I had to show him. Let him know I made something of myself even without his help. I wanted him to know that I wasn't rotting in an unmarked grave like my mother."

She flinched.

"I even entertained the notion of taking revenge on him."

Her expression must have revealed some of her disapproval. She regretted that. She shouldn't judge. She couldn't know what he'd endured. She couldn't begin to understand how he felt. Then or now.

"Should that surprise you?" he asked, that corner of his mouth kicking up, tempting her with his non-smile. "I thought marrying some fine blue-blooded lass would be the final revenge. Flaunting her in my father's face . . . going to all the same functions that he and his *real* family attended. I thought about doing that very thing for a long time. Even after I learned my father was dead, I thought about it."

For some reason this confession made her feel a little hollow inside. "You're looking to marry an aristocrat?" she asked numbly, feeling awkward and inadequate sitting across from him. She twisted her hands in her lap. A poor shopgirl like herself shouldn't be worth his time and yet here he was stuck in a carriage with her.

"*Thought* as in past tense. Not anymore." He chuckled harshly. "I shook off that fit of madness, thankfully. Can you imagine? I was contemplating shackling myself to a blue-blooded miss simply to prove that I was as good as my sire. And he's dead." He laughed roughly. "I suppose I thought he could see me from where he's burning."

Relief coursed through her. And sadness. She was perversely and selfishly and *wrongly* glad that he still wasn't on a mission to marry, but she felt sorry for him, too. He seemed so . . . alone. For all his money and power, he was alone.

She studied the big shape of him across from her. His legs took up a great deal of space, nearly touching the bench where she sat. It was difficult to reconcile such a brawny man with the words she was hearing from him. He looked invulnerable, but he was so obviously embittered.

She moistened her lips before speaking. "It can't be good for you to keep this festering inside you."

He was silent for a moment. His eyes black as a graveyard in the confines of the carriage, and she was quite certain he did not appreciate her advice. He leaned forward slightly, propping one elbow on his knee in a gesture that felt faintly menacing. "My mother took me to him once, you know, as I mentioned. Presented me as though he might be proud at the sight of me." He laughed harshly again. "I was the spitting image of him. Resembled him even more than Marcus. Ironic that."

So Autenberry saw his dead father when he looked at his bastard half brother? That must be a struggle. What else did he see when he looked at Struan? His father's infidelity? The sting of betrayal? Suddenly the fight outside Barclay's made a little more sense. As difficult as Struan's life had been, this couldn't be easy for Autenberry either.

Struan continued, "My mother wanted him to acknowledge me. Take me home with him. Can you believe that? She still believed in fairy tales after everything that happened to her."

"She was your mother," Poppy said slowly, thoughtfully. "She loved you and wanted the best for you. Yes. I can imagine that."

"Well, that didn't happen. Instead he left us to starve and freeze through a Highland winter. My mother was already weak. Too few meals over a long period of time . . . years. She would always see to me first. Food and clothing, shoes, went to me first."

Poppy nodded slowly, tears clogging her throat as he uttered all of this so impassively, his face a stone mask. Wouldn't she do the same if she were a mother? Would she not do the same for Bryony?

"She never saw the spring," he finished.

She inhaled, uncertain how to proceed after his admission. She had to tamp down the urge to reach across the space separating them and touch him, to offer some measure of comfort. *For him or yourself?* She shook off the question, pushing it down deep inside her.

Undeniably, she did not trust herself with him. Not after last night. There was too much tension between them, too much temptation wrapped up in him. He was a magnet for which she could not resist.

"You do have family that cares about you or you wouldn't be on the way to Autenberry Manor. The dowager duchess, Clara, Enid . . . she's your half sister," she reminded him.

"I scarcely know them."

"As of now," she acknowledged. "But they clearly have no wish to remain strangers."

He chuckled, still managing not to smile as he studied her contemplatively. "You are full of sunshine. I wager you've never met a soul that didn't like you. You're a rare thing, kitten. Not everyone is like you." He exhaled. "I'm on the way to Autenberry Manor because my half brother is in a coma. When the duke wakes, that invitation shall be revoked and I'll be cast out and heading back to Town." He shrugged. "Or Scotland. A stranger yet again to the Autenberry clan."

She shook her head. "Lord Strickland thinks when His Grace awakes you two could put everything behind you and become at the very least friendly—"

"Does he now?" Amusement laced his voice. "I'm the bastard son. The dirty evidence of the late duke's indiscretion. Autenberry admired his father greatly and I'm evidence that his lauded father was far less than the great man he believed him to be. Trust me, my brother didn't want me around before his coma. He won't want me around after."

She lifted her chin, thinking of the duke coming into Barclay's every week. His ready smile and kind words didn't match the man that Struan was describing. "I think you're wrong."

"Oh, that's right." His lips curled in a sneer. Something sparked in his dark moss eyes that made gooseflesh break out across her skin. Her stomach quivered and her breath caught. He leaned forward, draping his wrists on his knees so that his big hands with their long, tapering fingers dangled loose on the air. She tried not to stare hard at those hands, those fingers. Tried not to remember how they felt on her. "He's your perfect prince of a man," he bit out, his brogue hard and clipped.

"I didn't say that. No one is perfect." Autenberry just happened to be close. At least the *notion* of him that she had created in her head was close to perfection.

"Oh, you'll admit that? I'm shocked. Your fiancé isn't perfection?"

She flushed, not about to malign a man in a coma . . . especially one to whom she was supposedly affianced. "That's not what I said either. You're twisting my words. Autenberry is quite nearly perfect."

"*Quite* nearly? So he's imperfect?"

"Stop it!" she snapped.

"Is it his kissing technique?" He angled his head. "Is that where he falls short?"

She flushed hot. "I didn't say he falls short and his kissing is . . . is perfectly fine."

"Fine?" Mockery again. "Well, that's a ringing endorsement."

"He's splendid! Brilliant!" She tossed her hands in the air, astonished that she was even having this conversation. Why was it that around this man all sense of propriety failed her? "A glorious kisser!"

"That a fact?"

"Yes." She should stop now, but she kept going, the words flying out like barbed arrows. "Who do you think taught me to kiss? The duke is more than adequate." She didn't know where these lies were coming from. Mackenzie did something to her. Made her not even recognize herself.

"Oh?" The word was uttered with such stillness. Almost too quiet. It should have warned her. "And what else did that brother of mine teach you?" he growled, reaching across the seat to seize her waist with both hands.

Before she could get out a word, he plopped her on his lap, her skirts a froth of fabric around them.

She squeaked, her hands coming up to balance herself on his shoulders.

"I have an idea." His brogue, deep as the forest of his eyes, dragged across her skin, a physical caress. "Why don't you just show me?"

Chapter 17

*H*is mouth slanted over hers. Liquid heat rushed through her as his hand curled around her jaw. His other hand slid inside her cloak, the broad palm spanning her back.

Air escaped her nose in rapid little pants. The sound was embarrassing. It gave away just how affected she was, just how devastated she found his mouth on hers . . . his hand on her . . . his voice—

"No running away this time, kitten. No interruptions," he growled against her lips. "We've plenty of time in this carriage for you to show me everything my damn brother taught you."

His growly words should offend her. Outrage should have her pushing him away, but the way his mouth worked over hers, hot and punishing, hungry, as though she were the last meal he would ever eat, had her hands doing other things.

Instead of pushing him away, her fingers relaxed and crept up his shoulders to curl around his neck and tangle in the too-long strands of his hair. The dark gold strands felt like silk, the ends soft as feathers brushing her palms. Did Vikings have hair this soft?

She ran her fingers deeper into his hair, her nails scraping his scalp, and he gave a low sound of pleasure. "Keep touching me," he breathed into her mouth, his air filling all the little hollows inside her.

She reveled in him. A deep throb of pleasure spread through her, arrowing with thrilling precision directly between her legs.

He was right. She couldn't run away. There would be no Watch interrupting them now. Just as he said. They were in a moving carriage, and unless they capsized, they had only each other for company for the duration—however much longer that was. Plenty of time to thoroughly ruin her if she allowed it.

His tongue licked at the seam of her lips and she opened her mouth, letting him in. He stroked the inside of her mouth, tasting her, touching her tongue with his. She copied the move, surrendering to the madness and the demanding throb at her core.

His hand traveled around her ribs and slipped upward to cup her breast over her dress. Her face flamed and she moaned into his mouth as he pressed the palm of his hand into the slight mound. She was suddenly conscious of how small she was in that arena. She dressed and undressed daily beside her sister, so she knew the difference between amply endowed and simply . . . not.

He kneaded her breast, fondling her until she had to bite her lip to keep from crying out. "Did he teach you how good this felt, hmm? Did he make you moan?"

She clenched her teeth harder into her lip in an attempt to stifle her moan, scarcely understanding what he was saying but knowing it was wrong. She was supposed to be affianced to his brother. She shouldn't be letting him do this to her. She shouldn't *want* it—him—so much.

"Does that feel good?" He chafed his thumb back and forth against her nipple through the fabric of her dress.

Releasing her lip, she moaned, leaning into him, feeling drugged, slave to the ache in her clenching core.

"That's what I thought," he said, his voice smug, satisfied.

He tugged down her bodice, growling only to find the barrier of her corset. "You're wearing far too many clothes."

She opened her eyes to find him gazing back at her, his eyes laden with hot promise. "I—I'm wearing what every lady wears."

"I don't care what every lady wears. I only care what you're *not* wearing."

A shudder ripped through her at his words.

She grasped the edge of her corset and tugged it up, making certain it was still secured over her bosom. "It's for the best." She leaned back, withdrawing. "We need to stop before this goes too far."

"And what would be too far?" He still clung to her waist, holding her in place over him, not letting her climb off him.

"I think stopping just shy of ruin is best."

"Is that all? I can promise not to ruin you. What happens in this carriage need never be known . . ." His voice faded as his hand moved to her hem, inching her dress up her leg, his short nails scraping against her stocking and eliciting shivers.

She grabbed his hand, halting him at her knee. "What are you doing?"

His heavy-lidded gaze fixed on her. "Not ruining you, kitten."

"It doesn't feel like that to me." She moistened her lips, grasping for the twisting ribbons of her resolve, hoping to crush them. She couldn't do this. Couldn't be with him. *So where was her voice?*

Clearly sensing her reservations, he lowered his mouth to her neck and she shivered at the glide of his lips. His voice husked over her ear. "I promise only to touch."

"I'm w-with Autenberry." Blast her less than convincing stammer. More than ever she needed him to believe that. She needed that to matter.

He tensed beneath her and for a moment she thought she'd said the thing to make him give up. "I can make you forget Autenberry."

Oh, what a wretched web. She was certain he could make her forget, too. Especially considering she had no exceptionally remarkable memories to forget. She did not think she and the duke had ever even touched. Not even in the most harmless of passing.

His lips closed on the lobe of her ear and her breath caught. His teeth scraped the sensitive skin and bit down gently. A sound strangled in her throat and his teeth let go, which only had her leaning in and grasping the edges of his coat, clinging to him.

His brogue purred into her ear. "Touch and

taste you." The hot drag of his tongue followed that comment.

She was lost in a muddle of sensation. It didn't matter what he was saying anymore. His fingers moved up the inside of her thigh.

"What are you doing?" she gasped even though she had a fairly decent idea. She knew there was a good amount of wickedness that went into bed sport.

"I thought that would be obvious. I'm making you feel good."

"It's not proper," she insisted, diving for his foraying hand beneath her skirts.

He laughed against her mouth. "Is kissing your fiancé's bastard brother proper?" he challenged. "Perhaps we should ask the others in the next carriage to weigh in with their opinions. Face it. You're not a proper female, kitten."

She gasped and without any forethought brought her palm cracking against the side of his face. He reared back, fingering his cheek. Even in the shadowy carriage, her handprint stood out starkly against his skin.

"What was that for?" he growled.

"You disgust me."

He stilled over her in a way that made the tiny hairs on the back of her neck stand on end. "Indeed?"

She nodded jerkily even as she knew that was not the precise word. He made her feel things, but disgust was not one of them.

"Ever a liar, aren't you?"

"I'm not."

"Let me tell you something about myself, Poppy. There's not much that bothers me, but lying ranks high. And you know why?"

A sinking sensation settled over her. "Why?" she whispered, the word barely a sound.

"My father. He was many things to different people. He showed one face to his family, but there was another side of him. The side he only showed to my mother and me. He promised her the world and then he destroyed her. He *lied* to her and she paid for it every day."

"And you," Poppy couldn't help pointing out. "You paid the price, as well."

He shrugged. "I'm still alive. She's gone." He pinned her with his hot gaze. "So, liars? I don't have any tolerance for them."

Those words echoed through her. He had no tolerance for liars.

Lying was all she had done since they first met each other. Someday he would know that. Then there would be nothing stopping him from hating her. Granted, her lies weren't destroying him— Lord Strickland had persuaded her into believing that they weren't hurting anyone—but Mackenzie would still not appreciate the deception. Her stomach twisted.

It was merely a matter of time. Soon he'd know the truth and whatever admiration or attraction he felt toward her would die a swift death. He hated liars.

He would hate her, too.

He took her by the shoulders and pulled her closer, still talking. "So don't tell me I disgust you when I don't. I think perhaps you're disgusted with yourself. Not me."

She started at that accusation. "That's absurd."

He nodded as though she had not spoken. "You can't be disgusted too much if you let me do this."

His mouth covered hers, silencing her attempt to withdraw. This kiss was different. Tender and coaxing and it weakened her knees. "You taste of lemons, Miss Fairchurch," he murmured against her lips, giving her bottom lip gentle nibbles before kissing her fully again.

Now he addressed her formally?

"Poppy," she sighed in relent, breathing into his mouth, shaking from the battle of resisting him, from fighting herself.

His hand skimmed over her stockings and her limbs turned to pudding.

He kissed her again. She kissed him back, but

the more intimate his touch, the more ragged and sloppy their kissing grew. She moaned into his mouth when his fingers slipped through the slit in her drawers to brush her sex.

"Oh," she cried into his mouth as his finger eased inside her. He pushed deep and held his finger there for a moment, letting her get accustomed to the fit and sensation of him.

He shifted and she felt him, his erection hard underneath her bottom. She couldn't help herself. She ground down against him.

"God, you're tight, Poppy." He withdrew his finger and thrust it back inside, curling it as he did so, hitting her in some invisible spot that brought forth a rush of bewildering sensation. She started shaking, feeling herself coming apart.

"Struan," she whimpered.

He groaned and stroked deeper.

The drag of his finger against her oversensitive flesh was driving her to the brink of something. The tight ball coiling inside her broke, bursting into tiny pinpricks of sensation.

She shuddered, dropping her face into his neck. His finger remained lodged in her for a long, breathless moment as the tremors ebbed from her body.

His mouth moved against her hair as he spoke,

sliding his hand out from under her skirts. "That's going to feel even better when it's me inside you."

She stiffened, equal parts horror and delight sizzling through her at his bold words. This couldn't be how a gentleman spoke to a lady—and that shouldn't titillate her. She was a good, Christian woman. How could she have reveled in him touching her like that?

Shoving her skirts down, she scrambled back across the opposite seat and glared at him. She dragged a trembling hand down her throat. Her skin felt pulsing. He did that to her. Blast him. She *let* him do that. Oh, very well, then, blast *her*!

"That's not ever going to happen. This was a fleeting lapse."

"Is that what you're calling it?" His brogue seemed thicker as ever as he echoed, "A fleeting lapse?"

"You seduced me," she accused. "From the moment I stepped inside this carriage . . . ever since last night!"

"You offered to show me what my brother taught you," he said evenly.

She hissed. "I never—that's not how it happened and you know it." Hot shame flushed through her. Her voice shook out of her with bewildering emotion. "Stay away from me."

"Are you certain you want that? That's not what you were saying a moment ago when you were crying out my name."

She lifted her hand to strike him again and he caught her wrist, his eyes glittering black. "You've struck me once. Never again."

She yanked her hand free and glared at him. She didn't even know herself around this man. She'd never felt moved to violence before. *You'd never been moved to passion before either.*

How could she have allowed him such liberties after so short an acquaintance? Heaven knew Edmond had pressed her for more and she had stood firm against him. Over professions of love and promises of marriage, she had resisted.

It was this man. Struan Mackenzie. Edmond possessed a nice enough face, but he did not look like Struan Mackenzie. Nor did he talk like him. Or kiss like him. Or infuriate her like him.

"I am certain of what I want. Leave. Me. Alone."

He gazed at her and a ghost of a smile curved his mouth, taunting her. She could still taste him on her lips. Still feel his expert touch. Angling his head, Struan looked so insufferably enticing right then, and she knew she was in serious trouble.

He was correct. She was ever a liar. Because she

wasn't certain what she wanted anymore. To curl right back up in his lap or strike him squarely in the nose?

Autenberry had been her dream. Mackenzie was a brute. She shouldn't be feeling this way.

"You don't want me to do that." That brogue of his only stoked the flames higher inside her.

She scowled and pressed back into the carriage squabs, shrinking like a wilting bloom against a frigid wind. Frustration rose up and squeezed inside of her. "Very well. My body is a treacherous and weak thing and isn't repulsed by you." She sniffed. "Is that what you want me to admit?"

He nodded. "It is a start." He leaned forward as though he would join her on her side of the carriage. She held up a hand to ward him off.

"That admission is the *end.*" She inhaled through her nose thinly. "The *end* of *me.*" She flattened a hand against her chest. "If I were to let this happen between us, I could not like myself." Silly as it sounded, she had always *liked* herself. She had always been able to look at herself with pride in the mirror each day. Thanks to Papa. Not a day passed where he had not told her how clever she was, how lovely and special. How loved.

"I cannot engage in a strictly physical tryst—"

"Oh, you could," he said with maddening surety.

"People do it all the time. It's the giving and receiving of pleasure. There is nothing wrong about that, lass."

Preposterous. He was a sinful, debauched creature who would drag her down to the very brink of depravity if she let him.

"I *could* do that," she allowed. "And then I would despise myself. I can't have this—" she motioned between them "—without affection. Without . . ." Her voice faded and heat slapped her face.

"Love?" He snorted. "Don't tell me you're one of those?"

"One of what?"

"An idealist. A romantic." He made it sound like a dirty thing. "Don't tell me you love Autenberry?" The scorn in his voice cut like a knife.

She nodded even if her conviction wasn't nearly as strong as it once was. "Of course I love him," she whispered, telling herself it was the necessary falsehood. "I'm going to marry him." Never since she started this charade had the lie felt more necessary than in this moment. "I love him. I've loved him since the first time we met."

"Bollocks."

She pulled back, a hard breath escaping her. "I beg your pardon?"

Did he know? Had he seen through her ruse?

"Love at first sight? Bollocks!" A muscle in

his jaw twitched. "I don't know if you're lying to yourself or me, but you're a liar nonetheless."

Oh, he simply refused to believe the sentiment was genuine. "You arrogant—"

"You couldn't kiss me like that and open yourself to me and be in love with him. That much I know about you, Miss Fairchurch, foolish romantic as you just professed yourself to be."

The carriage seemed to be slowing. Either that or it was wishful thinking on her part. She slipped a hand between the curtains and peered out. They were definitely slowing. The landscape no longer whipped past as quickly.

She patted her hair and straightened her garments, hoping the damage not too great and no one would make anything of her untidy appearance. Hopefully, they would just chalk it up to the rigors of travel.

"You, sir, are a blackguard and I demand you keep your distance from me henceforth." He stared at her for a long moment and she could not help but notice no such promise was forthcoming. "I'm waiting, Mr. Mackenzie."

"Then you'll have to wait forever, kitten, because I'm not in the habit of telling lies."

Not precisely what she wanted to hear from him.

The carriage rolled to a stop. "We're here. Time to get out."

He opened the door and climbed down. She followed, hovering in the open doorway and peering out. He waited for her, one hand proffered, ready to assist her down. Beyond him loomed Autenberry Manor, the grandest residence she had ever seen, a vast gray edifice of stone that was home to the Duke of Autenberry and a countless line of dukes before him. A steady stream of liveried servants spilled out of the house to form a receiving line, ready to greet the dowager duchess and her family. And Poppy—the fraud.

Instantly, she knew. She would never belong here. She had thought she loved Autenberry—or rather, she *could* love him. As handsome and kind and charming as he was, it would not be difficult to fall for him. She had thought that perhaps he could love her, too. Perhaps. If he only knew her. Now she knew that would never be.

Life wasn't some fairy tale. She loved the *idea* of the Duke of Autenberry. The myth. Confronted with this mausoleum, she knew that the reality was far, far removed from her.

She had made a mistake in coming here—in ever perpetrating this charade. She needed to go home at once, and put all of this—*him*—behind her. Easier said than done. Unfortunately, for the time being, she was trapped.

She lifted her chin in resolve. There would be

no more stumbling into his arms. No more kissing. No more anything. She didn't have to be so weak-willed again.

No more future trysts. He saw too much.

She had to make certain that he did not see all . . . everything. *Her.* The man had not lifted himself from poverty to such heights without a keen gift of scrutiny. She would be cautious and have a care around the man.

Struan Mackenzie dropped into step beside her. The large shadow of him fell over her just as it began to snow in earnest.

Trapped with a wolf breathing down her neck, ready to devour her if she made one misstep. Maybe her life was a fairy tale, after all.

Chapter 18

The next few days for Struan passed in a blur of frustration.

Poppy avoided him. He never caught her alone. After their carriage ride, he supposed it was inevitable that she would wish to avoid him. She had yet to realize. She would be his.

Even if she would never be his because she belonged to his brother.

He shoved the unwelcome reminder aside. He didn't want to *keep* her. He didn't want forever. He simply wanted her. One time and he would rid her from his system. One time and both of them could move on.

Only they would need to be alone for that to happen.

If she wasn't surrounded by a gaggle of women, then she was sitting by the duke's bedside—and that, too, she never did alone. There was always a maid in the corner or the dowager or Lord Strickland with his knowing, watchful gaze.

It was a damnable situation.

She might be avoiding him, but the dowager and Lady Enid were not. They were interested in knowing him. Naturally, Lady Clara was more interested in spending time with Bryony. He saw the girls rushing about the grounds, playing with the hounds, walking the snow-draped gardens and building puny-looking snowmen that collapsed by the following morning.

Enid showed him around the manor, from the grounds to the vast house. She took him down the portrait gallery, pointing out their ancestors. That was a strange experience. One predecessor in particular, his great-grandfather, bore a striking resemblance to him. Their eyes were the same. Same green. Deeply set. Enid remarked on it.

"See. You belong here. Your roots are here." She smiled mildly at him.

He nodded once in acknowledgment. Not agreement. His roots were in poverty. In Glasgow. In bastardy. He was the son of a prostitute, a woman bought and abused daily. There was no shaking that past.

"I'm glad you came," Enid said, moving along the gallery. "I didn't think you would."

He strolled beside her, hands clasped behind his back. "No?"

"Marcus . . . your arrival to Town, your existence, has been difficult for him."

Struan laughed harshly. "*My* existence has been difficult for him? Somehow I doubt it was any more difficult than growing up unacknowledged by our father."

"Marcus loved our father. He thought him everything good and noble. That's how Papa presented himself. Learning about you, learning your beloved parent was another person entirely . . . it's disillusioning to say the least. Marcus was worried you wanted to hurt us."

Struan stopped to face her. "What about you?"

"At first I worried that you were out for revenge, too." She studied him thoughtfully. "Then I learned more about you." She shook her head. "I waited, but you never attempted to see us. That didn't sound like someone who wanted to hurt us." She laughed lightly. "I was actually bothered because you didn't want to meet us. I—I . . ." She stammered in a way that seemed uncharacteristic for her. "I wanted to meet you."

They stared at each other for a long assessing moment. "And now that you have?"

She lifted one shoulder in a half shrug. "I have another brother. I want you in my life. Whatever happens with Marcus, I want you in my life."

He shifted his weight on his feet, feeling unaccountably abashed. "Yes. I would like that."

She smiled again, her lips curving widely, taking her from plain to strikingly pretty. "Splendid. Now. Would you like to join me in the kitchen? Cook makes the best gingersnaps. Your life is truly not complete until you've tasted a least a score of them."

He smiled slightly and motioned ahead. "Then by all means, lead the way."

STRUAN OWNED SEVERAL properties. The aristocracy was renowned for living beyond their means and that had a way of catching up with one. Generations of living like royalty without paying for it eventually came to an end for all.

Eventually, *someone* had to be paid, and Struan was often that someone. He was the man scooping up properties that weren't entailed to ancient noble titles—property that had to be sold off to honor outstanding debts.

That said, even as many fine, resplendent homes as he had acquired, restored and sold again over the years, Autenberry Manor was the finest he had ever seen. He tried not to let the old feelings of inadequacy creep over him as he sat at the centuries-old dining table. A dining table that had fed his ancestors. Men and women of his bloodline sat at this very table and feasted.

And yet he didn't belong here. Despite how welcoming the dowager was. Despite Enid escorting him through the gallery and pointing out his resemblance to his forefathers, he felt like an interloper.

Then why are you still here?

Of its own volition, his gaze drifted toward Poppy Fairchurch. She wore an elegant gown of blue silk that he knew she could not possibly own. Clearly they'd been here long enough for the dowager to find appropriate dresses for both Misses Fairchurch. Young Bryony preened in a peach-colored gown like she was born to wear such finery. Poppy appeared less comfortable and he wondered, again, at her relationship with Autenberry. Why had his brother not showered her with silks? Why should she sit in this dining room and look so ill at ease if she was to marry into this glittering world?

He forced his gaze away from her and back to the others at the table.

"Thank you, Darby," the dowager said in that effusive manner of hers, her elegant hand brushing the server's arm in additional thanks. "And how is your grandmother?" She shifted in her seat to more fully face the servant and hear his response. That in itself was singular. A duchess that gave a damn about someone stations under her.

His gaze drifted to Poppy. She watched the exchange, too, looking equally mystified, that delicious mouth of hers that filled far too much of his thoughts parted slightly in wonder.

"Much improved, Your Grace." The man bobbed his head, his eyes adoring but reflecting no surprise or bewilderment. Because this was normal. The young dowager, caring for those lesser than she, was normal. "Thank you for inquiring."

Her dark eyes flashed in Enid and Clara's direction. "We must call on her tomorrow. Have Cook prepare some of my *abuela*'s magical *caldo*. It cures all ailments."

"All?" Enid dryly interjected.

The dowager fluttered a hand in her direction dismissively. "Indeed, yes. I know what I speak."

Struan gave his head a slight shake. He wanted to dislike her. She was the woman his father had remarried. Even when his own mother had still been alive, he had chosen her. *Married* her. Forgot about him and the woman he'd seduced and discarded in Scotland. He'd chosen a young foreign beauty. Even if born to a noble Spanish family, the English peerage couldn't have fully embraced her. And yet none of that had mattered to the late duke. He'd chosen her.

Struan wanted to hate her and yet he could not find it in him. The noblewoman was an anomaly—warm and welcoming. The fact that he and Poppy were even here was a testament to her kindness and openness, a definite eccentricity among the ton.

He glanced around the table and caught Lord Strickland gazing at the dowager in a way that was *more* than friendly. The earl was affable if not guarded. Struan usually found him unreadable. Except for right now. For a brief moment, that wall came down and Struan read the admiration in the young man's eyes. Hell. More than admiration. If the man wasn't in love with the dowager, he was certainly in lust.

Struan observed her as she accepted a refill of Madeira in her glass. Unlike many English ladies of her class, she did not eschew spirits. She drank deeply from her cup. Her upswept hair gleamed like a moonless dark ocean. Her golden skin beckoned a man's fingers. What sane man wouldn't want her in his bed?

She laughed gaily at something Clara said to Bryony, tossing her head back with abandon. Lord Strickland watched her hungrily and Struan almost felt sorry for the man. He was her stepson's best friend, several years younger than she and of lesser rank. The poor bastard did not have a chance.

Sane or not, Struan did not want his late father's wife. His gaze drifted again to Poppy Fairchurch. He wanted *her*. He supposed that proved his desire for her was genuine and not something fleeting or driven by revenge—because what better way to satisfy his deep-seated resentment of his dead father than by taking the man's woman? Too bad he didn't want her. Too bad he burned for someone else.

He tore his gaze away and endured the rest of the dinner, chiming into the conversation when appropriate. Unlike Poppy. She hardly spoke.

"I never imagined Marcus would find himself such a shy little dove," Enid remarked.

"Perhaps she is simply overwhelmed," the dowager defended.

"Overwhelmed? Of us? *You?*" Enid said drolly, and contemplated that prospect with an exaggerated air. "Not possible." Enid sipped from her glass. Not Madeira. She was not quite as eccentric as her stepmother, but then her roots were English, after all.

Poppy never responded to their questioning, simply managed a tight smile. They scarcely finished their meal before Poppy excused herself.

She didn't have to say where she was going. He knew.

He remained with the rest of the party, joining them in the drawing room, trying not to think about her upstairs with Autenberry. Since they'd arrived at the manor it's where she always went. Tending to the duke. Hiding from Struan.

No more.

He was done letting her hide from him. Tonight they would speak.

She would talk to him. He'd make certain of it.

Chapter 19

*H*e was waiting for her when she emerged from the duke's bedchamber. At least it felt that way. Struan Mackenzie spoke her name as she gently closed the bedchamber door on the duke. Strange, she supposed. It was as though she feared waking the unconscious duke.

At the sound of her name she startled and whirled around, a hand flying to her throat. "Mr. Mackenzie. You startled me."

The hour was late. She'd hoped he, along with the others, would have retired for the night by now. She'd done an estimable job avoiding him since she arrived at Autenberry Manor. It wasn't too difficult. She was here as the Duke of Autenberry's fiancée. It made sense that she should want to sit with him as he convalesced. No one questioned it. Even if Struan Mackenzie's gaze watched her darkly when she joined them for meals, he dared not voice disapproval. It wasn't his place. Despite what had happened between them in Town, and in the carriage . . .

Good heavens. That was sordid. Her face burned as it did whenever her thoughts roamed in that direction. How did she go from the over-looked sister, grateful for the attention of the village baker, to this? A female who engaged in wicked trysts with smoldering, unacceptable gentlemen?

She knew this hiding was cowardly of her. She clung to the farce so that she could avoid Struan. Also, so she could hide from the overwhelming evidence of wealth and opulence that made up Autenberry Manor. It daunted her and made her feel all the more a fraud. Her sister might be utterly at home in this world, but she felt like an interloper. Any moment she would give herself away.

He strode toward her with effortless grace. It was odd. For a man his size, he moved like a predator strolling at ease through the jungle. "Are we still exercising formalities, Poppy? I've heard you use my Christian name. On more than one occasion." The slight smirk to his lips told her he was remembering how she had uttered his name. When and what they were doing.

She inclined her head slightly in acknowledgment of that truth and glanced up and down the length of the corridor, confirming they were well and truly alone. Not the best idea.

"You are up late," she went on to say, turning in the direction of her bedchamber on the *opposite* side of the house in the opposite wing. It was several corridor turns and rooms from here— unfortunately. She couldn't escape him so easily. Blast, why did this house have to be so colossal?

She began walking, pausing when he fell into step beside her.

"The same could be said of you," he returned.

"I was checking on His Grace."

"Yes, very attentive of you. And how does your *beloved* fare?"

She did not mistake the mockery in his voice.

"There has been no change," she replied, sliding him a cautious look.

"I am certain with you sitting vigil at his bedside there soon will be."

She eyed him, attempting to assess whether he mocked her or not. It was difficult to know.

"I know a thing or two about caretaking." Her voice rang out defensively.

"Do you now? And how is that?"

"Before Bryony and I moved to Town, I cared for my father for the better part of a year. Before he passed away."

"Did you? You are a regular angel of mercy, Poppy."

She stopped and faced him. "I cannot infer if you are toying with me or not, Mr. Mackenzie."

"I would never toy with you, kitten." And yet as he uttered this she did in fact *feel* like he toyed with her. As though she were in reality a kitten and he her tormenter, dangling a ball of yarn before her. "I am most convinced before you relocated to Town you were a devoted and attentive daughter to your ailing father. Just as you are a most devoted sister. That much is obvious. The people in your life are lucky to have you."

She slanted him a suspicious look. "Thank you?"

"I mean that in all sincerity. You needn't say 'thank you' like a question."

Not certain what to do with this complimentary Struan Mackenzie, she resumed walking down the corridor. "Bryony requires looking after."

He stopped her again, placing a hand on her shoulder and turning her around to face him. "And what of you? Who looks after you, Poppy? Autenberry?" Skepticism dripped off the question.

"Why is that so difficult for you to believe?"

"Because so far I'm not impressed. I see little evidence that Autenberry cares for you as a man should care for his woman."

That is because I am not his. I belong to no one.

It was undeniable. His words sent a bolt of unfamiliar longing through her. Not just to belong to someone . . . but for someone to belong to her. The longing, however, was wrapped up in Struan Mackenzie. As he gazed at her with his green eyes as deep and dark as a night wood yearning seized her.

She shrugged his touch off her shoulder and started forward again. "You shouldn't say such things."

"I've nothing to gain or lose by speaking the truth."

"The truth as you see it," she tossed back.

"Before you moved to Town, you came directly from a small country village, I assume?"

"Yes." She nodded warily, wondering at the question. "Once my father passed we could not afford to stay on. We had to leave."

"Then your experience is limited. Allow me to enlighten you. A man provides room and board for his mistress—"

"I'm not any man's mistress! That is your problem . . . your insistence at identifying me as a kept woman. No one keeps me."

"Very well." He sent her a tolerant look that seemed to imply he thought she was in denial. "Fiancée, then." He shrugged. "You should expect a higher degree of consideration."

"You needn't concern yourself with me. I'm quite accustomed to taking care of myself and others."

At last, she stopped in front of her bedchamber door. He reached up a hand and brushed back a lock of hair off her shoulder, his fingers lingering on the tendrils. "Isn't that tiresome? Always taking care of others? Having no one to care for you?"

She twisted her neck so that his hand fell away from her. "I have someone." The lie was becoming quite a comfort, and easier to utter with every passing day, a defense that she clung to around him, something to put between them. A barrier of sorts. Not that he seemed to overly care at its presence. For whatever reason, he still pursued her even knowing that. Which was a curious thing. She had never been one to inspire great passion in the opposite gender. Edmond had made that abundantly evident.

His expression hardened at that reminder. "Indeed."

She had reached her room. She knew she could duck inside and close the door on his face, but still, for some reason, she lingered. "And who cares for you, Mr. Mackenzie?"

Some of the hardness eased out of his face, but his gaze was no less intent as he gazed at her. "No one, Poppy. I'm not so fortunate as my brother."

"I think that's not entirely true. You've won quite the admiration from the dowager. And your sister."

"And you?" He inched a step closer, eating up the air between them. "What of you, Poppy? Have you a care for me?"

She swallowed and reached behind her, her hand finding the latch of the bedchamber door and closing around it.

"What? No answer, kitten?"

"You're my fiancé's brother. Of course I have a care for you."

He moved quickly, suddenly, both hands flattening against the door on either side of her head. "Your feelings for me have nothing to do with him," he growled, his eyes flashing with a dangerous heat that she felt down deep in her bones.

She sucked in a breath and pushed her spine back against the door as far as she could go, the scent of him invading her, filling her senses.

"You're wrong. That's all there is . . . all there can ever be between us." She turned the latch. The door opened behind her. Before he responded, she plunged inside and shut the door on him with a snap.

Breathing raggedly, she collapsed against the door's supportive length. She waited, praying he did not attempt to follow her into her chamber. Several moments passed and she heard his steps fade away. Her prayer had been answered. So why was there that stab of disappointment in her chest?

Chapter 20

*O*n his fourth day at Autenberry Manor, Struan went for a ride, hoping to release some of the restless energy plaguing him even if the bitter-cold wind happened to freeze his face.

He wanted the chit. Badly. And if he was to take a clue from her continued avoidance of him—or her *continued* bedside vigil of Autenberry—she didn't want him back. She wanted his half brother.

Oh, he might possess the ability to arouse her, but that was merely the longing of her body. Desires of the flesh. Her head, her heart, wanted nothing to do with him—and that stung. It made him feel like the lad he was all those years ago standing before his father and facing his rejection. Who knew he could still feel so small and vulnerable?

He rode his mount into the stables, escaping the worst of the cold. The snow had ceased to fall, but the wind whipped bitterly. He waved off a groom who appeared to help him and unsaddled his horse himself, needing something to do with his hands and enjoying being alone with the animal that made no demands of him. Tension ebbed from his shoulders as he rubbed down the stallion, only to return at the sudden arrival of a feminine voice behind him.

"There you are. I've looked everywhere for you."

Bryony. Whereas her sister had avoided him, she had been his constant shadow.

He glanced over his shoulder at her where she stood at the stall's entrance. "Good morning, Miss Fairchurch."

She pouted prettily. "Please call me Bryony. Miss Fairchurch is my sister."

He inclined his head, but didn't utter her name. Poppy had her hands full with this one. The girl was very young, too pretty for her own good and a flirt.

"Did you go for a ride?" she asked in a singsong voice, reminding him that she was just a little girl, even if her face and body belonged to a woman.

"Yes." He turned to rub down the horse with a brush.

"How invigorating. I would love to go riding."

"Do you know how?" The rhythmic strokes of the brush filled the air.

"No, but you could teach me." She sidled closer.

He cast a quick glance over his shoulder. She affected a coquettish smile, her bottom lip thrust out.

Shaking his head, he returned his attention to his brushing. "It's cold. You should be inside."

"You're not," she returned pertly.

He shrugged. "I'm a man." He was on the verge of adding that he was also Scottish and accustomed to colder weather than this when she spoke.

"Of that, I'm *very* aware, Struan." Her fingers brushed the front of her bodice in a practiced move to draw attention to her bosom. She was brazen. Poppy needed to keep her on a tighter leash.

He shook his head, turning fully to face her and put an end to this. He doubted she would stop her antics until he made his lack of interest clear.

"Mr. Mackenzie," he corrected in a chiding tone. He spoke softly to lessen the sting, but he wanted to leave no doubt of where things stood between them.

She laughed. "So stern," she said mockingly. Not to be deterred, she flattened a hand to his chest.

"What are you doing, Miss Fairchurch? I'm old enough to be your father."

She made a tsking sound. "You're hardly *that* old."

"Close enough."

She batted her lashes. "Don't you like me?"

"You're very young."

"That's not an answer." Suddenly, she stood on her tiptoes and leaned forward to press a kiss to his cheek.

Damnation. He supposed this would not be a good time to let the girl know he preferred her sister. The notion made him smile. That would wound the girl's vanity, but then a little bit of wounded vanity might be a good thing for her. She was full of far too much confidence.

He cleared his throat to let her down in far firmer terms she would not mistake when a flash of movement caught his attention. He glanced up, his gaze colliding with Poppy's.

Hellfire. She'd chosen a fine time to stop avoiding him. He followed her gaze, looking down at where her sister stood inappropriately close to him, her hand on his chest, her soft kiss still palpable on his cheek. No doubt, Poppy had observed that little display. He looked back up, appraising her and not missing the flash of fury in her eyes.

Aye, she'd seen that.

He arched an eyebrow, suddenly, foolishly, glad to see her. He'd take this—a furious Poppy over the indifferent one who avoided him like a plague. This he could work with.

A SNEAKING SUSPICION led Poppy to the stables.

For all her avoidance of Mackenzie, she was achingly aware of his every movement. She had to be in order to effectively avoid him. She had vowed that his presence would not catch her by surprise and she would not be forced into close quarters with him ever again. She had to remain vigilant.

Of course, then, she knew when he left for a morning ride. She eyed him through an upstairs window as he headed out to the snow-draped stables. She maintained her position by Lord Autenberry's bed, the window in full view so that she would not miss his return.

She did not see him return. Indeed not. Instead, quite some time later, she watched her sister scurry out along the path to the stables. Her sister without Lady Clara beside her was a rare sight. The two had been inseparable over the last few days. And it was not as though Bryony possessed any affinity for horseflesh. What could be drawing her to the stables?

What indeed?

A slow trickle of dread coursed through her and she rose to her feet, departing Autenberry's chamber. She scarcely took the time to don her cloak before hastening outside to investigate.

Upon entering the shadowy interior, she followed the murmur of voices to a stall at the far end of the aisle. The door stood open and Poppy identified her sister, young and fresh in her pink dress, standing before Mackenzie.

She was oblivious to Poppy, all her attention focused on the man beside a massive stallion. She tossed back her head with soft, throaty laughter, showing off the lovely arch of her throat. Poppy felt a stab of an unfamiliar emotion. Her sister really was lovely. For all her little-girl ways, she didn't look like a little girl anymore. No, indeed not. She and Poppy looked of like age. It was deceptive. They could both be twenty years old. With one exception—Bryony was the beautiful one. The one men stared at wherever they went.

Poppy narrowed her gaze, taking in the cozy scene. A scene that only grew cozier as her sister's hand fluttered to her chest and the décolletage so modestly on display.

Struan murmured something that Poppy could not hear. She glared across the distance, imagining it to be vastly inappropriate. And why wouldn't it be? He had been inappropriate with her at every turn.

Whatever he said, Bryony found it exceedingly

amusing. She laughed again, this time lifting her hand off her bosom and pressing it to Struan's broad chest in a move that looked practiced and expert. Poppy gawked.

The chit was too bold! Where did she learn such things? In that moment, Poppy recognized Bryony's every movement and gesture for what it was intended—enticement.

Clearly certain females were born with an abundance of feminine wiles. It must be writ within their composition. Sadly, that trait must have skipped right over Poppy and landed on her baby sister.

Suddenly Bryony sobered, her laughter fading. She leaned closer, brushing her hand in little circles over Mackenzie's chest in a far too familiar manner. Then, before Poppy had any idea what her sister was about, Bryony stood up on her tiptoes and a pressed a lingering kiss to his cheek.

Poppy saw red. She couldn't breathe. She thought her head was going to explode. Her sister needed a good thrashing for such forwardness.

And what of you and the intimacy you shared with Mackenzie?

She shoved the voice aside with a mental snarl. It was not the same. For one thing, she was a woman of twenty. Not ten and five.

An uncomfortable sensation—the same she had felt moments ago only more pronounced, more painful—prickled in her chest as she stood watching her sister.

Struan stared at Bryony, the barest smile on his face—a face Poppy suddenly wanted to scratch to ribbons. How dare he toy with her and then move on to her sister?

Oddly, his face wasn't the only one she wanted to attack. For years she had indulged her sister, feeling guilty because Bryony had no memories of their mother and Poppy was Papa's favorite. That had left an uneasy guilt within her. She was always trying to compensate by sacrificing whatever she could for Bryony. She had never been jealous or wished her sister ill.

Until now.

Poppy pushed the ugly thoughts aside. Bryony was her sister. She was young and naïve and didn't know what game she played at—or that Struan Mackenzie was a man far out of her realm. Poppy knew. She knew that firsthand. She needed Poppy's understanding and guidance now—not some foolish, misplaced jealousy.

Poppy narrowed her gaze back on the lothario in question. What was he thinking as he looked at her much too impressionable sister? The reprobate! He was likely thinking how quickly he might find his way beneath her skirts.

Over my dead body.

As though he could feel the knife of her stare, he turned and his gaze landed on her. For once it wasn't hard to maintain his gaze. Acid churned in her stomach and her fingers curled at her sides, itching to sink into his too-handsome face.

He arched an eyebrow at her.

She arched both eyebrows back at him and crossed her arms.

"Bryony," she called.

Her sister looked at her and took a hasty step back, proving she wasn't entirely oblivious to the inappropriateness of her behavior.

"Poppy," she greeted.

"Lady Clara is looking for you," she lied. It was likely true.

"Oh." Bryony cast a quick look at Mackenzie before stepping out of the stall. "I best see what she needs."

Poppy nodded, still not averting her gaze from Mackenzie. Not even when her sister hurried past, her footsteps fading out of the stables, did she break their gaze. She held his stare, not about to back down.

He strolled toward her, his gait indolent and unhurried. "Poppy," he greeted.

"Miss Fairchurch," she snapped.

His eyes darkened on her, the moss green deepening to a wooded night. "That seems silly, does it not? Given our shared intimacies."

Hearing him put that to words on the heels of his inappropriate behavior with her sister only intensified her temper.

"Stay away from my sister."

He smiled slowly then, actually showing a flash of white teeth. It was disarming. Enticing as sin. Her stomach muscles tightened.

Her hands curled tightly at her sides. She wanted to wipe that smile off his face. There was something sinister and manipulative in it. The seductive curve of those handsome lips made her shiver. Clearly he knew the appeal of his smile. It made her want to run after her sister and throw a blanket over her head. A man who looked as he did and smiled so wickedly couldn't be trusted in any proximity to Bryony. She already knew how weak she was around him. Her sister was made of far less resistance.

He stepped toward her and she took a step back. He kept coming, backing her up until she bumped the wall of the stall. His arms came up on each side of her, caging her in. It was a decidedly familiar moment.

Except this time she could see his face much clearer. She could practically count each and every one of his ridiculously long and lush eyelashes. She inhaled, scenting his maleness, fresh hay and horseflesh.

A sense of vulnerability swept over her. She hated that. Her eyes locked with his. "What are you doing? Anyone can happen upon us. Is it not enough that you risk my sister's reputation, must you—"

"Your sister is a little girl."

She paused, taken aback that he should agree on anything with her.

"Precisely," she said slowly. "For that exact reason, I demand you give her a wide berth. She doesn't need the likes of you to—"

"Your warning is needless. My appetites run to slightly more seasoned fare."

She paused, gazing into his eyes, feeling herself being dragged into the mesmerizing depths against her will. "Indeed," she managed to say in gratifyingly haughty tones.

"You, kitten," he replied easily, as though he were commenting on the weather. "In case there is any confusion, my tastes run to you." His gaze flicked over her. "You're no little girl."

"I b-beg your pardon?" she sputtered, not even bothering to remind him to quit with that infernal nickname. There was a bigger problem at the moment. Such as the closeness of his big body—and his words that wrought havoc on her senses.

He shook his head. "I see directness is required. My tastes run to *you*. In my bed. Under me. Over me. In every way possible."

An odd strangled sound escaped her.

She let out a frustrated sound that was part grunt and part groan. He was still at this ridiculous game of pursuing her. Blast him!

"Put that thought from your mind, Mr. Mackenzie. I'm engaged to your brother—"

"Are you now?" he mocked. His laughing eyes carried the reminder of the two times he had kissed her. When he had fondled her and touched her beneath her skirts. Damnably inconvenient history in a moment where she was trying to drive home the point of her unavailability.

"Yes! I am!"

"I have trouble recalling that fact at times."

So did she.

But no more.

She would not lapse with him again. She would not forget now.

She took a deep breath, filling her lungs to capacity. He *still* doubted her. He thought she was the duke's tart. Oh, it lit a fire inside her, stirring her ire. He thought she wasn't good enough to be Marcus's wife. Even more insulting, he assumed men were interchangeable for her and she would be receptive to his advances. Oh, the temerity.

"Stay away from my sister. Stay away from me."

The humor faded from his eyes and she was reminded of something she had already realized about this man—he did not like being denied.

"I've no issue with the first request. As to you, Poppy, you know where I stand on that matter."

He leaned in, those delicious-looking lips of his descending.

With a yelp, she ducked under one of his arms and darted forward, feeling quite smug at evading him so neatly.

That smugness died a swift death when he snatched her wrist and tumbled her back into his arms, his chest a hard wall at her back.

"Oomph!" she cried out at the impact, then stilled as his arm slipped around her waist, his big, warm hand searing her rib cage, directly beneath her breast. If she relaxed, she could rest his head on his shoulder. She could turn her face slightly and graze her lips to his jaw . . .

Only in no way could she ever relax like this.

Especially when he lowered his head and placed his open mouth just over the whorls of her ear. His hot warm breath tickled the sensitive skin. It wasn't a kiss, but it was just as distracting. Just as dangerous to her senses.

"You needn't be jealous, lass, it's you I prefer." His lips brushed over the lobe of her ear as he spoke and her belly clenched. "Just as you prefer me."

"I don't prefer you." Heat climbed up her neck as his actual words penetrated. Her face throbbed with mortification. "And I'm not jealous."

"Yes. You do . . . and you are, but you needn't be. Not when it's you I imagine in my bed." His fingers fanned out on her ribs, his thumb brushing the underside of her breast. "And you imagine it, too. Admit it."

"I'll admit no such thing! You arrogant—"

"Honest—"

"Insufferable—"

"Irresistible," he supplied.

"Oh!" Her cheeks burned with outrage. His head dipped even lower, his face turning so that his mouth grazed the side of her neck. He was going to kiss her. Again. Perhaps even bite her as he did that once. Heat throbbed between her legs.

Her chest squeezed, the air trapped inside, no longer flowing in and out of her.

She couldn't let that happen, not when she was so desperately trying to stand strong and show him exactly how objectionable she found him to be.

She was too late, of course. In a manner. He didn't kiss her. No, it was worse. He opened his mouth over the side of her throat. The velvet warmth of his tongue slid over her skin, tasting and turning her limbs to jam. She whimpered, her legs giving out. His arm tightened around her waist, holding her up, and then he bit down, his teeth scoring the stretched cord of her neck.

A strangled sound escaped her at the pleasure-pain of his teeth sinking into her. One of his hands lifted to her head. His fingers fisted in her hair, forcing her head back so that he had more of her to taste and bite.

If she had any doubt before that this man was wicked she no longer did. The things his hands and mouth did could only be called sinful. Perhaps even evil.

Before she could sink deeper under his spell, she lifted her foot and brought her heel down hard on his foot. Pain flared in the sole of her foot from the force of her kick, but she didn't care. Desperate times, desperate measures and all that.

He cursed, his hold loosening, and she bolted.

"Poppy," he growled as she raced down the wide aisle. She heard his steps fast on her heels and her heart hammered with equal parts fear and something else that felt horribly close to excitement. *Blast her contrary heart.*

It was the same sensation she had felt as a girl

when she would swing from a tree rope and drop into the village pond. The brief moment when she was airborne and falling, wind rushing over her as her stomach lurched up to her throat.

She dove outside, racing for the house. She burst inside, startling the doorman. She spared him only a quick glance before rushing upstairs.

The duke's bedchamber loomed ahead like a welcome beacon in the dark. He was never left unattended. Someone would be there to shield her, even if only a maid.

With that comforting knowledge, she plunged inside the room and let out a relieved breath. As expected, the room was occupied. Not only did a maid stand sentry in the corner but Lord Strickland was there, too, sitting in a chair by the duke's bedside and holding a newspaper.

"Lord Strickland," she exclaimed breathlessly, her voice louder than she intended. She winced and swallowed, fighting for some much needed composure.

"Miss Fairchurch." His gaze flicked beyond her as Struan emerged fast behind her. A small measure of satisfaction churned through her at the sight of him. He looked rattled, too, his cheeks ruddy with color, eyes bright as though suffering a fever. The effect was altogether shattering, making him only more attractive. Much too threatening to her senses.

"Mr. Mackenzie," Lord Strickland added in greeting.

"Lord Strickland," Struan greeted, his deep voice tight.

The earl looked back and forth between them. "Are we having a race?"

"A race? Y-yes, a race," she quickly agreed, releasing a single nervous titter of laughter. "I won."

Lord Strickland looked knowingly between them.

She smiled uncertainly as Struan stopped at her elbow. "Mr. Mackenzie challenged me. I could not refuse." She forced a smile, hoping that did not sound as ridiculous as it did to her ears.

Lord Strickland nodded, looking bemused and still much too knowing. He turned his attention to folding his newspaper and setting it aside.

Struan chose that moment to lean close and whisper for her ears alone. "This time you win. Enjoy it. For the next time the victory will be mine. You'll see what happens when you run from me."

She scoffed, crossing her arms in a gesture of bravado and ignoring how his promise sent goose bumps rushing across her skin.

"Laugh now, kitten. The next time there won't be anyone around to save you."

"Stop calling me that," she hissed uselessly.

Her face burned at his gravelly whisper so close to her ear. She knew she should be worried. Even a little scared. But the only thing she could wonder was how soon he might try to catch her again.

Chapter 21

She sat with Lord Strickland beside Marcus's bed for a good hour, listening with interest as he regaled her with stories of his boyhood with the duke, including their years together at Eton. Mackenzie left early in the conversation—no doubt he did not wish to hear of the childhood he was denied. Whatever the reason, it allowed her to actually concentrate on what the earl was saying and attempt to put the vexing Mackenzie from her mind.

When she emerged from the duke's bedchamber much later, she glanced around uneasily, almost expecting Mackenzie to pounce on her. After his warning, could one blame her? Things felt very unfinished between them.

Fortunately, she did not cross paths with Mackenzie. She was able to locate her sister without incident.

She found Bryony in her bedchamber, changing into warmer clothes to go on a walk with Clara and Enid. She tossed clothing from her armoire with frustrated tsks, as though she always possessed an extensive wardrobe and the addition of several new ensembles was not anything novel or spectacular. It occurred to Poppy that aside of being born to great beauty her sister was perhaps meant to belong to the upper echelons of Society. She had no difficulty navigating the social waters of the aristocracy. In fact, fourteen-year-old Clara seemed a bit in awe of Bryony.

"I've nothing to wear!" Bryony sighed, propping a fist on her hip.

"Try the plum-colored wool," she suggested.

Bryony seized the wool dress with undisguised glee. "We're gathering holly and mistletoe," she exclaimed excitedly as though they would be gathering gold bullion. It gave Poppy a pang to realize how very much her sister's life was lacking for her to take such intense pleasure in tasks that were very ordinary for others.

"Delightful," she murmured distractedly, trying to think how best to broach the subject of Mackenzie with her sister.

"Bryony," she began, deciding directness the best approach. Struan was not a man to be trifled with and her sister needed to realize that. "About Mr. Mackenzie . . ."

Bryony's cheeks colored prettily for a moment. "Spying on me, Poppy?"

"I just happened upon the two of you . . . as anyone else could do. The stables are hardly private. Not that you should be anywhere in private with that man," she said archly. "You really must have a care. He's not a gentleman. Once a lady's reputation is lost, it is no easy matter to repair."

"I'm not an idiot!" Bryony snapped. "I know about such things."

"Do you?"

"I know how to handle myself." She began brushing her hair, savagely pulling the bristles through the rich auburn mass.

"With the likes of Mr. Mackenzie? I fear you do not. You are quite out of your depths with him." *They both were.* "He is much more . . . experienced than you, Bryony."

"You don't think he likes me," she accused, propping her hands on shapely hips.

Poppy sighed. Did she think this would be a simple conversation? There was nothing easy about Bryony these days. "On the contrary, I fear he might like you *too* much, but you're much too young and he's not the sort of man to settle down and offer matrimony."

"If you, of all people, can win over a duke, I should be able to win over Mr. Mackenzie."

Poppy jerked at the not so veiled insult. "Bryony, I'm only concerned—"

"No, you're not! You're jealous!"

"Jealous!" She worked her lips but no other words would come out.

"That's right! Your duke is on his deathbed and you don't like that I'm the one getting all the attention from a handsome man." Her sister snatched up her muff and marched toward the door. "And don't think I haven't seen the way you look at Mr. Mackenzie either."

She gaped after Bryony, speechless. If her sister had noticed something afoot between Struan and herself, who else had noticed?

With one hand on the door latch, Bryony's razor-sharp eyes flashed with a fine fury as she accused, "You already have the duke, must you have Mr. Mackenzie, too?"

At that charge, Poppy found her voice. "Bryony! It's not like that!"

Shaking her head, the girl yanked the door open. Before storming out, she cast one last withering glare at Poppy. "You make me so mad! I can't wait until I'm married and you can't tell me what to do anymore!"

Poppy had never seen her sister look at her in such a way. It was definitely not sisterly. No, she glared at her like she was a . . . rival.

Poppy adopted a placating tone. "Bryony, you know I would never—"

"Clara is waiting for me. I need to go." She angled her chin at a proud angle. "I'm sure I'll forgive you later, but right now I don't want to talk to you."

That said, the girl flounced out of the room, slamming the door after her.

Poppy stood there, stunned, the sound of the door slamming reverberating in her ears. Never had she seen her sister in such a temper—and for what reason? Because Poppy had admonished her to behave herself with Mackenzie? Her own temper flared. The girl needed a good spanking. And Mackenzie! In her mind, he was equally to blame. If he was not . . . If he had not . . . not . . .

Been so handsome and enticing and intriguing?

She stomped her foot once, annoyed that it did not seem reasonable to blame him for merely existing and being himself.

Turning, she exited her sister's bedchamber and hastened to her own room. She was fuming and felt like throwing something. It was probably best if she did that in her own chamber.

She marched the half dozen strides that took her to her room. Opening the door, she stepped inside. For a moment, she collapsed against the door. Closing her eyes, she expelled a deep breath, her emotions still raging hot.

Blast Bryony! And blast Mackenzie, too! She would blame him if only because it made her feel better to do so.

After several more breaths, she pushed off the door and stalked toward the small side table on the other side of the room. When she had first spotted the tray of Madeira upon her arrival, she never thought she would have use for it. She had noticed every room in the house boasted a tray of Madeira. The maid, catching her gaze straying to the tray, had explained that the duchess had a penchant for the stuff as it reminded her of her country of birth.

It wasn't Poppy's habit to imbibe of spirits, but right now a nip of the stuff sounded just about right. Between keeping up the charade of being affianced to the duke, coping with her sister and fending off Struan Mackenzie, it seemed in order.

Her skirts swished as she made her way across the room and poured herself a measure of the drink. She swished it and stared at it a moment before tossing it back. She sucked in a breath as it went down in a scalding wash.

"Looking for some liquid courage, Miss Fairchurch?"

She whirled with a gasp, her now empty glass thudding to the plush carpet.

Struan Mackenzie stretched out on her bed, hands laced behind his head, bold as you please, watching her with hooded eyes that promised all manner of retribution.

"What are you doing in here?

"I told you there would be a reckoning."

She glanced to the door. "Anyone could enter my chamber. You cannot be here!"

"The duchess is having an afternoon nap. Everyone else is off holly gathering. However—" He swung his legs around, dropped his booted feet to the floor. She backed away as he rounded the bed, but he didn't approach her. He strode a direct, unhurried line for the door. Glancing back at her, he turned the lock on her bedchamber door. "If it makes you feel better, I'll lock the door so no one can walk in on us."

Panic swelled up inside her. "That doesn't make me feel better. Not at all."

That corner of his mouth kicked up as he advanced on her. She continued to back away, making certain that she moved in the opposite direction of that looming bed. She stopped when she reached the wall, her hands pressing, palms flat against the cool plaster.

He stopped, keeping a good space between them. It did little to comfort her. She still didn't trust him. Especially not alone with her in here.

"You won't quit," she stated flatly.

"It's not in my makeup."

"I'll scream," she warned.

He chuckled. "No, you won't."

She felt her nostrils flare on a breath. "Why are you so intent on pursuing me?"

He paused, giving her words careful consideration. "I don't rightly know. There's something about you, Miss Fairchurch. Something between us. I can't ignore it. Neither can you, if you'd be honest with yourself." He took one step closer and brought his hand to her throat. His thumb gently swiped over her pulse. "But honesty, I realize, is elusive for you."

Her pulse jumped from his touch. Or was it his words? She knew he was referring to her betrothal to the duke and the fact that he didn't believe it to be true. He wouldn't drop the matter.

"I mean it," she threatened.

He leaned in, still holding her throat, his mouth a hairsbreadth over her own. "Do it. Scream, then."

She opened her mouth, debating letting a

scream fly free. It'd be nice just to surprise him. To prove him wrong about her. Of course, there were other ways to do that.

Perhaps it was the Madeira swirling hotly through her blood, addling her thoughts, lending her courage.

She closed that last bit of space separating them. Wrapping her arms around his neck, she pressed her body against him and mashed her mouth into his. Perhaps if she shocked him, it would wipe that arrogant smugness from his face.

She succeeded in shocking him. He didn't move for a long stretch of moments, and then he did.

His arms went around her. She squeaked as he lifted her off the floor. Her feet dangled in the air. It added to the floating sensation his lips already stirred inside her.

They kissed until there was nothing but the combined frenzy of their lips and tongues.

She brought her hands up to his face, holding him and reveling in the sensation of his strong jaw as she explored the taste of him.

Suddenly she was falling. She grabbed onto his shoulders with a soft yelp as they fell back onto the bed.

The sensation of the brocade counterpane beneath woke her. She curled her hands into his shoulders and pushed. "No, stop!"

He froze, his chest panting with sawing breaths as he looked down at her with eyes gone dark and heavy. She felt an answering pull in her belly.

"You don't want me to stop," he growled, his brogue thicker than usual.

She moistened her lips. She knew she should probably be afraid. She was alone with him. He was big and strong, capable of overpowering her. He could easily do that.

"I'm in love with Marcus," she blurted.

A shutter slammed over his gaze. He sat back, lifting off her. "Of course you are. He's rich and powerful and titled. How could I forget?"

She flinched as his hand came down suddenly toward her. His eyes flashed, clearly aware that for a moment she thought he might strike her.

"You think I would strike you?"

She shook her head. Shame coursed through her. He lowered his hand the rest of the way to her. His fingers traced her kiss-swollen lips slowly. He merely wanted to touch her face. Not strike her. Never that. It wasn't in him to do that. Somehow she knew that much about him. The flinch had been a thoughtless instinct.

"Is lying so second nature to this mouth? I know you better than yourself."

"What's that supposed to mean?" she asked

against the brush of his fingertips. "I'm not frightened of you. I know you wouldn't hit me."

"That's not what I'm talking about."

"I don't understand, then."

"Whatever you feel for the duke, it isn't love."

She laughed weakly. "You know so much of love?"

He ignored the question. She was perhaps glad he did not answer her. She wasn't sure how she would feel to hear that he had loved someone else. The notion of it gave her an odd sensation in her chest. Almost as though a weight were there, pushing down. Which was ludicrous. He was close to thirty. Of course he could have loved a woman in the course of his life. She had no claim to him. On the contrary.

Instead he said, "You couldn't kiss me the way you do and love someone else. That isn't who you are, Poppy. You've more character than that. You look out for others . . . your sister, your father before you. You put yourself last."

"So?" She had to fight the urge to squirm beneath his praise.

"So you wouldn't hurt anyone. Least of all the man you love. You risk hurting the duke every time you've kissed me back. Every time you've let me touch you. You're not built that way."

She opened her mouth to deny the charge, but realized how foolish that would be. Who refused such an allegation? Everyone wanted others to believe that they were good and altruistic. She could not argue the point.

Without giving her time to respond, he climbed off her. She heard the lock click on her door as he opened it and stepped out into the hall.

He was gone.

She lay on her back, staring unseeingly at the ceiling. She brought her fingers to her puffy lips, still feeling him there . . . tasting him.

He was right. Whatever it was she felt for the duke, it wasn't love. She couldn't be in love with a man and crave Struan so desperately. She'd known this for a while but she hadn't acknowledged it until Struan said the words.

Groaning, she covered her face with her hands. She was vastly tempted to grab her sister and flee back to London. If it wouldn't raise so many eyebrows, if she couldn't be convinced that Struan wouldn't follow her, she would. He had proven exceptionally persistent in his pursuit of her.

Of course, you could tell him the truth. Admit who you are—or rather, who you're not.

And then he would hate her for the lie.

Or worse. He might not be interested in her at

all anymore. Perhaps he was only interested in her out of a misplaced competition with his brother.

There was no easy way out of this. Perhaps she could approach Lord Strickland tomorrow, explain how untenable the situation was becoming. She would leave out the part about falling in love with Struan Mackenzie—

She swallowed hard and shook her head against the mattress. Groaning, she covered her face with both hands. She was not falling in love with Struan Mackenzie. That would be madness. She didn't love the man. She wasn't that foolish. No, it was far safer falling in love with an impossible fantasy. A fantasy couldn't come true.

A fantasy couldn't hurt you.

Chapter 22

*S*truan reminded himself that there was a reason he only ever pursued women who clearly wanted his attentions. There was no confusion in those instances. None of this maddening rejection.

I'm in love with Marcus.

Even if she didn't mean it, even if he didn't believe her, she had said it. It was reason enough to leave her alone. He swallowed back an epithet. He should tumble the maid that changed the linens on his bed. She kept giving him inviting smiles and accidentally happening upon him while he was at his bath.

Instead of sinking between a pair of willing thighs, however, he found himself walking the corridor at the middle of the night. His feet moved, without conscious thought. Before he quite realized where he was going, he ended up in his brother's chamber. A groom sat in the corner, nodding to sleep.

"I'll sit with him," he spoke, his words jerking the servant awake. "Give us a moment."

The groom nodded and hastily left the room, no doubt sensing some of his dangerous mood.

Struan sank down in the chair beside the bed, gazing dispassionately at his slumbering half brother.

After some time, he spoke. "I know you hate me."

He waited a long moment as though he expected a response. "I suffered a great deal as a result of our father. You will never know how much." He shrugged. Specifics didn't matter. "He gave you everything and me nothing. Even so, I never blamed you. I never hated you or wanted anything that was yours."

Until now.

He didn't say the words. He simply let them hang in his mind, hovering like a great toxic cloud. Perhaps Poppy had the right of it and he needed to give her a wide berth. For the both of them.

"Funny thing. I actually admire you. I never thought I could feel like that about you, but choosing someone as special as Poppy. Hell, you're a lot more than I ever gave you credit for."

He released a shuddering breath and then jerked up from the chair. He stalked out of the room and found a groom waiting outside. One glance at his face and the groom scurried back into the room as though he feared Struan would level him with his wrath. He didn't have anything to worry about. Right now the only person he was angry with was himself.

He strode down the corridor, deliberately not glancing at the door to her room. He passed it without looking. If he was determined to banish her from his mind, he needed to stop giving her so much power over him.

As though the thought of her conjured her, he stopped hard. She stood ahead of him wearing nothing more than her nightwear. Her bare feet peeked out from beneath the hem of her night-gown and robe.

She hadn't noticed him yet. She knocked softly yet persistently at a bedchamber door. "Bryony? Please let me inside. I want to talk to you."

There was no response that he could hear. Apparently she heard nothing either. Her profile scrunched up in frustration. "Please, Bry. I don't want to fight with you."

"Go away! Ruin someone else's life and leave me alone."

He flinched and then wondered at that reaction. It wasn't as though the girl was attacking him. This had nothing to do with him. Poppy had made it clear they should have nothing to do with each other. He should turn and walk in the opposite direction as though he hadn't seen her.

Walk away, Mackenzie. Just walk away.

Poppy's shoulders slumped. She flattened her hand against the door and dropped her head, looking so forlorn that he couldn't move. "Don't be like that, Bry," she said so softly he could barely hear her.

More silence greeted her.

She waited as though hoping her sister would change her mind and open the door to her. Nothing.

She turned, wiping at her eyes. The fact that she was moved to tears made something shift inside him. *Hellfire.* He didn't like it.

She caught sight of him and froze. "What are you doing?" Accusation bit into each word.

"Returning to my room."

Her chin went up and she wiped at her eyes as though trying to hide the evidence of her tears. "I was just checking on my sister."

He advanced on her. "How is she doing?" An innocuous enough question.

She squared her shoulders. "Fine. Tired."

He stopped before her. "You're a terrible liar."

Those tear-soaked eyes widened. "Very well. She's upset with me."

"Why?"

She shook her head and turned, striding away from him with quick, little steps, her bare feet a whisper on the plush runner.

He followed. "What happened?"

"I don't want to talk about it."

"I assume it has to do with today in the stables. With me."

She spun around. "Because everything is about *you* with your stupid handsome face and your stupid brogue and your stupid . . . body." She gestured to him furiously. Tears clogged her voice and glistened in her eyes.

"I take it you had words with her about her boldness."

She sniffed back a sob. "Indeed. I had words with her about her boldness."

"And?"

"She didn't take it kindly. She had a few choice words for me in turn." She shrugged as though it didn't sting. "She's fifteen. The world revolves around her."

"Except it doesn't and you should make her aware of that."

She released a short laugh. "And you have a

great deal of experience dealing with young, over-wrought girls?"

"I don't," he admitted. "But maybe you're too soft on her."

"She's all I have."

Her words struck him right in the chest with a pang. Until he remembered. "You have Marcus."

She glanced away, avoiding his gaze. "Yes. That's right," she remembered. "How could I forget that?"

Why did she sound so unconvincing?

He stepped forward and brushed a loose strand of hair from where it clung to her wet cheek. "You should make your sister realize that you're a person, too. With feelings. And needs."

"I put those aside when my father died. My responsibility is to Bryony."

Her gaze drifted back to him and she looked so lost and sad that he couldn't stop himself. He glanced around and identified the narrow door of a linen closet. With a quick glance up and down the corridor, he took her hand and pulled her inside.

"What are you—"

"I'm taking care of you, Poppy," he said as he closed the door on them and doused them in the darkness of the closet, his blood pumping as he considered just how he would take care of her. "Trust me."

The soft scratch of her breath filled the space that smelled of fresh linens. He squinted, his vision growing acclimated to the darkness. A table full of bedding was propped against the wall. He knocked the blankets aside. Circling her waist, he lifted and plopped her down on the table.

He gathered fistfuls of her skirts and dragged them up her thighs. Her hands flew to his wrists, locking around them as though to shove him away. He crouched down before her knees, looking up at the shadow of her face. "Put your needs first for once, Poppy," he murmured, temptation laced in every word.

He felt her hesitation. She was at war with herself, debating the right or wrong of this.

"It will be all for you, Poppy." His fingers deliberately grazed the outside of her knees.

Only later would he acknowledge that it was just as much for him as it was for her. Tasting her was something he was aching to do.

Her hands relaxed and fell away from his wrists in consent.

With a growl of satisfaction, he shoved her nightgown and robe up to her hips. He cursed the darkness that prevented him from seeing her in her nakedness. He splayed her legs wider and pressed tiny kisses along the inside of her thighs.

"Struan," she sighed, her fingers lacing through his hair and sending ripples of sensation down his spine.

"Poppy," he breathed directly against her sex, his hands sliding around to grip her bottom and pull her toward his face. He tasted her with a slow, savoring lick. She was exquisite. Sweet and earthy and he wanted to dive into her. Drown himself in her essence.

She jerked, clearly startled at the sensation of his mouth on her. "Struan, I've never done this before . . ."

"Relax," he murmured, pausing only for a moment as her words sank through him with a shudder.

She'd never done this before.

Autenberry had not been here before him then. In this, he was her first. He pushed the gratifying thought away, relegating it for later pondering. Right now there was only this. Tasting Poppy, feeling her shake and rock against his questing tongue. He settled himself deeper between her thighs, nestling his face close, adjusting his hands and lifting her higher for him.

"Oh, this is wicked," she gasped, her fingers tightening in his hair as he increased his mouth's pressure, his tongue finding her sweet spot, playing with it and sucking the tiny nub between his lips.

She cried out, pushing into his mouth wantonly.

"Shhh," he said against her as he brought his fingers to that small pleasure button. He rolled it, pinching and then taking it between his lips again, scraping the nub with his teeth and thrumming his tongue over it until she released a muffled shriek, convulsing all around him.

He slipped a finger inside her, pushing deep, curling inward, reveling as she came apart a second time for him, her channel tightening around him and making his cock swell against his trousers. It would be so easy, so sweet. He need only free himself and ease inside her. She was wet and ready. She'd take him.

This was for her. That was your promise. It's not about your needs.

He lifted himself up. She shook, clinging to his shoulders. Her gleaming eyes locked on to his in the darkness.

She wasn't the only one shaking. His hands trembled and his jaw locked tight against the ache to take her, finish this and slake his lust for her.

"Struan," she whispered, her hand lifting to fall on his chest, fingers splaying wide, each one a singeing imprint that he felt through his clothing.

He straightened, brought her to her feet and yanked her nightgown back down, covering her limbs. "Go to your room."

She stiffened and he cursed himself. His words came out too harsh. He'd hurt her feelings. She didn't understand.

He grabbed her hand and forced it between them over his swollen member. "Go to your room before I break my word to you and make this about me . . . about my pleasure."

She gasped. Even in the darkness, he could identify the shock in her eyes, the tremor of her hand on him.

Her lips parted on a hitched breath. "I—I did that to you?"

He said nothing for a moment. Just let the sound of his labored breath crash between them. "Kitten, you have no idea what you do to me." He forced her hand to rub up and down against him.

He dropped his head with a groan as she curled her fingers over him through the fabric of his trousers, exploring his shape as much as she could. She squeezed him and he jerked.

She yanked her hand away. "I'm sorry. Did I hurt you?"

"It's only the sweetest torment." He took a step back and inhaled a shuddering breath. "Go, Poppy."

She hesitated, and he knew she was considering breaking her resolve. He glanced around the darkened closet. He hadn't brought her in here for a quick romp. He'd wanted to make her feel better, to give her something with no expectations for himself.

"Go," he barked.

She vaulted from the closet. The door clicked shut after her. He stayed in the closet for several moments after she left, taking bracing breaths, fighting to compose himself and willing his raging erection away.

He clenched his hands into fists. Since when was he in the habit of giving and not taking? Especially when it came to a woman he wanted. Especially since he'd never wanted a woman as much as he wanted Poppy Fairchurch.

For the first time, he entertained the notion of leaving her alone—even if her responses to him had been ardent and welcoming and seemed in direct opposition of wanting such a thing.

He had not lifted himself from the dregs of poverty by turning away from every challenge.

Giving her a wide berth seemed like a sound plan. For her. For him. He couldn't promise her forever. He needed to kill this hunger for her once and for all. Forget it before they reached a point in which neither one of them could return.

Chapter 23

*I*t was a perfect evening.

The kind of Christmas she had when Papa was alive and they would sit in front of the fire and sing carols. Just the three of them—Poppy and Bryony and Papa. They'd eat oranges and mint scones and read from the Bible, a tradition Mama had started and they maintained even after her passing. Her present reality felt like an echo of those times and made her feel warm and fuzzy inside.

Those were good times. They were by no means well-off then, but she didn't have to worry about money. She didn't have to worry about how she and her sister were going to survive. She didn't have to worry about any of those things at all.

Just as she did not have to worry about them right now, sitting with this wonderful family. True, it would all come to an end, but for however long it lasted, she would enjoy her time here and evenings like this.

This was the kind of evening Poppy had imagined for herself when she was a girl weaving fantasies of a life with Edmond and a gaggle of children gathered before the fire at Christmastime. It hadn't taken long for her to replace that fantasy with another image—one of her with the Duke of Autenberry. Only that image was so embedded in fantasy it embarrassed her now.

Sitting in the drawing room and listening as Lady Enid played carols on the pianoforte, she wasn't sure what perfect was anymore. She rather suspected that perfection did not exist. She only knew that in Struan Mackenzie's arms, she had felt something far more real than anything she ever had with Edmond or the Duke of Autenberry.

Lady Enid's performance came to an end. The dowager duchess, resplendent in an emerald green gown that set off her dark hair, clapped happily. "Beautifully done. You've improved so much, Enid. A shame your brother is not present to hear you." It was as though she was determined he not be forgotten.

"Indeed," Lord Strickland said. "The only thing

missing is Autenberry hale and hearty and over-seeing the festive occasion."

For some reason his stare fell on Poppy. She smiled and held his gaze, struggling to show no reaction when he swung his gaze to Struan. Lord Strickland's eyes narrowed and turned far less kind as he considered the Scotsman. Almost as though he knew something had transpired between them.

Struan stared back at him unflinchingly, his stare bold, as usual, and unapologetic. One corner of his sensual mouth tipped in a smile. She felt an answering clench in her stomach. The man was in her blood. As alarming as that was, it was even more troubling to think he also knew that fact.

He'd met Poppy's gaze directly when she first faced him over breakfast—and every time since. Even so, his presence didn't detract from the pleasure of the evening. He gazed on her more than once as they nibbled on desserts and sipped their after-dinner drinks, adding to their much too full bellies. The meal had been unimaginable excess. Roasted pheasant and goose. Savory pies. Sauces and puddings and decadent breads. She could quite happily never eat again.

Struan had been quite civil with her on their rare moments of conversation. His gaze at times lingered, but as long as he didn't touch her she could maintain composure. His hot-eyed stare didn't fill her with the previous panic or frustration. No, indeed it did not. It filled her with longing. She didn't feel nearly so hunted by him. The game he had made of pursing her had evidently come to a halt. At that, she felt oddly disappointed. Gone were the long stares in which she felt herself sinking into his pirate's eyes.

Ever since their tryst in the closet, they'd reached an unspoken truce of sorts. He kept his distance. Their conversations were limited. He was polite yet distant, cool. It was everything she had demanded of him.

And yet she missed it all. She missed *him*. It was damnably bewildering and made her feel the most contrary of creatures. She had demanded he leave her alone, and now that he had, she was forlorn for the loss of him.

For once she wished he would stare at her with that feral look in his eyes. Oh, what a terrible contrary creature she was. She had warned him off time and time again and yet now she missed his attention.

"Marcus shall be with us soon," the dowager duchess proclaimed to the room at large.

Everyone nodded and murmured agreement, for once appearing to mean it. And with good reason. That very afternoon, Lord Strickland had reported that Marcus stirred and even mumbled a few words. Heartening signs, according to the physician, and the dowager duchess couldn't stop talking about it.

It was yet three days before Christmas and the dowager was hopeful that the duke might yet awaken and join them for the celebration.

Lady Enid finished at the pianoforte and they moved into a game of charades.

"Poppy! It's your turn! Your turn!" Lady Clara clapped excitedly from where she sat after Bryony finished her turn.

Poppy stood from the chaise lounge, dusting her lush purple skirts free of invisible lint. She selected a slip of paper from the bowl, studied it, folded it back up and then set it down on the glossy wood table that held their cups of steaming chocolate.

She moved to stand before the fireplace, her mind already feverishly working on how she would perform this charade when the doors to the drawing room burst open.

All heads swiveled at the intrusion, wide eyes staring at the breathless maid. "It's the duke! His Grace! He's up!" She shook her head as though jogging loose the proper words. "He's awake! Awake!"

Precisely five seconds of silence met her vivid declaration before the room exploded into chaos.

TO DESCRIBE EVERYONE as joyous would be a gross understatement. There were tears and laughter and hugging. The dowager duchess, someone Poppy never suspected as being particularly devout, clapped her hands together and began praising and thanking God with all fervency and sincerity.

The somewhat taciturn Enid was wiping tears from her eyes and Clara was bouncing with more vigor than usual even for her. Even Bryony, who had never met Marcus, participated in the happy melee.

"Let us go!" Lady Autenberry exclaimed. "Come, everyone!"

"Wait!" Lord Strickland waved his hands in the air. "He might not be quite ready for a bombardment of such biblical proportions." Lord Strickland's gaze seemed to land on her, conveying some manner of message. He was the only one present who knew the truth of her ruse, after all. He had to know the duke would want an explanation for suddenly finding himself with a stranger for a fiancée.

"Oh." The dowager's hand fluttered to her

mouth. "Yes, I see your point." She glanced around the room, gnawing on her lip thoughtfully. "Yes, that would be a bit much."

"Overwhelming indeed." Enid nodded in agreement. "Strickland, you should go."

Everyone else nodded, too. Except Poppy. She couldn't move. And neither, evidently, could Struan. He held himself stiffly. Only his eyes showed any movement, looking only at her, sliding over her face, assessing her expression.

"I'll just start weeping. Yes, you go and explain what has happened." The dowager waved him on. "You'll be the most levelheaded and you can best assess whether or not he can cope with the lot of us."

"Very well, then." Lord Strickland strode from the room, addressing the maid. "Send someone to fetch the physician from the village."

As soon as he left, merriment returned again.

The dowager duchess grabbed Poppy and pulled her into her embrace. "Oh, Poppy! I knew he would wake. I knew it."

She nodded, a lump lodged in her throat, threatening to choke her. "Yes, you did."

The duchess pulled back to look at her, her hands cupping her cheeks warmly. "You believed it, too, my dear girl."

"Yes." Poppy nodded, blinking suddenly stinging eyes. "I did believe it. I knew he would be well."

Then they were hugging again and Poppy's heart was breaking. Not because the duke was recovered. For that, she was elated, her chest lighter, expanding with relief. She'd prayed for his recovery.

No, it was because this would all come to an end now. The duke was awake. He would tell everyone that she was a fraud, that she was no one to him. They would all know she was no one.

She and her sister would have to leave this place and this family for whom she had come to care. Worse than leaving them, worse than never seeing them again, was knowing that they would hate her—despise her for the liar she was.

She looked over the duchess's shoulder to find Struan Mackenzie staring at her intently, his gaze unreadable as his eyes drilled into her.

Soon he would know, too. He'd have the truth at last. Not that he ever thought she was good enough for Autenberry in the first place. He always thought her a liar.

She pulled free of the duchess's embrace. "Excuse me," she murmured. "I need a moment . . ."

The trail of her words was hardly noticed. Lady Autenberry turned to the rest of her family to celebrate the return of their loved one.

For a moment, Poppy stood there, feeling once again every inch on the outside. Now more than ever. Even though her sister was in the room, as well, clinging happily and obliviously to the new best friend she found in Clara, Poppy was achingly aware of how very alone she was. She didn't belong here and soon all of these kind people would know that within minutes.

The sting in her eyes returned with a vengeance and she turned, slipping from the room without a backward glance, determined no one see her cry.

Chapter 24

$\mathcal{H}$e watched her go amid the happy and noisy exchange. No one else seemed to notice but he did. He was attuned to her every movement.

His skin felt too tight, like it didn't fit his body anymore. Autenberry was awake.

He'd lost her.

A muffled curse burned on his lips. *She was never yours.*

It went without saying that Struan would be leaving soon. His half brother would never tolerate his presence. He would have to say farewell to the family he had come to know and, admittedly, come to care for.

He'd have to say farewell to Poppy.

Whatever he had been doing with the girl

would come to an end now. Hard to seduce a female when she was no longer in such easy proximity.

Seduction. It didn't ring right. The word made what they were doing sound tawdry and dirty. Somewhere along the way their trysts had come to mean more than that to him. *She* had come to mean more.

With one last glance at the preoccupied family, he slipped from the drawing room. His steps thudded over the parquet floor as he moved across the foyer and down corridors. Somehow he knew where she would go. Ever since they arrived she took many a morning stroll in the conservatory's orchard. He wound down the stairs to the bottom floor. The corridor that led to the conservatory stretched long and hollow as he walked its length.

When the double doors came into view he spotted the green leaves of the lemon trees pressing against the glass.

He opened the door and stepped inside its balmy warmth. He closed the door softly behind him, cocking his head slightly. He thought he heard a slight snuffle from somewhere deep within the enclosure. He stepped off the pebbled path, his boots sinking into the lush carpet of grass.

He walked through the gloom, through a warren of hedges and trees and shrubs, past flowers of incomprehensible colors. The only reason he could see at all was due to the paltry red light emitting from strategically placed coal-burning grates. It might be winter outside but in here plants and vegetation thrived.

He found her near an orange tree, her back to him. The moon gleamed down through the glass ceiling. It did not feel like winter. In this conservatory, it felt as though they were trapped in their own private bubble of spring.

He watched her in silence for a long moment, the squeeze he had felt in his chest ever since the maid burst into the drawing room coiling ever tighter.

"It must be difficult for you to wait here instead of rushing to see your duke right now."

She stiffened, her shoulders pulling back. He studied the enticing fall of her hair. It was pinned up at the sides, leaving the rest to fall in artfully arranged waves down the center of her back. His palms itched to touch it and gather the mass up into his hands.

Without turning around, she demanded, "Do you mock me? Please do not. For the life of me, I cannot endure it. Not tonight."

He flinched at her husky plea. He had bred such distrust in her. "No. I'm not."

He moved closer, drawn to her as if an invisible

thread pulled him in. His boot steps struck the ground silently.

He stopped behind her, leaving space between them. He studied the back of her hair, the loose arrangement of waves. He wanted to touch that hair a final time, lose his fingers in the soft strands.

"You shouldn't be in here."

"I know." Now more than ever he knew.

"Why are you?"

"Isn't it clear? I'm here because you're here." Because he wanted to see her one more time before he left.

"So you'll still continue this game with me, shall you?"

"And what game is that?"

"Hunting me."

"No." He almost smiled. Hunting her. Yes, he couldn't deny that he had done that. Except it wasn't a game for him. Perhaps it had started that way, but no longer. "I'm leaving."

"You won't stay to see Autenberry?"

Staring at the back of her, a groan of frustration welled up inside him. He swallowed it back. It was easier as long as he didn't see her face. Her eyes. Her mouth. He could do this. Leave without touching her.

"You and I both know he won't want to see me.

Now that he's awake, his hospitality toward me comes to an end."

"A great many things come to an end tonight."

"That is true." He turned and started walking, putting some much needed distance between them.

"Struan!" The desperate cry warbled on the air. *Don't turn around. Don't look at her.*

Stopping, he held himself motionless. He never should have gone after her.

"Struan," she said again, this time her voice demanding, pleading.

He had to turn. Had to look. His hands opened and closed at his sides, groping for control. *Just walk out and don't look back.* He'd be glad later. Glad he was free of her and this place.

Glad he hadn't been a prize idiot and looked at her a final time.

Slowly, he turned and faced her. "Poppy . . ." He put a wealth of meaning into her name. It was a warning and a plea.

Her face was ravaged. Her big eyes glistened with tears. Wet tracts lined her cheeks proving she had already been crying. The sight broke something loose inside him.

Damnation. It wouldn't be the first time he acted like a prize idiot.

It took three long strides for him to reach her.

After that, there was no going back.

SHE SHOULD HAVE let him go. He had tried to leave. She didn't know why he had followed her in the first place. Perhaps to say good-bye in his own way. It didn't matter. He was here, standing before her, and he would know everything soon enough.

He'd know she was a liar. A fraud. He would hate her. Whatever he saw in her now . . . the way his eyes turned warm and molten. That would be over. Done. Gone forever.

His hand reached up to cup her face. His thumb grazed her cheek, catching on a tear. "Are these tears for him? Tears of joy and relief?"

She shook her head. "I don't know . . ."

"I hate it."

"Wh-what?"

"The way you weep for him."

She knew he only cared because of this petty rivalry between him and Marcus. "Would you rather I weep for you?"

"No," he growled, his hand reaching out, curling around her neck and hauling her closer until his mouth ghosted over her own. "I'd rather you scream for me."

Her heart took off, wild as a bird set loose from

inside her too-tight chest. His eyes, bright and dark, fastened on her.

Everything slowed. Blood rushed, a dull roar in her ears. She imagined she could hear the muffled thump of her own heart.

Then everything leapt to action. They moved in unison, coming together. Their mouths fused, lips breaking only for the time it took them to tug their clothes free in a blur of motion. Everything was frantic. Desperate. Violent in its fierceness.

They kissed and kissed and kissed.

Hot and feverish, tongues and clanging teeth. It was fierce and wild. There was nothing smooth or civilized about it, but it shattered her completely.

His free hand tugged down her bodice until there was just her corset-covered breasts. He pushed the low-cut edge of her corset down with a savage yank until both breasts spilled over the top. She gasped at the brush of air on her exposed flesh. His hands grazed over the crests, rough palms abrading the tender skin as his mouth ravaged hers. He wasn't gentle. He didn't treat her like some fragile piece of crystal.

His hand settled on her right breast, closing over the small mound and squeezing, making her feel voluptuous and beautiful.

"You're wearing entirely too many clothes," he muttered, his hands untying the laces at the front.

Then she was free. Her loose chemise gaped open, exposing her breasts. His head dipped, taking her into his mouth. She cried out, her fingers latching on to his head.

They sank to the base of the tree, the carpet of grass the softest of beds as his hardness fell over her. He pulled back, looking down at her, his hand skimming her face, hard fingers burying into her hair, scattering pins. He gripped her scalp as his hot mouth crashed over hers, consuming.

Her hands dove for the front of his trousers, eagerly unbuttoning the falls of his breeches to free him. He pulled back to shuck off his jacket and shove his trousers down his hips.

She watched, devouring the sight of him. They came together again, bare skin sliding sinuously against each other. He shoved the skirts of her gown to her waist and settled between her thighs and it felt so right, like two puzzle pieces locking together.

He kissed her breasts again and she whimpered, arching her spine, wanting more. His mouth closed around one nipple, pulling deep, and she moaned, her fingers clenching in his strong biceps. He shifted his weight and brought his manhood directly against her opening.

She panted, her fingers moving to clutch the back of his neck, clinging, straining against him, pulling him closer as she rotated her hips, needing him inside her like a body needs air.

"Poppy? Are you certain?"

Yes, yes, yes. This would be all she would have of him before he learned the truth. Before she was cast out from his life.

Gasping, she shifted her hips and pushed up against him. "I want this. I want you, Struan."

His eyes gleamed fiercely as he wedged himself between her parted thighs. She looked down between them, watching as he took himself in hand, gripping his hard member and guiding it toward her. Her mouth parted in a small O, fascinated and aroused at the sight.

He wrapped an arm around her waist and hauled her closer, holding her steady as he began to sink inside her. His eyes locked with hers.

It was a dreamlike moment, staring into the depths of his eyes, feeling his body joining with hers, stretching and filling her with a burn that wasn't entirely comfortable.

Her body stretched to accommodate him. Gasping little breaths escaped her as she molded to fit him.

"You're so bloody tight, Poppy," he hissed.

Her eyes flared wide, and she whimpered as he pushed inside another fraction.

He stilled, his biceps tensing, muscles bunching tightly. "Am I hurting you?"

Just when she thought he was done, he pushed in deeper and she cried out, partly in pain and partly in relief to have him buried so deep—an answer at last to the clenching ache.

He froze again. Her grip tightened on him. "Don't stop!"

The arm at her waist pulled her closer, mashing her breasts to his chest as he thrust himself fully inside, finally seating himself and wrenching a sharp gasp from her.

"Oh, my," she choked.

"Poppy?" he growled, his voice bewildered. "Are you . . . have you done this before?"

She met his gaze and gave a swift shake of her head. "No."

He stilled, his manhood lodged deep, pulsing inside her. Myriad emotions flickered across his face. "Why didn't you—"

"I never said I wasn't a virgin."

He shook his head, his eyes anguished. "But you let me think . . . I called you—"

She leaned forward and wrapped her arms around his neck. She pressed her mouth to his and kissed him for all she was worth, silencing what she knew he wanted to say. He felt remorse for judging her, for assuming she was something other than what she said. Given the lie she had been perpetrating, he'd reached only reasonable conclusions.

But this wasn't supposed to be about revelations. Soon enough he would discover that he had *not* been wrong about her. She was a deceiver.

For now, in this moment, she would have this. Hunger. Raw desire. *Struan.*

She wiggled beneath him, gasping into his mouth as shards of pleasure spiked out from where they were joined.

"Keep going," she commanded, her nails scoring his back through his shirt.

He rocked his hips against her in reflex and she cried out, arching against him.

"Oh, hell, Poppy, you feel good." He withdrew and drove back inside her. "I'm sorry. It will feel better next time."

It felt amazing now. An aching pressure built inside her as he moved faster, increasing the delicious friction and tightening that invisible coil low in her belly. It was like before, when he made her fly apart just by using his hand and mouth. Only better. Everything more intense.

She writhed against him, desperate to reach that climax. He hooked a hand under her knee and wrapped her leg around his waist, angling her for deeper penetration.

The next thrust shattered her and she cried out hoarsely. She never felt anything so amazing. So good. Her vision blurred as he pumped inside her again. He continued to move against her, working a steady pace. She dragged her nails through his hair, loving the absolute freedom to touch him, to love him with her hands. His name ripped from her lips.

"Poppy," he growled in her ear. "Let me hear you scream again."

She was almost there. Shudders shook through her.

Her head nestled in the warm nook of his neck, muffling her moans. His hand rooted in her hair, pulling her head back to look at him. He held her there, watching, peering into her eyes as he moved inside her, and it felt like he was looking into her soul right then. "I want to see you."

She nodded jerkily. The familiar burning ache seized her, tightening, bigger, deeper. It made her arch up against him. "Ohh!"

"That's it, Poppy." He drove harder into her and she cried out, every nerve ending sizzling and then bursting. She went limp.

He came over her, his lips seizing hers. She

groaned into his mouth, feeling his own release follow and shudder through him.

They collapsed down to earth together, his weight on top of her. As heavy as he was, she didn't want him to ever move. She could stay like this forever.

Chapter 25

After they set their clothes to rights, Struan helped her to her feet. She wobbled a little, clearly unsteady. He grasped her elbow to steady her. She pulled away, putting a circumspect step between them. It almost made him laugh. A little late for propriety.

He should feel bad . . . ashamed even. He'd taken her maidenhood on the ground of the conservatory like any well-used tart.

"Why did you let . . ." His voice faded. He didn't know what he wanted her to say. What he wanted her to hear from him. Despite everything, he didn't regret it. He couldn't.

She shook her head and averted her gaze.

"Poppy?" He took her chin and forced her to look at him.

She moistened her lips. "I wanted it to be you."

Something unfurled inside him. She'd chosen him. She didn't have to. She had Autenberry, but she chose him. He waited, hoping she would say more. Hoping she would say that this changed things for them.

"Why?" he demanded. Autenberry was awake now, and yet she gave herself to him. It could mean only one thing. She had to see that. "I'll tell you why," he snapped when she didn't respond. She eyed him warily, but said nothing. "You don't love him as you think you do."

She inhaled a deep breath. "Struan, I can't do this right now. Soon it will all make sense and then you'll . . ." Her voice faded and bleakness flashed across her face.

"I'll what?" he pressed.

She closed her eyes in a tight blink. "You'll understand."

"I understand you, Poppy. I see you," he whispered, desperate for her to hear him, to believe. She had to know that this had meant something to him—that *she* did.

Poppy stopped abruptly and turned to face him.

His heart hammered a wild drum as she gazed up at him.

"No." She shook her head and tore her stare away as though his eyes, his face, were too much.

"I see the real you. You're kind and selfless. You put others first before yourself—"

She shook her head. "Stop. No."

He continued, "You don't like attention. You don't want the light to shine on you, but I see you."

"No." She pressed a hand to her stomach almost as though his words made her sick. "You don't see me. You can't. You think you do, but you're wrong."

The sharp edge of something sliced through his chest.

Lifting her skirts, she headed across the grass toward the path leading out of the conservatory.

He fell into step beside her. Something ugly started brewing inside him, threatening to boil over. He had just come as close as he ever had to laying himself bare for a woman. And she was walking away from him.

She glanced at him. "We should not emerge together."

"Yes. Mustn't besmirch your reputation. Your duke wouldn't like that. Tell me, how will he feel when he finds out he didn't have you first? Will you tell him it was me? Perhaps I should be the one to tell him that."

She stopped and faced him, her expression stricken. "Is that what this was about for you? Beating your brother?"

He glared at her, the blood rushing in his ears. He longed to say yes. He wanted to fling that lie at her so she could feel as miserable as he did. "No," he managed to get out. "I can promise you that Autenberry was the last person I was thinking about while shagging you."

She flinched, her eyes wounded as she held his gaze. Turning, she moved swiftly from him, disappearing amid the hedges.

This time he did not go after her.

He waited several minutes, inhaling the sweet aroma of flora, letting her proceed far ahead of him and giving himself time to compose. At last he moved, striding from the conservatory and toward the study, eager for a drink. Or four.

He entered the room lined with bookcases and poured himself a brandy. He was on his second when the door to the study opened.

Lord Strickland's voice rolled across the air behind him. "He wants to see you."

Struan paused only a moment before downing the rest of his drink. "I imagine he does." Turning, he departed the study and made his way upstairs to the duke's chamber.

SHE EASED INTO the chamber she had occupied so often over the last week, her slippered feet falling softly on the thick Aubusson carpet.

After she fled the conservatory and Struan last night, she had gone to bed without seeing the Duke of Autenberry. No one visited with him the previous evening save Lord Strickland and the physician. The physician agreed it was wise not to overwhelm him just yet.

She could only hazard a guess that he knew now of her charade. He couldn't have been awake this long and not learned that he had a fiancée. Aside of an evening spent with Lord Strickland, the dowager had spent nearly an hour with him before breakfast. There was no way he could be unaware of her existence.

Poppy gazed across the great length of space to the bed, verifying he was awake. She didn't want to disturb him if he slept.

Her pulse thudded in hard beats. The coward in her begged for her to turn, grab her sister and run. Leave this place without ever facing the duke. But she couldn't do that. She owed him an explanation. Hopefully, he would bear no grudge. She had saved his life, after all. That must count for something.

He was not asleep.

"Miss Fairchurch." He smiled at the sight of

her, sitting up a little higher and waving her forward. "Lovely to see you. Come inside."

She inched deeper into his chamber, immediately feeling at ease in the face of his welcoming manner.

"You look much better." She could not disguise the relief from her voice as she rounded the bed. He looked the picture of health with his dressing robe parted at the front, revealing a vee of broad chest faintly sprinkled with hair. He might not be as muscled as his brother, but he was nonetheless a well-formed man. "There's color in your cheeks again."

"All thanks to you," he returned with that smile she had forgotten. Sweet and tender as though she and he alone knew a secret. He had that gift, the ability to make others comfortable. That's what had drawn her to him in the beginning.

But then she met Struan, and nothing was comfortable anymore.

Indeed, Struan did not make her feel comfortable. He made her feel like she was on fire from the inside out.

He made her feel necessary.

When he looked at her she felt as though she was the center of his universe. When he touched her she felt like she was everything to him—the difference between life and death.

Pushing thoughts of Struan away, she stopped at the foot of the bed. She and the duke stared at each other for an awkward moment, the duke seeing her, perhaps truly, for the first time and she seeing him with fresh eyes.

This was the man she thought she loved, whom she had built so many fantasies around. It had been a girl's whimsy. She didn't know him. She never had.

She *knew* Mackenzie. *Struan.* She knew how his mind worked. She knew how important family was to him for the very reason that he didn't have any left. She knew how important *this* family—the dowager, Enid, Clara—had come to mean to him.

He was kind and generous even if he didn't want people to know that about him. He never forgot where he came from or all he had suffered and he was compassionate to others.

And there was the way his mere gaze could light her afire.

She knew how he tasted. How he felt . . . the sounds he made when—

She gave herself a swift mental kick, killing such disturbing thoughts.

"I owe you an apology," she began.

"You do?" He blinked. "For what? Saving my life?"

She inclined her head, feeling all kinds of awkward. "For coming here under false pretenses. For permitting your family to believe we are . . . closer than we, in truth, are." Good heavens. She couldn't even bring herself to put the awfulness of her deed into words before him. She sucked in a breath. "I'm fully prepared to explain everything and apologize to your family. Hopefully, they won't hate me too much."

He looked at her kindly. "I doubt anyone can hate you."

Struan's face flashed before her. He would hate her when he discovered that she had been lying to him this entire time.

The moment had come and passed for her to admit the truth. Lying in his arms, when there had been nothing between them, she had her chance and she let it slip between her fingers.

"You'd be surprised." Again, she thought of Struan and how he would view her when this was all over and done.

He shook his head. "Impossible. It appears *everyone* has fallen in love with you while I lay like a slug in this bed."

Not everyone. She wasn't the only one who had an opportunity to make a confession. Struan had said nothing of love any of the times they had been together, but there had been those moments together in the conservatory last night.

He had claimed that he knew her, that he understood her. She could have shown him who she really was. She should have tried to explain then.

"Your family is very kind and generous. It's no more than that."

"Oh, I don't know about that. My sisters can be tricky creatures, and yet they adore you."

"Sisters often are tricky," she agreed, thinking of her own. Bryony would never forgive her once everything came to light. She was planning on a future as a sister-in-law to a duke. She would not enjoy returning to their humble life.

He continued, "Strickland is in your pocket, as well. He's a hard man to win over, but he is a staunch admirer of yours."

A blush heated her face. "Lord Strickland is a gentleman."

"A gentleman enamored of you, and trust me. He's a hard man to impress. In fact, you've won him over so much that he thinks that I should in truth wed you."

She laughed.

Marcus stared back at her soberly, his expression not cracking with humor, and her laughter faded. "Oh. I thought you were jesting."

"He brings up a valid point. My entire family adores you, and I cannot remain a bachelor forever. I've heirs to produce, after all."

She stared at him a long moment, certain she had walked into some dream where dukes proposed to shopgirls who had lied to them—about them. "That is hardly reason enough to enter into matrimony," she whispered.

"People marry for far less."

She winced. "I was hoping for more."

"Ah, you're a romantic. That's fine and well. I don't mind that. It means you have a tender heart."

He didn't mind it? But she did. She wanted more.

She wanted Struan.

"Come now, Poppy, let's make my family the happiest people in the world this Christmas."

She opened her mouth, knowing she should jump on such an offer. Any sane woman would. For Bryony, she should. Still, it was very confusing why he should want to marry her. "I don't know if I can—"

"Is it because of Mackenzie?" he asked, a sudden hardness entering his voice.

She froze. What did he know of her relationship with Mackenzie?

He continued, "Strickland told me, of course. The man has been showering you with his questionable attentions, sniffing about you like the randy mutt he is. I questioned him myself, of course."

Her head snapped up at that. "You talked to Struan?"

"Struan," he echoed, his lip curling with distaste. "Yes, I spoke to him. You know better than to trust him, I hope." His gaze turned flinty. "Any overtures he's made have been done clearly to thwart me. They are not genuine. He is not a gentleman. I'm most alarmed that he had been under my roof all this time."

She laced her fingers together, uncertain how to respond.

"I hope you have not fallen prey to him," he added. "I know he can be persuasive. He is quite the rogue and has ruined many a chit since his arrival in Town."

She bristled, wanting to defend Struan. She did not like the image of Struan with other women even if he was free to pursue whomever he chose. "He's only ever conducted himself honorably with me, which is more than I can say for myself."

The words did not feel like a lie. He'd only ever been honest with her. She was the one who had lied.

The duke waved a hand, clearly pardoning her behavior.

"I would *hope* that he had the decency to conduct himself honorably with you—he did not confirm or deny on that score when I pressed him."

No, he wouldn't. She could well envision him holding himself silent on that matter.

The duke continued, "I wouldn't put it past him to pursue what is mine as I was bound helplessly to this bed." His hands fisted at his sides, and suddenly she understood that this wasn't about *her* for the duke. It was about this war he waged with his half brother.

"I'm not yours," she mumbled, casting her gaze down.

"But you could be."

Her gaze snapped back to his handsome face. Something gleamed in his eyes. It was the hot need to claim, to possess. "Why are you doing this?"

"I told you." He shrugged. "My family loves you."

"But you don't," she returned.

Again, the shrug. "I wasn't expecting love in my marriage."

"There's something else motivating you." She scrutinized him, for once not feeling self-conscious. "It's because of your brother."

He snorted. "He's the last person I care about making happy."

"Precisely," she returned. "That's why you'll marry me. You think it will hurt him and you want that."

"So you don't deny, then, that he cares for you?" Satisfaction gleamed in his eyes. "Very good. That will be one perk." His stare refocused on her. "But what of the perks for you? I know your situation. I know of your sister. A young girl with no prospects. No money. No male to look out for her. The world can be a frightening place for such a girl. Especially in London."

Her throat thickened and her eyes burned. He was right. She should not dismiss his offer. In fairness, she could not.

Still, she hesitated. She couldn't help thinking about Struan . . . about what this would do to him. She didn't imagine he loved her. He wanted her, she knew, but love had never been uttered between them.

"He's gone," the duke declared.

She blinked. "I beg your pardon."

"Mackenzie." He pursed his lips as though he had difficulty saying the word. "He's gone. He left early this morning."

Struan was gone?

"I see." And she did see. It was crystalline clear for her. Struan wanted her. He had her. Now he was gone.

"Thank you, Your Grace." She squared her shoulders to face him. "I'd be honored to wed you." No more would she let herself worry about what this would do to Struan. She had to look out for Bryony. For herself.

Later, she would worry about what this would do to her.

Chapter 26

*T*hat evening the duke himself joined them for dinner. His color was high as well as his spirits. The dining room was beautiful, decked out in holly and garland and ribbons. Candlelight glistened throughout the vaulted-ceiling room. All the ladies were resplendent in bright silks, Poppy included. The dowager insisted she wear one of Enid's gowns, a confection of gold silk trimmed in jet beads.

Autenberry was most attentive, occasionally brushing his hand against hers resting on the table's surface, listening when she spoke. As though what she had to say mattered. As though he truly cared for her.

His stepmother beamed. Lord Strickland looked

on like a proud papa who had brought them together—and, in a way, she supposed he had. Everyone was overcome with joy and good cheer. The duke was alive. Engaged to marry Poppy. It was a happy yuletide. All was right.

She had landed a duke. Her sister would never go without again. It was almost enough. Almost.

Blast. *It was enough.* She pushed the petulant thought from her head. This was all she had ever wanted and more. Belonging. Her charming duke. An instant family. Everything she had dreamed to the letter.

Only now she realized that getting what you want wasn't all she thought it would be. Sometimes other things exist. Better things. One couldn't dream it because they didn't know it.

"As soon as Christmas ends, it's back to Town," the dowager was saying. "We'll have to meet with Madame Stefana about your wedding gown." She bounced in her seat, her breasts jiggling dangerously in the daring cut of her bodice. "And, oh, the church! St. Paul's must be booked at once. Do you think we have enough time to plan a spring wedding? Perhaps it should be in the fall?" She blinked her lush dark eyes and stared back and forth between Poppy and Autenberry expectantly.

Her head spun. She brought her fingers up to massage her temples. A dull headache had started to throb there. To be fair, her head had been throbbing ever since she left the duke's bedchamber this morning. Ever since it became clear she would be marrying him.

Ever since it became clear that Struan was gone.

Poppy's gaze drifted and locked on her sister. For once, Bryony didn't seem quite so focused on Clara. She stared at Poppy with a slightly cocked head as if mystified.

She quickly looked away, glancing down at her plate, afraid her sister would see something in her expression that revealed just how unhappy she was.

"Poppy?" the dowager pressed. "Did you not hear me? I was suggesting you honeymoon in the Mediterranean. You can visit with my family there. They will make certain you see everything you should see . . . and give you the desired space. They will understand the needs of newlyweds."

Lady Clara grimaced, clearly not relishing the idea of her brother's *needs*. To be fair, Poppy had to fight her own grimace.

She opened her mouth and nothing came out. She tried to form words, but nothing happened. She felt like she was drowning. Sinking through fathomless water and unable to breathe.

"Poppy?" Bryony's pretty face scrunched in concern. "Are you well?"

"Of course she is," the duke assured, skirting the food around on his plate with a fork, presumably looking for the perfect bite.

Perplexed, she watched him. Was he indifferent or simply did not care about the state of her heart and mind?

Her gaze lifted, colliding with Bryony's again. Her sister looked at her in concern, her lips mouthing, "What is wrong?"

What is wrong?

Everything.

Her gaze slid to where the duke sat at the head of the table, handsome as ever. She could not stomach the idea of being his wife, no matter how much she tried to deny it. No matter how much she tried to talk herself into doing this.

"I can't," she uttered. No matter how much it could benefit her sister, she could not.

"I beg your pardon?" the dowager asked, sipping from her glass.

"I can't . . ."

"What did you say?" Lady Enid asked. "We can't hear you."

"Poppy?" Bryony frowned at her from across the table.

She couldn't bear it anymore. She flung her napkin down on the table. There came a time when enough was enough. The madness had to stop. It was time for her to be honest. With herself and everyone else.

She pushed up to her feet. "I'm sorry." She looked at the duke. "I can't marry you."

He reached for her hand, frowning and appearing suddenly alert. "What is wrong, Poppy? You agreed this morning—"

"No." She shook her head and slid her hand free.

The dowager stood and rushed to her side. "What do you mean? Is it because of me? Am I overwhelming you with wedding plans? I can stop."

"She does tend to be overbearing," Lady Enid interjected dryly, stabbing at a bit of potato on her plate and bringing it to her mouth to chew.

The dowager nodded in dogged agreement. "I do."

"No. No, it's not that. I'm sorry all of this has become so complicated. I'm not His Grace's fiancée. I never was. He never proposed to me. Well, not until this morning, that is."

"What?" The dowager duchess swung to glare at her stepson as though he were somehow responsible for this matter. "Of course he proposed to you before today."

"No! He didn't . . . he wouldn't have. I made it all up. I'm a mere shopgirl. Your stepson and

I have never been romantically involved. I work in Barclay's flower shop. That is the only way he knows me. As the shopgirl that sells him flowers. I saved his life that day, but that's all. That's the only bit of truth that I've said to you, and I'm so very sorry for deceiving you."

Everyone gaped. Lady Enid glared, actually looking unfriendly. Lord Strickland shook his head, looking disappointed. Presumably with her.

As for Bryony, Poppy couldn't meet her gaze. She wasn't prepared for the hatred she knew she would find there. She would be lucky if her sister even accompanied her home. She wouldn't want to leave this place, but she wouldn't have a choice. The Autenberry clan would hardly want to keep Bryony considering what Poppy had done.

"I'm sorry. Truly. You've all been so kind to me. You treated me as one of your own and I'll always be grateful to you for that." She shook her head and sucked back a sob. She inched away from the table, pausing at the dining room threshold, her grand skirts swishing with a whisper on the air. "I'll pack now."

She fled, glad to escape. She felt only relief in that moment. That confrontation wasn't as hard as she feared. Staying, living a farce, that would have been immensely more difficult.

"Poppy! Wait."

Stopping, she turned to face the duke striding toward her. She braced herself, squaring her
shoulders. His handsome face was locked in a
scowl.

"This is because of him? You're throwing everything away for him? That degenerate?"

She flinched and had to resist an angry rebut-
tal. Lacing her hands together in front of her, she
managed an even tone. "You don't know your
brother at all, Your Grace." Her voice rang with
satisfying conviction.

He stared at her for a moment. For the first
time, he looked a little uncertain as he gazed at
her. "You really believe that?"

"Yes. And if you did, you would want him in
your life. You'd regret the lost years and try to
make up for them." She moved away, stopping to
add, "Someday I hope you have that chance."

The chance she wouldn't have. The chance she
had lost.

Poppy wasn't certain if she ever really had
such a chance. She'd never presented her true
self to him, so had there ever been any hope for
them?

Almost as though he could read her mind, he
uttered, "Struan Mackenzie is my father's by-blow.
My father abandoned him." His jaw clenched at

this admission. "There is no component of that scenario in which my half brother and I could be friends."

Poppy shook her head, feeling immensely sad for the duke right then. "You're better than that . . . than this."

"And now you think you know *me*?" He angled his head. "They're right about you. You see the good in everyone. You even managed to fall in love with my brother." He snorted. "While I was sleeping, no less, and according to everyone, you spent the majority of your time sitting vigil at my bedside. Impressive feat. I have to hand it to him, he works fast."

"It wasn't like that. It *isn't*."

He shook his head. "It's fine. I'm not angry." He gestured for her to continue on. "Go, Poppy. Live your life. I wish you well."

Turning, he walked away. She watched him for a moment. There was something lost about him— the duke she thought had everything. He was as sad as she was.

A LITTLE OVER an hour passed before Bryony entered Poppy's chamber.

Poppy turned, halting her packing as her sister strolled into the room. Facing her, she squared her shoulders and braced herself for the verbal barrage she was certain would come. She would deserve no less.

She had just destroyed her sister's chance for a privileged future as the sister to a duchess. All the advantages, all the opportunities such an existence could bring, were gone, lost because she couldn't bring herself to marry a rich, handsome duke.

Because she was in love with his brother . . . a man who clearly didn't love her back.

She waited, ready for her sister to call her selfish. Ready and willing to accept all the names she would hurl upon her head.

Bryony propped her hands on her hips and glanced at Poppy's open valise and the clothing strewn about the bed. "Can I help you pack?"

She could say nothing for some moments. Poppy only watched as her sister stepped forward and began folding her stockings and tucking them inside the valise.

She choked back a sob and nodded, tears burning in her eyes. "Thank you, Bry. Yes. That would be nice."

IT WAS THE day before Christmas and Struan had nowhere to go. No family. No friends noteworthy or special enough that they would miss him. He

wasn't even certain what home was to him anymore. England? Scotland?

Home was Poppy.

He banished the thought. How wrong was it
for that thought to enter his head? He'd clearly
gone mad. Poppy belonged to Autenberry. Autenberry had made certain he understood that when
they spoke—along with the fact that Struan was
not welcome in his home. Ever.

Poppy wanted the duke. She loved him. She
flung herself in front of a carriage for him. Or believed herself to love him at any rate. In the end,
the distinction didn't matter.

He stopped at the first village and ordered himself a meal of mutton stew.

Before departing Autenberry Manor, he'd said
his farewells to everyone except Poppy. He'd
spared himself that. He didn't care that his brother
demanded he leave immediately. He owed proper
good-byes to the dowager, Clara and Enid. They'd
welcomed him as family.

"Is this Marcus's doing?" Enid had demanded.
"Oh, he can be such a stubborn mule."

"It's simply time for me to move on," he'd explained. It wasn't his intention to sour Enid on her
brother. To a degree, he even understood Marcus's
motivation. He'd do the same thing in his position.

The ladies had refused to let him leave without

exacting a promise from him to call on them when they were next in London. He'd made the promise, although he wasn't certain he could keep it. The very idea of visiting them and seeing Poppy as Lady Autenberry, knowing she was his brother's wife, was too much to stomach.

Struan sat at a table by himself near the window, eating his dinner and sipping his whiskey, scowling at any of the serving girls who dared approach. Through the mullioned glass, he watched people scurrying about with their full and busy lives.

This was all he had. A life of plenty. Wealth and whiskey.

A life without Poppy.

Nothing.

He poured another whiskey and contemplated drinking himself into oblivion. He might as well get a room for the night. He had nowhere to be, after all.

Chapter 27

*P*oppy? Did you hear a word I've said? Come away from the window."

She shook her head, not fully processing her sister's voice. She fixed her stare on the busy street below. Her gaze scanned the crowded village, her mind spinning and heart aching.

She thought she'd seen Struan out there in the village. Of course, it couldn't be him. It was just the longing of her heart, addling her vision and confusing her.

She covered her heart with her hand, pushing against the dull throb. She imagined her heart would do that for quite some time. Still go on. Still continue to beat even though it ached and twisted inside her chest.

Blinking several times as though to clear her vision, she focused her gaze again, narrowing it in on the hatless man walking in the opposite direction, away from the inn where she and her sister had taken lodgings for the night.

"It's him," she whispered.

It wasn't her imagination. She'd know him anywhere. The shape of him. The set of his shoulders. His long stride. The glint of dark blond hair in the paltry winter sunlight. If she closed her eyes she could still feel him, taste him . . .

"Who?" Bryony came to stand beside her, startling her from her thoughts and making her jump a little where she stood.

"Struan," she murmured, facing the mullion-paned window again. She had not expected to see him again. She didn't know what was crueler. Never seeing him again or seeing him again and not having him.

"Uh, Poppy? You might be hallucinating."

"No. It's him. There." She pointed, tapping the glass.

Her sister fell silent as Poppy's gaze followed Struan weaving between people. She only caught glimpses of him here and there, but it was undeniably him.

Suddenly, her sister spoke up. "What are you waiting for, then?"

Poppy turned to gawk at her. "What do you—"

"He's the reason we left. The reason you couldn't marry the Duke of Autenberry." At Poppy's shocked look, she laughed. "Come now, Poppy. I might be young and, at times, not the best sister to you, but I'm not unintelligent. So what are you standing here for? Go after him."

"It's not that simple."

She lifted her shoulders in a single shrug. "Isn't it?"

"I rejected him, Bryony. He won't be kindly disposed to me at the moment—"

"And what is the worst that could happen, Poppy?" She tsked. "He could reject you? You've already faced that before and by someone you didn't love. This man you *do* love. I daresay he's worth the risk."

She opened her mouth to deny that she loved Struan, but what would be the point? It would only be a lie. She loved him. What she felt for Edmond was a pale shade of what she felt for Struan. There could not even be a comparison. One had been real. The other an illusion.

Shaking her head, she smiled at her sister. "When did you suddenly start becoming such an adult?"

"I have eyes," she retorted. "I can see you both belong together—that you *want* to be together."

She snorted. "The man did not even respond to my flirtations and not many men can do that, let me assure you."

Poppy sighed in exasperation. "Bry," she said in warning. "I feel as though I need to deposit you in the nearest convent."

"Go. Lecture me later. Catch up with him before he's gone."

Poppy nodded slowly as her sister's advice stole over her and took root. She had nothing to lose. If she didn't do something, Struan would be out of her life forever. She'd lose him anyway. "Very well." She glanced at her sister in concern. "You will be well here?" She wagged a finger in warning. "Do not leave this room. I'll be back shortly—"

"Go." Bryony pointed to the door with a huff of breath. "I'll be fine."

Nodding decisively, Poppy snatched up her cloak and hurried out into the hall, down the stairs and outside in the direction she had seen him striding.

The streets were crowded with people bustling about, intent on their shopping. A long line stretched outside the butcher's shop. Apparently everyone was attempting to buy provisions for their Christmas day feast. She closed her eyes in a pained blink. She and Bryony would be alone Christmas morning.

Looking both ways, she stepped out onto the street to go around the winding line of people and dodged a single rider. The gentleman scowled down at her from his mount and tossed out a terse, ungentlemanly reprimand. She supposed, dressed once again in her shabby garments, she looked to be a female of no account or worth.

Ignoring him, she narrowed her gaze ahead to the red-bricked inn at the end of the lane. It was a far more prosperous-looking establishment than the one she and Bryony had let for the night, well out of their price range. Her limited purse required they stay at the village's far more meager inn.

A delicious aroma of roasting meat drifted out the front door and carried across the distance as someone passed through it. Her stomach grumbled, reminding her that she had not yet eaten for the day. Perhaps Struan was staying at this establishment? The smells were certainly an enticement and far better than anything she had smelled in the kitchens where they were taking lodgings.

She was about to cross the street when she spotted him emerging from the inn. He wore his great coat with the collar hiked up to ward off the worst of the frigid wind.

She froze, unable to move or speak. Someone

jostled her rudely from behind and it was as though the movement served to wake her up.

Sucking in a deep breath, she waved her arm wildly. "Mr. Mackenzie! Struan! Struan!" she called.

He heard her.

He stopped and looked around. She called his name again. His gaze found her. Surprise and something else flashed across his features before his expression settled into an impassive mask. For a moment, she thought he would continue on his way and ignore her altogether. Instead he shook his head and stepped toward her, resignation in his steps. Not the most promising reaction, but at least she would see him again. Hope swelled in her chest. He would give her a chance and hear her out. A chance. She sucked in a stinging breath. A chance was all she could ask.

The snow-slickened sidewalk grew more crowded as a parade of women hefting their Christmas geese, fractious children in tow, blocked Struan from view.

She craned her neck, losing sight of him in the melee. Suddenly, a fight broke out among the children. A mother cried out and grabbed for one of the squabbling boys, swinging her enormous goose as she went. The slippery boy dodged her hand and collided into Struan, casting him out into the street and propelling his great body directly in the path of that peevish rider who nearly struck Poppy earlier. Struan backed away hastily to avoid the horse and rider, hitting on an icy patch that sent his feet flying. He landed hard on his back in a great heap. Poppy winced.

The frazzled mother called out an apology, seizing her child as she did so.

Struan regained his footing, shaking his head as though to clear it. He beat his hands against his breeches, trying to rid himself of mud and snow.

That wasn't all she saw.

A carriage was bearing down. Fast. It was like déjà vu.

Everything dragged to a crawl as she watched its speeding approach.

The driver struggled with the reins, trying to slow the racing carriage. People standing in its path dove out of the way, but Struan wasn't looking. In the din of the busy village it was just more noise. Struan bent to pick up a goose that had tumbled into the street with him.

Her heart dropped to her feet as she watched the carriage and horses with their steaming breath and wild eyes closing the distance, mud and snow spitting up at their hooves. Struan called something to one of the mothers, holding up that blasted goose, oblivious to the impending collision.

No. God, please, no.

Again, as before, she didn't think, simply reacted, rushing straight into the street. Except
unlike before, her chest actually constricted so
much it hurt. And that would be just the beginning of her pain. She knew her life would be shattered if anything happened to this man. There
was no doubt of that.

She knew because she loved him.

She loved him.

Cold washed through her. "Struan!"

His gaze lifted, eyes widening as he spotted
her, and she knew she must look like a mad-
woman. She vaulted the last bit of space separating them, flinging her body against him. A cry
escaped her as they flew through the air, clearing the carriage's path. They slammed together
on the ground. They collapsed on the other side
of the street the precise moment the carriage
roared past. Hard arms wrapped around her, the
big body cushioning her.

Hopefully she had pushed him to safety without harming him too much. If the result wasn't
death or coma, she could count herself successful.

The horses screamed in protest nearby as the
driver pulled hard on the reins, still trying to get
them to stop.

She looked down at Struan beneath her.

The big, fuming Scot glared up at her, his face drawn tight in lines of pain. "What the hell was that?"

The air left her in a rush and she couldn't even make herself move for a moment. She let out a great exhale, assessing herself for injuries. Everything felt fine. Nothing broken.

"You're welcome." She clambered off him.

"Are you trying to get yourself killed?" he demanded.

"No, just saving your life," she returned.

"At risk to yourself?" He closed his eyes and let loose a curse. "You did it again, Poppy."

"That's right, you oaf. I did." She propped her hands on her hips. "I did it for you because I didn't relish you being flattened and killed."

She noticed then that there was a deathly pallor to his face—as though all the blood had been leeched from his body. "Are you hurt?" Dear Heavens. What if he was harmed?

She quickly looked him over. She didn't note any obvious injuries. His broad chest rose and fell with labored breaths but he appeared otherwise healthy.

"You'll be the death of me yet, but I'm well. You can't take such risks—"

"People take risks for those they care about," she shot back, only realizing she had said that once before. When he'd criticized her for shoving Autenberry out of the way, she had said the same thing. *People take risks for those they care about.*

It was the truth then and now. Now more than ever.

He stilled, a strange look coming over his face. They locked eyes and she knew he was remembering that, too. He hadn't forgotten her words either.

"Poppy." He whispered her name almost in reverence and she shivered. Clearing her throat, she glanced around and noticed they were the subjects of many fascinated stares. "What did you say?"

His question drew her gaze back to him. "I said: People take risks for those they care about."

Silence met her reply. Although there was all manner of people and sounds around them it was as though they were the last two people on earth. A muscle feathered in his cheek, ticing madly.

His lips quirked and he finally found his voice. "So you care about me?"

She felt her heart pound savage and wild in her chest, desperate to break free.

This was it, then. The moment of truth. *Her* truth. She moistened her lips but before she could form the inevitable answer, he continued. "Poppy, what are you doing here? Shouldn't you be with Autenberry?" There was some scorn in his voice as he asked this, as though he had thought to grab the question and arm himself with it at the last moment.

"You left . . ." she began.

"You didn't think the duke would want me to stay, did you? You know I would have to go once he woke." His lips twisted. "Even if he hadn't demanded it of me, it was for the best. All things considered."

She nodded. *All things considered.* Meaning her lie.

He still thought she was Autenberry's fiancée. He thought she wanted his brother over him.

She sucked in a deep breath. That was why he had left. He thought that now that Autenberry was awake she belonged with him.

"I lied to you," she blurted. Finally, she said it. She said it and she could only hope he would not hate her. That he would understand . . .

He angled his head, looking at her intently as though he were trying to pull back all her layers and see to the core of her. "What do you mean?"

"Forgive my boy, sir." A red-faced woman pushed close to interrupt them. "I've my hands full with—"

"Quite all right," Struan replied, not even

glancing at the woman as he seized Poppy's hand and pulled her after him, charging through the gathered crowd and cutting a direct line for the inn—*his* inn. He marched them through the main door and up one flight of stairs. A small group was singing carols in the taproom and their discordant rendition of "Old King Wenceslas" followed them.

Her feet raced to keep up with him. His longer strides ate up the floor. He thrust her ahead of him into his room and slammed the door behind them.

Propriety didn't even signify in this moment as he towered before her, larger than he had ever appeared.

For a moment, her mind reeled with the knowledge that she knew him. In the carnal sense. She had taken this man into her body and felt him unleash himself inside her. They had been as close as two people could physically be. Heat clawed her face and he must have interpreted some of her inner thoughts for his eyes darkened and his gaze dropped to her mouth in that way that reminded her of the moments before he kissed her.

He took a step and she retreated back another. She could not permit him to touch her again until she told him everything. Until everything was out in the open between them. Then, after she stood before him with no lies hovering, if he still wanted to touch her, he could. He could have all of her—heart, soul, and body. *If.*

"As I was saying, I haven't been honest with you."

"I know." His deep brogue rolled over her.

"You know?" She blinked.

"Aye. From the start I've known you don't truly love Autenberry. I've always known that, lass."

She nodded, wishing that were the all of it. "Yes, you thought that—"

"No. I've known. Because I know *you*, Poppy."

He closed the space separating them, which brought her hand flush with the hard wall of his chest. "Very well, that is true," she admitted. "But there is more."

He stared at her, waiting as though he finally understood she had to say it all—*everything.* Deep breath. No matter the cost to her, he deserved to know. "I was never engaged to the duke. Was never even his mistress as you suspected. I was nothing. I am nothing." She flapped her arms helplessly at her sides. "No one to him. Just a girl who sold him flowers and harbored a schoolgirl crush for him."

He was silent for a moment before asking, "And you just made up the whole betrothal?"

She grimaced. "Yes. I'm sorry. I never meant for it to go so far." It wasn't worth mentioning Lord

Strickland's involvement. She went along with everything—she was the one at the center of the deception.

He let out a breath and looked down before lifting his gaze back to hers. "So we have a problem, then."

Her heart stalled. He couldn't forgive her. He didn't want her. "What's that?" she asked, hardly breathing.

"You said people take risks for those they care about." She nodded in response. "Meaning you care about me?" he pressed.

"I do," she whispered. "Yes."

"That's not good enough for me, I'm sorry," he replied, his expression hard and unyielding.

His words stung like a slap. Her throat clogged tight with emotion. "I understand."

She couldn't even think. She only knew that she felt like she was splintering apart. Her chest grew so tight it hurt to breathe. She turned to go, but was seized suddenly by his arms and forced around.

"It's not good enough because I need more. I want everything from you, Poppy Fairchurch. Your whole heart." His fingers flexed on her arms and she felt each one like a singeing brand. His moss green eyes scoured her face. "You lied about loving my brother, about being betrothed to him?" He shook his head side to side. "That's the sweetest lie I ever heard."

She choked back a sob. A happy sob.

He continued, "I want your love because God knows you have my heart. It's yours. I love you. I love you more than I thought I could ever love a person."

Her gaze flicked over his face, so harsh and unrelenting in the absolute intensity of his declaration. She smoothed a hand over his cheek.

She shook her head, her eyes blurring. "I love you, too. Almost from the start, although I didn't realize what was happening." The words burst from her in a choking torrent. "I loved the idea of the duke. He was a stranger that I built a romantic ideal around, but it wasn't real. That was never more obvious to me than when the duke woke and proposed in truth—"

"Autenberry asked you to marry him?" He stared at her in something akin to awe.

She nodded. "Yes, in a strange turn of events. I think he thought it would make his family happy—"

"And thwart me." He grunted, his eyes glinting with anger.

"Perhaps, yes. That, too," she allowed, covering his hand with her own.

"And you didn't want that? Your duke? The fantasy? Being a duchess?"

She shook her head. "The reality of you is better than any fantasy I've ever had."

"You choose me," he said, and his voice sounded faintly constricted. "Aside of my mother, you're the first person who ever chose me."

He was thinking of his father . . . of his rejection. She moistened her lips and swallowed. "I choose you. I'll choose you every time, Struan. You came along and the reality of you is so much more . . . you made me feel so much *more*. You woke me up to how love can truly be. Things I never thought I could feel." She lifted her shoulders, a sob catching in her voice. She motioned between them. "I didn't know this existed."

He swept her up in his arms, lifting her feet off the ground. "It exists, kitten. This is real. And it's forever."

She wrapped her arms around his neck and clung, hanging on, never wanting to let go. He kissed her then. A long, breathless kiss that tasted of forever.

And she knew it would be.

Epilogue

Four months later . . .

 Poppy brushed her hair in long strokes, pausing in front of her dresser mirror as the bedchamber door opened. Smiling, she watched as Struan entered their chamber and approached. She parted her lips to greet him, but her words twisted in a yelp as he bent down and scooped her up from the dresser bench and tossed her onto the bed like she weighed nothing at all.

He followed, dropping down beside her and tugging her closer with an arm around her waist.

"Struan!" She laughed, her hands splaying against his chest. "I'm trying to get ready. The guests will be here soon."

He groaned. "Do we have to go downstairs?"

"You were the one who wanted to have this little soiree," she reminded pertly, rolling onto her side to face him.

They'd been in London for several weeks now after taking some time for themselves and spending a fortnight in Scotland. Bryony had spent that time with the dowager and her family, reveling in her new family and not missing Poppy in the least.

Now her sister was settling in quite happily into her new home with Struan and Poppy—even if that meant enduring a governess and tutors. It was more than Poppy had ever dreamed for her sister. Her gaze roamed over her husband's face, reveling in every line and hollow, in the well-sculpted mouth she knew so well. *This* was more than any dream she ever had for herself.

"Do you blame me for wanting to show off my beautiful wife?" Their noses practically touched as they reclined side to side on the bed. They were so close they shared each other's very air.

"And that's the only reason?" she asked. "I thought this was to satisfy the dowager?"

"Well, she was rather angry that we did not invite her to the wedding," he mused.

"No doubt. We didn't invite anyone." The dowager duchess had been most displeased that they had eloped. She insisted they do something to commemorate their nuptials, so Struan had arrived at this solution. "I don't think we'll ever hear the end of it. Even after this party."

She smiled at the thought of their wedding day. They'd married privately in a small village in Scotland. Just the two of them, the minister and his family as witnesses. In all her imaginings of a grand church wedding, nothing could have been sweeter or more intimate or more perfect than the two of them staring into each other's eyes, uttering their vows and knowing that the other one meant every word with every fiber of their being. She savored the memory even now, and she knew that she would savor the memory in years to come, alongside all the memories they would have of their lives together. Their story was just beginning.

"Do you think your brother will be here?" she mused.

His brow furrowed and she reached her fingers up to smooth away the tension lines. "There's been no word from him."

"Where can he be?" She shook her head. "The dowager is beside herself. He didn't even leave a note. Just left without a—"

"He's a grown man, Poppy. He can look after himself. He nearly died. That can change a person and alter their perspective. He'll come back when he's ready."

She nodded, and shoved away the troubling thoughts. Struan was right, of course. Autenberry was probably having the time of his life somewhere on the continent sipping champagne with a bevy of beautiful women. She liked to think that at any rate. Any alternative to that scenario left her apprehensive.

Struan leaned in and pressed a slow, savoring kiss to her mouth.

"Our guests . . ." she murmured, not very insistently.

"Can wait," he finished for her.

"Very well," she agreed, sinking into his kiss. "We can be quick."

Struan's mouth roamed, nibbling down her throat. "Quick?" Her fingertips walked up his chest to rest against the warm skin of his throat. "What I have in mind is going to take some time. An hour . . ."

"An hour?" she squeaked as he pulled open her dressing robe. Chill air skated over her, making her shiver. He ducked his head, his bigger body shielding her and suddenly her shivers had nothing to do with the cold. His warm mouth closed over her breast, and she arched with a moan.

"Or two," he came up to say, his green eyes darkening.

"Two?" she breathed, her heart palpitating the way it did whenever he looked at her like that. She doubted that would ever change. Even when she was gray-haired and doddering, one look from him would serve to do that to her.

He nodded once. "At least."

She burrowed her fingers through his dark gold hair, tugging him closer to her again. "At least," she agreed, no longer caring that they would be late to their own party. "We have time."

All the time in the world.

Next month, don't miss these exciting new love stories only from Avon Books

Taken by Cynthia Eden

Bailey Jones survived her abduction by the infamous Death Angel, but although she's healed, she can't stop wondering about the woman she helped to escape. When LOST agent Asher Young is assigned to her case, Bailey instantly feels an attraction to the ex-SEAL who has his own secrets. As corpses begin surfacing, Asher must race to stop a killer who wants to claim his next prize: Bailey . . .

Good Vampires Go to Heaven by Sandra Hill

Two-thousand-year-old vampire demon Zeb is supposed to spend eternity turning mortal sinners into bad guy Lucipires like himself. But Zeb is a bad boy in a good way—secretly working as a double agent for St. Michael the Archangel in hopes of one day earning his wings. But when his betrayal is discovered, Regina, a foxy, flame-haired Vangel witch on a rescue mission, busts out Zeb. Hello, temptation!

Wild at Whiskey Creek by Julie Anne Long

Glory Greenleaf is ready to leave Hellcat Canyon with her guitar and her Texas-sized talent. Only two people have ever believed in her: her brother, who's in jail, and his best friend . . . who put him there. Eli Barlow has always loved Glory, so he knows she can't forgive him . . . or forget the night they surrendered to passion. But when Glory's big break is threatened, Eli will risk everything to make it right . . .

REL 1116

THE SMYTHE-SMITH QUARTET BY
#1 *NEW YORK TIMES*
BESTSELLING AUTHOR

JULIA QUINN

JUST LIKE HEAVEN
978-0-06-149190-0

Honoria Smythe-Smith is to play the violin (badly) in the annual musicale performed by the Smythe-Smith quartet. But first she's determined to marry by the end of the season. When her advances are spurned, can Marcus Holroyd, her brother Daniel's best friend, swoop in and steal her heart in time for the musicale?

A NIGHT LIKE THIS
978-0-06-207290-0

Anne Wynter is not who she says she is, but she's managing quite well as a governess to three highborn young ladies. Daniel Smythe-Smith might be in mortal danger, but that's not going to stop the young earl from falling in love. And when he spies a mysterious woman at his family's annual musicale, he vows to pursue her.

THE SUM OF ALL KISSES
978-0-06-207292-4

Hugh Prentice has never had patience for dramatic females, and Lady Sarah Pleinsworth has never been acquainted with the words *shy* or *retiring*. Besides, a reckless duel has left Hugh with a ruined leg, and now he could never court a woman like Sarah, much less dream of marrying her.

THE SECRETS OF SIR RICHARD KENWORTHY
978-0-06-207294-8

Sir Richard Kenworthy has less than a month to find a bride, and when he sees Iris Smythe-Smith hiding behind her cello at her family's infamous musicale, he thinks he might have struck gold. Iris is used to blending into the background, so when Richard courts her, she can't quite believe it's true.

JQ4 0515